Unspoken Promises

A BAILEY ISLAND ROMANCE

SKYE TAYLOR

SandCastleBooks

Copyright 2025 by Skye Taylor

Print ISBN: 978-1-7347431-8-0

Sand Castle Books

Skye Taylor enjoys hearing from her readers. Visit her at: www.Skye-writer.com

Cover design by Carrie Schachter – The Monkey Factory

Upscaling, optimization and the creation of parts or all of the cover art was processed with tools or software using AI-driven technology.

Interior design by Nancy Quatrano

Praise for Skye Taylor Books

"Skye Taylor's **Worry Stone** is a deeply emotional tale. Authentic and evocative, this love story between a veteran and a one-time war protester makes us appreciate the healing power of love. I loved it!" Eve Gaddy, National Bestselling author of **Trouble in Texas**

"**Falling for Zoe** is a deftly plotted and delightful story of family, of real life, and love, and trying to do the right thing. **Falling for Zoe** is a romantic gem." Cheryl Reavis, Best-selling, Award-winning author

"**Keeping His Promise** - A compelling tale of love, compassion and being true to your heart." NY Times and USA Today bestseller, Caridad Pineiro

"Bravo Zulu for **Healing a Hero,** filled with turmoil, tenderness, and painful secrets from the past. Will Gunnery Sergeant Philip Cameron have to choose between the Corps and the woman he loves?" Heather Ashby, author of the Love in the Fleet series

"In *The Candidate*, Matt Steele could be the White House occu-pant we all wish for, running a strong campaign with a platform the country sorely needs. But Steele's past comes back to meet him in a way he never imagined, via a photograph and a stranger. In a time when an honest candidate is almost a myth, Steele has the option of being true to his past, or saving his political career. An enjoyable read that will renew your sense of patriotism." C. Hope Clark, Bestselling author of the **Carolina Slade** and **Edisto** mystery series

"*Bullseye* is a fast-paced whodunit with lots of surprises! Deputy Jesse Quinn is a welcome new addition for mystery lovers." A.E. Howe, author of the **Larry Macklin** series

U nspoken Promises is about Kenzie and Eleanor, one rebuilding her life in the present day, and one left waiting during WWII. It's about the promises both women made to themselves and about the unspoken ones they made to others. It's about love, loyalty and starting over.

Reeling from the loss of her job, the end of her marriage and an empty nest, Kenzie Ross decides to fill the void temporarily by traveling to Bailey Island Maine to check out the cottage her old college mentor had bequeathed to her, accompanied by Duffy, the shelter dog the woman had adopted only months before her death. Stunned to discover Bailey House is far more than the rustic seaside bungalow she envisioned, Kenzie ends up deciding to stay and fix up the 150-year-old mansion big enough to shelter three or four families with ease.

Kenzie, determined after a marriage of always giving in, promises herself that she is going to be her own woman, learn to make her own decisions and not fall for the first man she meets. Then, she nearly trips over the dangerously charming Sam Phillips who has his head under an old truck he's trying to fix.

While poking through the dusty old attic, Kenzie finds boxes of old puzzles, books it will take years to read, and a wedding dress that had never been worn. On a whim, she tries it on, admiring the lovely dress in front of a tall oak mirror as old as the house.

Then it's 1943 and Eleanor Murray is happily planning her wedding. Her aunt is pinning up the hem of her gown while Eleanor smiles at her reflection. Then her fiancé barges into the room to announce he's just enlisted in the Army to join the war in Europe and their wedding will have to wait. Crushed, Eleanor hides her sense of aban- donment, plants a Victory Garden and knits socks for Red Cross care packages for soldiers on the front lines.

Her fiancé's letters become more and more distant and her brother's best friend, home to recover after his plane is shot down, starts wooing her. Eleanor accepts her aunt's invitation to stay with her in New York. She finds work at the Brooklyn Navy Yard, a job critical to supporting the war, in an effort to keep the unspoken promises she made when it all began.

To MacDuff, aka Duffy

And all the wonderful dogs who spend their whole lives bringing love, joy, fun, and unwavering companionship to our lives. They are gone way too soon, but all of them leave their pawprints on our hearts.

"You can't go back and change the beginning, but you can start where you are and change the ending." C.S. Lewis

I didn't have a chance to tell you, Patrick, but in my heart, I promised to wait for your return, however long it might be.
Anna Murray

CHAPTER ONE

Kenzie Ross – Present Day

My heart plummeted as my boss outlined his plans for the company. Bill had just pulled the rug out from under my feet. My head buzzed making me wonder if I was about to faint. I felt like crying. I didn't do either, but still . . .

I loved my job and my place in this little cottage industry company that made beautiful things of wood, from one-of-a-kind pieces of custom furniture to unique swag and promotional items by the hundreds bearing company logos. I'd been with Bill and Sara nearly since the beginning. Havelocks sort of felt like my own company. Of course, it wasn't and the decision they'd had to make for family reasons was the best for them. But it wasn't best for me. Not now. Not after the week I'd just barely managed to survive.

A week in which I'd discovered that having an empty nest was more painful than I'd expected following the whirlwind of packing and preparing to drive my twin sons to New England for their freshman year of college. With Luke happily getting to know his new surroundings at Brown in Rhode Island and Liam thrilled to be studying at Suffolk University in Boston, my home now felt more than just empty. It felt dead and way too quiet. I had comforted myself with the thought that with the boys on their own, Garrett and I could begin planning what to cross off our bucket list first.

That solace ended two nights ago when Garrett packed his clothes and a few essentials he needed for the next few weeks and left. Without me.

How had it come to this? No marriage. No boys to busy myself with. And now, no job.

No job, that is, unless I wanted to move across the country to a city I had never even had a desire to visit.

"No need to give me an answer right this minute, Kenzie," Bill said, his voice coming from a long way off. "Think about it. You might want a change considering everything . . ." He trailed off, probably not wanting to contemplate how devastated I might be by Garrett's defection.

But what about my boys. Sure, they were in college, but they were still on the east coast. They were all I had left. My heart felt like someone was squeezing it in a vice.

My one-time mentor, then long-time friend, Maggie Shaw, had been killed in a car crash in August. My next-door neighbor and coffee buddy had just moved to Florida. My very best friend was Garrett's sister. How a divorce would impact that fun, easy relationship I didn't want to contemplate.

Yet another blow the week had delivered was that Garrett's leaving was only temporary. Our home, the dwelling we'd shared for our entire married life, where our boys had grown up, was Garrett's. He'd grown up in that house, and though he'd carried me across that threshold after our wedding, we'd never added my name to the deed. I had never imagined any need to go through whatever legal hoops might be required.

Garrett had been generous by his standards. I had a month to find a new place before he returned, bringing with him the woman he'd been seeing behind my back for more than two years. I had pictured myself dandling grandchildren on my lap in that house. Growing old and maybe even having to install one of those walk-in showers advertised on TV when Garrett and I got too old for a tub.

"Kenzie?"

I'd totally zoned out and hadn't heard Bill's last comment.

"Sorry. You were saying?"

"We'll be at least three months before we're up and running again. I'm giving you a nice package. Call it severance if you decide to stay here in Virginia where you . . . have roots. Or call it continued employment if you want to come to Dallas with us. Except you won't have to do any work for a few months. You could take the time to find an apartment, get moved and settle in."

Bill held out an envelope. I took it automatically, numbness settling in. I let my hand drop to my side without even glancing at it. Bill fidgeted with a pen laying across a stack of papers on the crowded space he called his desk, and I suddenly realized he was eager to get back to his current task, whatever that was. Handing me a pink slip surely hadn't been a highlight of his day either.

I thanked him. At least I think I thanked him, as I turned to leave. My mind had gone blank. Better mute than tears. That would have been awkward beyond anything.

Bill's wife and business partner looked up from a recent project she was packing into boxes and smiled. "I sure hope you decide that Dallas is your next stop. Having you to keep the books straight and inventory in order has been priceless, as the saying goes. You'll be a hard woman to replace."

I shrugged. "I need to think about it. See you tomorrow?"

The woman shook her head. "Not unless you have stuff still hanging. Doors close today. I'm just getting the last of this stuff ready to ship. I know it's kind of sudden, but we kept waffling until Bill's mom had her fall. Tomorrow, we start packing up the shop. I guess Bill explained about his mom and why we decided to move our fun little company to Dallas?"

I nodded and turned toward my tiny office to start gathering my personal belongings. Bill had explained, and I understood, but I was still in denial. It had been a week of blows I struggled to comprehend. I stared at the family photo proudly displayed on the corner of my desk. A photo taken less than a year ago on our last family trip to Hawaii. The ledgers and catalogs that had been my domain lined neatly along the shelf above the desk. I touched the letters carved into the wooden name plate Bill had made for me, then picked it up.

Pens protruded from a mug I'd purchased in the bookstore when Liam and I had visited Suffolk while he was scouting colleges. Without caring where any of them ended up, I dumped the pens on the desk and pulled the mug to my chest along with the nameplate. Then, ignoring the photo, I grabbed my purse from the bottom drawer, turned and walked blindly out of the building, barely noticing the lovely aroma of raw wood. Cedar and fir and so many agreeable scents that had filled my workspace for all these years, and part of what had made coming to work a pleasure.

I was sitting in my car before I remembered the envelope I held, still unopened. I slid my finger under the flap and peeked inside.

No way!

Another shock.

Bill and Sara couldn't afford this. Surely an extra zero had been added by mistake. I started to open the car door to go back in and talk to Bill but then noticed a small bit of paper still inside the envelope. I pulled it out.

Written on the back of an old design sketch in Bill's cramped hand, were just three words.

YOU DESERVE IT.

I drove home on autopilot. Unfortunately, that didn't include a follow-through to fix myself something to eat, so when someone rapped on the door I was still sitting on the bottom step in my spacious foyer. I tried to ignore the rapping, but when it got more insistent, I finally dragged myself to my feet and answered it.

"I was about ready to knock the door down, or at least call 911 for a wellness check," Jaycee Westman announced as she strode into the hall. She stopped short and gazed around. "No lights? Are we still in mourning for my two-timing louse of a brother?"

"Mourning my loss of home and employment."

"You're kidding. Tell me you're kidding." Jaycee paced back to square off with me. "Wait. You aren't kidding, are you? But I don't get it. Explain."

I waved a hand like Vanna White on Wheel of Fortune. "This is Garrett's house. He asked me to leave by the end of the month."

"He can't do that, can he? I mean, you've lived here forever. It's as much yours as his. You need to get a lawyer."

"Doesn't work that way in Virginia. You guys grew up here, and Garrett inherited it from your grandfather before I even met your brother."

"But your name's on the deed." Jaycee nodded her head. "Right?"

I shrugged. "Never thought I needed to. We were just supposed to grow old . . . together."

"Well, that sucks. Maybe, we should just kill him off. I bet he hasn't had time to change his will yet."

I gasped. "Jaycee! That's not even remotely funny."

Jaycee's mouth pressed into a hard line before she sighed and changed the subject. "And what's this about your job? No way you got fired."

"Havelock Memories is moving to Dallas Texas. Lock, stock, and barrel. It closed shop as of . . ." I consulted my watch. "Two hours ago."

Jaycee wrapped me in a tight hug, then pushed me away to ask, "Why Dallas?"

"Bill's mom can't live alone anymore, but she's lived in Dallas her entire life. All her friends are there, and her clubs and her life. With her possible diagnosis of Alzheimer's, they didn't want to drag her east and confuse her any more than she already is, so they are moving the company to Dallas." I fought a wave of vertigo, still trying to take it all in myself, never mind explain it to my sister-in-law. "I'm invited to go with. Or not. My choice."

"Are you going to go?" Disbelief now colored Jaycee's voice as well as my brain.

I wordlessly handed Jaycee the check.

She whistled. "Is this a bribe?"

"Severance, if I don't go. Salary if I choose to stay on since they think it will take a few months to get the company moved, set up and running again. And I'd have to get moved and settled in, too."

"This calls for a drink," Jaycee announced surging to her feet and dragging me with her. "Grab a coat. It's getting chilly out."

CHAPTER TWO

Kenzie Ross – Present Day

My head throbbed. My eyes ached. This had to be the worst hangover of my life. At least the worst since my college days. I couldn't remember how I'd gotten home, and prayed it wasn't in Jaycee's car because, near as I recalled, she had matched me drink for drink.

I lay, an arm over my eyes trying to blot out the brightness of the day and the insistent call of some darned bird outside my window, recalling the bender we'd been on. Now that I thought about it, I'm pretty sure Jaycee's husband had come for us and dropped me off. He'd been good about his rescue, and at least in my presence, had not berated his wife for her indiscretion. Likely, he was just thankful Jaycee had the good sense to call him for a ride. Vance was one of the good guys.

Careful to keep my eyes shielded, I slid from the bed and headed to the bathroom where the slosh of the flushing toilet added to my throbbing head. More of last night's events began to return. Jaycee's advice. At least the sound advice that came before the alcohol took effect when she'd begun to outline several plans for Garrett's discomfort. Some of them had probably been illegal. Some just downright fiendish. Thankfully, she hadn't returned to the idea of knocking him off. If anything happened to Garrett, who knew how many patrons at O'Malley's might have overheard us and been quick to point fingers in our direction.

I needed coffee. Black, and strong and a lot of it. Or maybe I needed some hair of the dog. Bad idea. If I kept this up, I'd be looking for AA meetings.

Finally, dressed in jeans and a sweatshirt, I waited while the coffeemaker gurgled away. My cell phone buzzed, rattling itself across the kitchen counter. No caller ID. I should just ignore the call, but the coffeemaker was still spitting out the caffeine laden brew, so I answered.

"Hello?"

"Is this Mrs. Kenzie Ross?" A pleasant female voice asked.

"It is, but I'm not buying." I started to pull the phone from my ear to hang up, but the woman stopped my intent before it became action.

"I work for Jason Bissell, attorney for Miss Margaret Shaw. Are you aware that Miss Shaw mentioned you in her will?"

That opened my eyes, even without the caffeine fix. Maggie had mentioned me in her will! I definitely hadn't seen that one coming. "No. I was not," I finally replied.

What could Maggie have left me? Maggie was all about charities. She had no children and her husband had died when they were still newlyweds. So far as I knew she didn't have any living relatives, so I'd assumed she'd left her estate to all her favorite causes, mostly those involving dogs in some way or another.

"Mr. Bissell was wondering if you could make it into our office sometime soon. Perhaps today after lunch. Would that be possible?"

"Sure." Not like I had anything else on the schedule. At least, not unless I was of a mind to put any of Jaycee's diabolical plans into action. "What time?"

"One thirty?" the pleasant female voice suggested.

At precisely one thirty, the owner of the pleasant voice ushered me into Attorney Bissell's well-appointed office. The lawyer got to his feet and came around his desk to offer me a hand.

"First let me offer my sympathy for your loss, and thank you for coming so promptly. I tried to reach you last week, but your husband said you were out of town."

Bastard! Garrett hadn't even bothered to mention that to me when I got home from Boston. He was so wrapped up in his own plans he hadn't even cared to pass on a message regarding mine.

"Please. Have a seat." Bissell gestured to one of the two leather bound chairs facing his desk, then took his own seat behind it. He shuffled a few papers to the side and opened another folder. "I assume from what my secretary told me, that Miss Shaw did not discuss her will with you." A statement instead of a question.

I shook my head, then voiced the lack of foreknowledge. "Maggie and I were friends of long standing, but she never mentioned her will. I'm not family, and I don't guess she had any suspicion she was going to die like that. I only learned she'd gifted her body to science when the priest at the church explained why there was no casket." A drunk driver had taken the life of a woman who still had a lot of years left in her.

Bissell looked suitably saddened. "Most people aren't truly prepared but let me get to the meat of the matter.

"Miss Shaw had no surviving siblings, nor any family close enough to have a claim. She has made significant bequests to a number of charities." He began listing them, all ones that were no surprise to me were aimed at rescuing dogs and other critters. A sizeable one to my alma mater where I had first met Maggie when she had been a professor and I a fledgling co-ed. Two others to St. Jude's and Habitat.

"Which leaves just two items that she bequeathed to you," Bissell went on. "The first is her family home on Bailey Island, Maine, and _"

The lawyer was still speaking but his words were lost to my shocked reaction.

Maggie's cottage in Maine. The place I'd been invited to visit but had never managed to tear myself away from Garrett and family obligations to honor the invites. I'd never even seen a photo of the place, although I had once done a google maps search to see where it was.

When I dragged my attention back to the lawyer, he was discussing the transfer of ownership, deeds, taxes, and the like. And offering to handle all the paperwork for me once I decided what I wished to do with the inheritance.

"That brings me to her second bequest. Really more of a request that she hoped you would honor should something happen to her while any of her rescued dogs were still living."

Duffy!

My heart lurched as the soft cadence of Maggie's voice reached out to me over the void that now separated us. We'd finished dinner and were settled in the cluttered but cozy living room of her apartment with Duffy stretched out between us. Had she a premonition about her death? No one expects to die in an auto accident, and it wasn't like she had cancer and knew the end was approaching. But still she'd asked, as if she'd known.

"Should something ever happen to me, I hope you'd come to Duffy's rescue and give him a home. He'd be so lost and confused to lose another person he counted on." She'd gone on to remind me of how she'd come

to rescue the gentle, loving dog after his initial family had abandoned him at a dog park. I'd made sympathetic sounds, but now that I thought about it, I'd never made her any promises. At least not in so many words. The likelihood had seemed so remote.

I nodded my head, too sad to reply. How could I have forgotten that heartfelt request until the lawyer brought it up?

"Where is Duffy now?" Maggie had been aware of Garrett's aversion to dogs, but still she'd asked this of me. Clearly the woman had been clairvoyant if she had guessed my first thought would be of Garrett's response, and of the fact that his opinion wasn't going to matter anymore.

"He is being fostered by a volunteer family under the auspices of C.A.R.E out in Sandston. If you are willing to take him on, I will let them know you will be calling to set up a time to meet the dog. They will have the foster family bring him to the center."

"Of course, I will take him. Maggie would be crushed if I failed to honor her last wish." Maybe I hadn't made the promise she'd asked of me, but I was certainly going to keep it.

Jason Bissell looked like he might be ready to embark on a lecture about dog ownership, but I got to my feet, and he shut his mouth. I had never had a dog because Garrett insisted he was allergic to them. But I'd liked all the dogs Maggie had rescued over the years. How hard could it be?

"How soon can it be arranged?"

I left the lawyer's office with a letter from Maggie that I was saving to read later, and a smile tugging at my lips for the first time in days. Just the thought of this small act of defiance in bringing Duffy into Garrett's house made the grin widen. Tomorrow, the lawyer told me, after he'd gotten off the phone. Tomorrow the family would bring the dog to the shelter, and I could take ownership there. He'd had to explain to the shelter worker that I already knew the dog, and therefore would not have to be introduced first.

I detoured to PetCo to purchase food and a bed, then realized I had no idea what Duffy ate. Or, for that matter, what I might need beyond food or even what belongings he might bring with him. Okay, not a problem. PetCo allowed dogs on a leash in their stores, so I'd been told. I could stop on our way home tomorrow to pick up anything he might need.

With yet another grin, I called Jaycee. The sun might be waning, but at the moment it seemed a lot brighter than it had just a few hours earlier.

"Of all the things you thought up to do to Garrett last night, you didn't think of this one," I began as soon as she answered. "I inherited a dog. And I'm picking him up tomorrow. He'll have three weeks to leave fur and dander all over the house before Garrett moves back in."

Jaycee's peal of laughter echoed the fun in my heart.

"So, who left you a dog?" she asked once the gales of laughter had died down.

"Maggie Shaw."

"The lady that died in the car crash?"

"Yes. And it gets even better. She left me her cottage in Maine."

CHAPTER THREE

Kenzie Ross – Present Day

Duffy sat proudly erect in the passenger seat, a sloppy smile on his face while wind coming in the half-lowered window of my RAV tugged at his ears. I'd had my doubts while watching him being hugged by each member of the foster family. He'd looked so comfortable with them and kept giving me sideways glances as if he knew I hadn't a clue about dog parenting.

He'd been trained to ride with a harness that got buckled into a seatbelt, I was told, and he seemed to be totally okay with it. That was a good thing, or I'd have become the world's worst distracted driver.

A box containing all his earthly possessions sat on the back seat. He was a wealthy dog if the size of the box was anything to go by. His bed was stuffed into the rear compartment; a huge fluffy thing that I had already decided to set in front of the gas fireplace Garrett had installed in my now temporary home.

"You're a good boy, Duffy," I said, glancing over at my new co-pilot. "We are going to have such adventures together. I hope you're up for more new places."

His tongue lolled and the doggy grin remained in place. He appeared to be up for it.

Good grief! I'm carrying on a conversation with a dog. What did that say about me?

Without the need for a pitstop at PetCo, I pulled into my driveway sooner than I'd expected and was surprised to find my sister-in-law's minivan parked in her usual helter-skelter fashion.

I unbuckled and slid from the car, then went around to unhook Duffy. Not sure if he'd automatically follow me to the house, given it was a place he'd never been, I snapped on one of the leashes I'd been given and invited him to jump down.

"About time you got home," Jaycee called out as she took the front steps two at a time. She enveloped me in a bear hug.

"And this must be Duffy?" Jaycee released me and fell to her knees. She offered Duffy a hand to sniff, which he dutifully did. Then without another thought, she wrapped her arms about his neck and gave him a thorough hugging, too. She looked up over the dog's head with a mischievous grin on her face. "Does Garrett know about the dog?"

"Not yet. I just picked him up. I should probably let him explore the back yard before we go inside."

We detoured around the side of the house to the backyard where Duffy did a lot of sniffing before finding several places that needed his mark. All Garrett's severely trimmed shrubs got a healthy squirt. Made my heart happy. Then we went into the house where Duffy checked out everything in the kitchen to his satisfaction before collapsing into a comfortable heap on the rug by the door while Jaycee pried all the details about the rest of my inheritance out of me.

"So, when are you going to check out this cottage you now own? Is it just a summer place or could you live there if you wanted? I know Garrett is kicking you out. I'd fight him for this place if it were me, but then, we've been fighting since I was old enough to realize he wasn't God."

I laughed. "Jaycee, you are good for the soul, but no, I'm not going to fight him for the house. You guys grew up here. I didn't."

I held up the tea kettle. "Want a cup?" Jaycee nodded so I filled the kettle with water and set it back on its base to heat. Then I filled the teapot with my latest favorite tea, set two mugs and sugar on the table and reached into the fridge for the milk.

"If you need company on your trip to Maine, I'd be happy to take some time off," Jaycee offered just as the tea kettle shrieked its readiness. I took a moment to pour steaming water into the teapot and plopped the cozy on top before carrying it to the table.

"I think I could probably find the place on my own," I started but was cut off.

"But just think what a great co-pilot I'd make. And I'm funny, too. When traffic gets bad or you're just getting down over Garrett and missing the boys, you might not like being alone."

"I have Duffy."

"He's not going to reply to anything you might tell him."

"Means he'll keep my secrets."

"I'll keep them too. If you think I'm giving that idiot brother of mine any ammunition for when you two face off in divorce court, then you have seriously misjudged me."

"Won't Vance miss you?"

"Vance is up to his eyeballs with work. He won't notice I'm gone until dinner doesn't appear on the table by magic."

"You really are good for my spirits, Jaycee. How does two weeks from today sound?" It would be nice to have her along. Not counting Maggie or my coffee buddy, Sue, who were already gone from my life, Jaycee had been my best friend for more years than I wanted to count. I would miss her unannounced visits and crazy humor if I moved away.

"I'll help with packing too. How much are you planning to keep and how much do we dump on Garrett?"

I walked Jaycee to the door when the tea pot was empty, and she decided it was time to head home to prepare Vance's magic supper. As we said goodbye with another rocking hug beside her minivan, she whispered into my ear, "I can't wait for Garrett to find out you have a dog in *his* house." Then she hopped into her car and gave me a thumbs-up as she cranked the engine.

After she'd pulled out and the taillights were disappearing around the corner, I glanced at the house to see Duffy watching me. Only his head showed in the bottom half of the storm door, but I could tell he was wagging his tail. He was good for my spirits, too. I hadn't even known I was going to become a dog owner, but already I sensed we were going to be best buds.

I collected his bed from my car and dragged it along with the box of his things into the house. The big fluffy bed looked right at home in front of the fireplace. As did his food and water bowl beside the counter in the kitchen.

"Just you and me, now, Duffy," I said as I moved things around to make room for his kibble and treats on one of the shelves and began fixing his dinner following the instructions the foster family had shared with me.

I half expected an angry phone call from Garrett about the dog, but Jaycee was as good about secrets as she'd promised. I was sure she'd tell Vance, but it was unlikely Vance would have any reason to report to

Garrett. All I needed was two weeks. And Garrett would never know about Duffy until he began sneezing. That is, if he really was as allergic to dogs as he'd claimed every time the twins had begged for a dog.

All my married life, I'd considered myself an independent woman capable of choosing my life goals and lifestyle, but now the reality that Garrett had been making decisions for me all along hit home. Worse, I'd let him.

I bent down to wrap my arms around Duffy. He licked my face. Garrett would be appalled. I felt empowered. I plopped onto my butt and pulled the dog into my lap. All seventy pounds of him. I scratched his ears and he continued to clean my chin and cheeks. Go me!

CHAPTER FOUR

Kenzie Ross – Present Day

My Rav's smooth ride gave way to a not so gentle rumble as I pulled into the dirt lot next to a sign advertising kayak rentals. Duffy whined in the rear seat as I unbuckled my seat belt and slid out. It had been a while since our last pit stop, and he probably needed to pee. "In a minute," I promised him as I shut the door.

"Why are we stopping here?" Jaycee climbed out after me and frowned at the barn-red building with a rack of kayaks next to it.

"This bridge," I said drawing her attention away from the kayaks, and toward the bridge stretching out across the channel separating Bailey Island from the rest of the Harpswell peninsula. "Is supposed to be the only one like it in the world." I'd been reading anything I could find online about Bailey Island and this bridge had aroused my curiosity.

"Really?" She turned to study it. "It's pretty, but what's so special about it?"

"All those slabs of granite and not a speck of cement anywhere. I read that the idea was to let the tide come and go through it and the slabs are heavy enough to just sit there and not move. Amazing, right?"

"Are you sure it's safe?" Her brow furrowed.

As she asked the question, a half dozen cars and two pickup trucks streamed off the bridge, heading north while a beverage delivery truck waited for them to pass before starting onto the approach.

"Guess we're going to find out," I answered as I climbed back into the driver's seat.

I pulled back onto the paved road and following the truck. The bridge suddenly felt a whole lot narrower than described in the article I'd read. Would I ever get used to sailing over this magnificent bridge without cringing at every car that passed going the other way? My knuckles turned white as I gripped the wheel tighter, doing my best not to cringe. Finally, like the last bit of toothpaste squirting out of the tube, I exited the bridge and sighed with relief.

Jaycee twisted to look back over her shoulder. "Wow! That's an awfully skinny bridge. I wonder why they didn't make it wider."

"It was built in the nineteen-twenties. Cars weren't so big. It might even have been just horses pulling wagons for all I know of Island history. Before the bridge, people rowed across."

"But why not make it wider now?" Jaycee asked turning to face forward again as I headed up the hill.

"It's listed on all kinds of historic registers," I parroted what I'd read online. "Engineering being one of them. Maybe they can't widen it without losing some of the bragging rights." I shrugged. "Keep an eye out for a sign that says Captain Patrick Murray House. It's on your side according to my GPS."

"I see it," Jaycee said a moment later.

I'd seen it, too, and turned on my blinker.

"The agent said I'd see the sign first then the cottage," I told Jaycee as I turned and began rumbling over a gravel drive.

"Hey, whoa!" Jaycee gasped. "That can't be your cottage."

I put on the brakes and stared.

A low wall of irregular slabs of stone ran along the edge of a vast spread of vibrant green grass. The wall curved around at both ends to disappear down a gentle slope. A couple shallow steps bisected the wall in the middle leading up to a path of flagstones that curved across the amazingly green expanse of lawn. Bright fall plants bloomed around the fieldstone foundation of a charming old mansion that would have been better described as an uber generous bed and breakfast than a mere cottage. A glimpse of the ocean peaked out from behind the house.

Strangely enough the only picture Maggie had ever shown me of the place she'd grown up, was of herself and her playmates sitting on a wide step to what looked like a porch. Well, this place did have a porch. One that swept across the front of the building, wrapped around the corner, and might even continue around to the back with a full view of the water.

A beaten down grass verge along our side of the wall was currently occupied by a green Land Rover. I pulled in behind it. Maybe my cottage was around back. Or even a little further down the gravel lane where it disappeared between a stand of tall spruce trees.

A woman waited, hips propped against the side of the Land Rover, her face shaded by the floppy brim of an enormous beach hat. She pushed herself off and headed our way, so I turned the engine off and got out. This time Duffy whined more insistently. He'd have to wait a tad longer.

"Kenzie Ross?" The woman held out a hand.

I took her hand in mine and nodded. "That's me, but—" I struggled to remember her name.

"Welcome to the Captain Patrick Murray House," she said with a sweep of her arm toward the beautiful old home with the endless porch.

My breath felt trapped in my lungs, unable to exit. I took the two steps up through the wall and gaped in awe at the enormous house with several peaked dormers on the second floor and windows everywhere. Two massive chimneys suggested cozy fireplaces within. The porch did, indeed, wrap all the way around to the back, and a widow's walk perched at the peak. Still wordless and stunned, I walked past the woman to study the house. A white spindle railing punctuated by tall columns finished an enclosure large enough to host a major gathering. Elegant and timeless. But definitely not a cottage.

"Is this what you were expecting?" Jaycee appeared at my side.

I shook my head, desperate to find breath enough to speak again. "Not even close."

"Garrett will be sick with envy," she replied. "Wait, he can't claim it in the divorce, can he?"

Again, I shook my head. I doubted it, given he was keeping his house, but in reality, I wasn't sure.

"Would you like a tour?" The agent had caught up with us. "Or maybe you need to let your dog out first? I heard him whining."

"I'll get him," Jaycee offered. "Then I'll catch up."

"I switched the reservation for our best suite. I assumed you would want it for yourself. It was supposed to be booked through the end of next week but there was another suite available and the renters were first timers so they were fine with the change, especially when I offered them a discount," the agent was babbling on, and I was only half listening as she led me across the porch to the front door.

Before we got that far, however, I was distracted by the view to my left.

Another breath-stopping moment.

The ocean sparkled in the sunshine and an old-fashioned sailing ship leaned into the wind as it gracefully made its way out to open ocean. At the moment, at least, there was not another boat in sight. I might have stepped back in time.

"Stunning, isn't it?" The agent was at my side again. "Wait until you see the sunsets." She nodded her head vigorously to emphasize this was a 'not to be missed' event.

I hadn't even begun to see all there was to see, yet I already knew I wanted to stay here. Like live here. I'd be close enough to see both of my boys, and far enough to never see Garrett again. But more importantly, I just had a gut feeling about this house. Like I belonged here. Where had that certainty come from? I hadn't even been inside. And the upkeep had to be costly.

"Okay, I'm ready for that tour," I turned away from the sparkling sea and the old ship. Just as I was about to admit to having forgotten her name and accept the embarrassment of having to ask, it came to me. . . Donna.

"Seven bedrooms and five bathrooms. Three rooms have ensuite bathrooms, and two have small sitting rooms. One full kitchen and two kitchenettes, two dining rooms and four living spaces. Where would you like to start?" Donna asked as she ushered me through a front door as impressive as the house and into a great room so elegantly decorated I could have been featured in a Regency romance.

I wondered how much of the furniture was actual antique and how many reproductions, given the place had been a rental for years. The far end of the great room was dominated by one of the fireplaces I'd guessed at based on the chimneys on the roof. Built of fieldstone with a raised hearth, it begged to have a fire burning in its depths. Paintings graced the walls that I had to assume were of local interest, but I didn't have time to look closer as Donna bustled on, outlining all the amenities.

Next we toured the main kitchen, a room that appeared to have been updated sometime in the last ten years but still showed evidence of that second chimney. No fireplace or stove connected to it, just a small round cover where a massive kitchen stove must have once dominated the room. At the far end, four doors led to a walk-in pantry, a room that doubled as storage and laundry, a half bath and a rear exit. I especially liked the kitchen island that had been added in the middle of the room with stools lined up along one side.

The downstairs tour completed, we finally climbed the stairs to the second floor. The generous square landing at the top had very little wall and seemed to be made up of doors. Donna explained that the first door was to the room currently rented by the older couple she'd mentioned before. The second led up to the attic, she said as she passed it and reached to open the next one.

This door opened into a smaller landing with four more doors and an open stairway at the far side. She opened each in turn to reveal comfortably furnished rooms, two of which had views of the bay and two with windows that opened to the east. The stairway, Donna explained, went down to the door on the water side of the house. "It gives renters of these rooms their own entry." Then we retraced our steps back to the main landing.

"The smallest room in Murray House is just a single, but we rent it out more often than you might guess, perhaps because it has its own bath." she said as she opened the door on the far side of the stairway railing. "This one is also small but quite comfortable," she went on as she showed me a room with bunked beds and a single comfortable chair with a standing lamp next to it.

Then she gestured to the final door with a brass plaque that read *The Captain's Room.*

"You can always opt for a different suite, but I thought you would prefer this one. As I mentioned, it's the largest, has its own bath and sitting area and a small kitchenette so you'd be totally independent of the rest of the place should you wish. That would give you more privacy, as well. And it has the best view."

She opened the door with a flourish and ushered me inside.

The feeling of being home that had gripped me on the front porch clutched at me again. It wasn't the elegant old bed with turned posts and high headboard. Or the pair of easy chairs upholstered in a soft-hued plaid that sat in the little bay by the window. Not even the braided rug on the floor, or the bookcase filled with an eclectic assortment of books. Or the old fashioned, free-standing, full-length mirror made of burled oak. It was the whole of it. I crossed to the alcove with the chairs and peeked out the window to that same sparkling sea I'd glimpsed from the porch.

"Yes," I said turning back to Donna who still stood just inside the door, her hands clasping the hat no longer on her head. "It's perfect."

"Why don't I let you settle in and get comfy, then. I'm guessing it's been a long trip. You can come by the office tomorrow and I'll let you go over the books and discuss . . ." her voice trailed off. She was probably wondering if she was out of a lucrative client, or not. It was a good thing she didn't ask because I'm not sure how I'd have answered.

"Sounds good," I agreed.

Donna handed me her business card, pointing to the address. "It's just a short way south on the Harpswell Road, about a mile. On your left. If you get to the cemetery, you've gone too far. Give me a call when you want to stop in, so I'll be sure to be available." She turned to go, then jerked back. "Almost forgot. You'll be wanting these." She held out a keychain in the shape of a lobster with several keys attached. "One for this room, one for the front door. A spare for the back door and one for each of the other remaining bedrooms. This one is for the ensuite currently unoccupied and right across the hall from this room. Your friend will be comfortable there, I presume."

I accepted the keys and thanked her for meeting me and taking the time to show me around. She closed the door as she left and the sound of her footfalls on the stairs followed. Before I had time to even take a breath and decide what to do next, the door reopened, and Duffy charged in.

He headed for me, then stopped short and, nose twitching, checked out the surroundings. Jaycee was on his heels, or rather, paws.

"This place is a-maz-ing." Just as I'd done minutes before, she headed to the window to look out. Then back to the bed and finally to me. "Do we share the bed? Or do I get my own?"

I pried the last key pointed out to me off the ring and handed it to her. "Across the hall. Don't lose it."

She dashed out.

I sagged onto the edge of the bed. It had been a long day, but there were still daylight hours and I wanted to explore. But for this moment, I just wanted to savor the unexpected feeling that I'd come home. Odd that I felt such a strong compulsion given I'd never even seen a picture of the place, but the certainty grew stronger by the minute.

Duffy came over and sat, shoving his face into my lap, his tail swishing softly against the braided rug as if to add his approval.

CHAPTER FIVE

Kenzie Ross – Present Day

"I haven't slept so soundly in years," Jaycee announced entering the kitchen where I perched on a stool sipping my second cup of coffee.

An echo of my own revelation on waking a couple hours ago.

"Think it's the sound of the waves?" she asked as she poured herself a cup of morning brew.

I shrugged. "Could be. I think it's the unsullied air with a tang of salt."

Duffy appeared from the back stoop where he'd been soaking in the sun after our early morning walk. He ambled over to Jaycee and plopped his chin on her knee. She patted his head absently, her gaze not focused on anything.

"You're going to move up here. Aren't you?"

With not even a clue of the cost of upkeep for a house this old, or taxes and insurance, my main concern would be finding employment. But there had to be a way. Somehow.

"I am," I answered.

"Well, I'm going to visit every chance I get. She got up, dislodging Duffy's head, and walked over to the window, ignoring her just-poured mug of joe. "It's probably none of my business, but how are you going to afford the upkeep? Renting out space to summer visitors probably comes to a sizeable amount in the summer, but what about in the winter?"

Maggie probably never considered that when she willed all her investment assets to a dozen different charities. Of course, she had no idea Garrett would abandon me, so she probably didn't think the need would come up. Or maybe she just figured I'd continue to rent it out the way she had for the last twenty years or more.

"I'll figure it out. Somehow," I replied, praying I would. "Brunswick isn't that far away. Good office managers and accountants don't grow on trees. Or there's Bath where they build ships for the Navy."

"Don't you have to be in the Navy to work there?"

"They only build destroyers. They aren't Navy," I replied.

"So, here's my plan," Jaycee announced returning to her mug, taking a sip, and then setting it down. "Garrett wants to marry that twit, so he wants the divorce over as quickly as possible. Maybe if he never finds out about this place, or if he's like you, thinking it's just some old cottage from two centuries ago, he'll stick with the current split of investment assets. I'm going to play along and encourage him to just tell his lawyer to get the paperwork done."

I'd completely forgotten the investments Garrett had promised me if I didn't make a stink about the house. "Actually, it's me that needs to just sign the papers and get it done."

"Jeese! He didn't waste any time, did he? Bastard! I don't suppose you have them with you?"

"I do," I replied, setting my own mug back on the glistening white counter. "I couldn't leave them with my stuff in storage, so I stuck them in my suitcase."

"Well, what are we waiting for? I'll witness them and we can go to the post office today and send them overnight mail."

"I'll deal with that later. Right now, I want to walk down to Garrison Cove. We can take Duffy. He loves to swim. Donna says there's a restaurant called Cooks where we can get great seafood. They do take-out, too, so I thought we could amble over and check out the menu.

Coffee finished and sneakers on, we opted to try a little path I'd discovered that morning while giving Duffy a chance to explore the area and do his thing. I suspected the path might come out on Garrison Cove Road and I was proven right. We turned and headed for the cove.

The water side of the road featured a row of cottages, all looking as old as Murray House. I'd have been happy with any of them, but then I thought of the magnificent place Maggie had left me and sighed with pleasure.

Two dogs charged toward the edge of an unfenced yard but stopped five feet short of the road. "Guessing they have an electric fence," Jaycee commented as Duffy trotted over to sniff and get sniffed.

I left him to do his thing for a few moments, but with the cove now in sight, I whistled him back, and we set off toward the water. At first the road appeared to end in the ocean, but then I realized it actually curved around to the left while a paved launching ramp continued straight on into the water.

Duffy glanced back at me for less than a heartbeat, then charged into the water. He paddled happily in circles, before returning to the shore to shake all over Jaycee. Jaycee found a piece of driftwood and tossed it. Duffy obediently went after it and finding a spare one on his return, brought both sticks back and sat expectantly.

"I think he'd be happy to chase sticks all day, but my arm is killing me," Jaycee said after she'd played this game for a while. "Let's check out Cooks." I agreed, called the dog out of the water and we followed the final arc of road toward the restaurant.

Leaving a very wet dog outside with an almost as wet Jaycee, I went in to ask for a menu. Then we headed back up the hill to plan the rest of our day. In the end, we just sat on the porch admiring the view for the first half, and then unpacked my car.

The big fluffy dog bed that had so recently accented Garrett's fire-place, now sat in front of a new fireplace looking just as at home. I put Duffy's basket of toys next to it and plopped into one of the many overstuffed and incredibly comfy chairs to wait for Jaycee who was still doing God knew what in her room upstairs.

When suppertime arrived, we called in our dinner order, but we were both too tired to walk down to the cove again so I handed Jaycee the keys to my Rav, then fed Duffy and headed up to unpack my suitcase while I awaited her return. The smell of hot food brought me hurrying back downstairs just as Jaycee tossed my keys onto the counter and began unpacking the various options for dinner.

After consuming far too much of some very tasty Maine cuisine, I patted my stomach and sat back.

"A good day, wouldn't you say?" Jaycee asked, pushing her plate away and tipping the last of a bottle of wine into her empty glass.

"Definitely a good day," I replied, feeling more at peace than I had in weeks.

Even that peace was astonishing given the state of my life right now. Soon to be single, still struggling with the empty-nest syndrome, and unemployed. I should have been a basket case having been abandoned

by the man who promised to love me till death did us part and left behind by the young men I'd spent the last eighteen years raising. Never
mind adding the worrying about money and making ends meet.

The following morning, after consulting her phone, Jaycee brought
up a map and directed me to my agent's office. She needn't have
bothered considering I'd have had to be blind to miss it.

I spent an hour in the agent's office talking business and possibilities
going forward while Jaycee and Duffy visited a local point of interest
Jaycee told me was called the Giant Staircase. She promised to take me
there before I put her on a plane in Portland to get back to her life in
Virginia.

She'd also visited a tourist trap called Land's End and proudly wore
a neon orange sweatshirt with Bailey Island printed boldly across the
chest. Duffy sported a kerchief tied around his neck decorated with
lobsters. And I'd been gifted with an hourglass boasting that time
spent by the sea was never wasted.

Jaycee directed me to a little general store with a lunch counter
where we ordered lobster rolls at what I considered an exorbitant
price. But they were worth every penny and the ambiance of the rural
lunch counter was fun, all by itself. We spent the afternoon alternating
between naps and playing cribbage on my new porch that boasted a
view I'd never get tired of.

In the evening, I pored over the rental files Donna had given me
while Jaycee had her nose buried in a book about Bailey Island that
she'd bought at the gift store along with all her other purchases.

"Hey," Jaycee grabbed my attention. "Did you know this place is
supposed to be haunted?"

"Haunted how?" I asked.

Jaycee lifted the book from her lap and wagged the covers as if
releasing magic into the air. "Captain Patrick Murray's widow has

apparently never given up waiting for his return from the sea. People have seen her up on the widow's walk looking for his ship."

"Harumph," I responded. "The captain disappeared almost two hundred years ago, according to the agent, who, by the way, did not mention any ghosts."

"She probably didn't want to scare you off."

"I don't believe in ghosts to start with, but if all this ghost does is pace around the widow's walk looking for a long-lost ship, what's there to be afraid of?"

Jaycee shrugged. "Nothing, I guess. But it sounds like fun. Having a resident ghost, I mean."

I harumphed again and went back to my very real numbers and the business of running a guest house. Jaycee returned to her book to see what other gems she could uncover about my new home.

When it was time for Jaycee to return to Virginia, I set Duffy's crate up in my room. He went in and laid down obediently while I prayed he wouldn't whine or bark and annoy any of my guests. The trip down to the Portland airport included a detour just long enough for Jaycee to see the real L.L. Bean and insist I purchase a pair of Bean boots that I'd need come winter. All too soon, I was hugging the last link to my old life goodbye and watching her enter the security lines at the compact little airport.

"I'll be back," she promised with a wave and a blown kiss before she disappeared toward her gate.

On the way home, I stopped for some groceries, but was eager to get back to my new home and my old dog.

Home! Odd, I'd been here just under three days and already it was home! Duffy had been with me less than three weeks and yet he was my old dog. Sometimes life turns on a dime. The thought hit me as I recalled the unexpected phone call from a lawyer that I'd almost hung up on.

After I stowed my groceries, Duffy and I went for a walk and found a new path that ended up on the shore of a sound bearing the Abenaki name of Merriconeag. I'd read that merriconeag meant quick carrying place in one of the indigenous tribal languages, but how that was supposed fit, I have no idea since the ocean, at least at the moment, surged lazily in over the rocky shore and retreated soundlessly. Duffy scrambled down over the ledges and probably would have gone for a swim if I hadn't called him back. He'd started hopping into bed with me at night and this late in the day, he'd never dry out and we'd both be sleeping soggy. He came reluctantly and after a short walk down the shore and back we headed up to the house.

I sat on the top step of the porch and gazed out over the water. With Jaycee gone, the loneliness finally hit me. I pictured my boys, busy in their new lives at college. I doubted they missed me nearly as much as I missed them. College was an adventure. A giant step into adulthood for my boys. For me, it was the end of an era. The end of what had defined my life for so many years it was difficult to remember what it was like before they were born.

I got up and shook myself. I was not going to become a maudlin wreck. Murray House was my new adventure. And it was time to get started. I'd already poked into every nook and crevice that was not currently occupied by my temporary guests, so I decided to check out the attic.

Another locked door beckoned. I rifled through the keyring I'd been given and found the correct one on the third try.

Duffy, faithful companion that he'd become, followed me up the creaking old staircase. Or maybe he was reluctant to let me out of his sight lest I disappear like Maggie had. I wondered how long a dog's memory was. Did he still miss Maggie? Or the temporary family with a raft of kids? Or maybe even the lonely nights in a kennel with no one he knew in sight? A question I'd likely never know the answer to.

Windows high up at either end of the space let in soft rays of late afternoon sunlight. A single bulb added a soft yellow glow and between the two I was able to make my way through the dusty room festooned with cobwebs without sneezing too many times. A row of boxes stacked near the top of the stairs held books. A lot of books. One day I'd haul them down and go through them. Maybe add more bookcases to the great room. Or maybe donate them to a local library. But that wasn't today.

A leather traveling trunk held uniforms from another era. I had no idea, but maybe even as far back as the Great War, as my great-grand-father always called WWI. A smaller leather suitcase was stuffed with letters that held a hint of roses as well as old paper. Those would be fun to read. I parked that case at the top of the stairs and continued my search.

A delicate old tea set. An entire set of Limoges porcelain dinner-ware. A box filled with candlesticks made of everything from wood to brass and a couple that might even be silver, given the coat of black tarnish. A trunk full of clothing from at least a century ago. Likely even longer. I sneezed again.

This place needed a good dusting.

Balanced across the arms of an old rocking chair, sat a very large garment box carefully tied with a faded blue ribbon that was as dusty as the rest of the place. I picked it up and sat in the rocker. Built by a craftsman who cared about his product, the chair was incredibly comfortable even bare, without a hint of padding.

I decided that chair was going down to my room today. I plopped the box back in the chair and dragged it to the top of the stairs. Step, by careful step, I finally inched the chair down to the landing.

Another sneezing fit forced me to stop and wait it out.

"I need to find a big shop-vac," I told Duffy, who wagged his tail and followed me as I hefted the chair into my room. Scooting one of the upholstered chairs aside, I went back to grab the rocker to place it where it would have the best view. As I set the chair down the box slid off and fell to the floor in another cloud of dust.

"What do you suppose is in this?" I asked the dog, as I pulled the faded blue bow free and lifted the lid.

I was greeted by the strong scent of camphor and at least a dozen layers of thin old tissue paper. I carefully peeled tissue away to reveal a sea of creamy white lace and satin.

A wedding dress!

How old was it, I wondered as I lifted the heavy fabric free of the box and a handful of moth balls rattled to the floor. I shook the dress out and the tissue paper joined the mothballs.

It was a stunning confection with hand beaded pearls across the lace bodice and satin train. I held it up in front of me and turned toward the old mirror in the corner. A beautiful vision from a bygone era.

Only God knows what imp possessed me, but I decided to try it on. It looked about my size. Stripping out of my sweatshirt and jeans, I lifted it to slide it over my head. That's when I noticed the pins.

Surprised, I laid the dress across the bed for a closer look. This gown, made with such care, had never been properly hemmed up and likely never worn. What could have happened to cancel that wedding? Had the groom cried off? Had the bride changed her mind?

Probably another answer I'd never have. I lifted it again, and careful not to dislodge any of the pins, I slipped it over my head. The velvety softness of satin slid down my skin like a caress. There was no way I could pull all the tiny satin covered buttons through the loops provided but even without it buttoned, it seemed like it might have been made for me.

I turned again to the old, burled oak mirror to admire the sparkling confection.

CHAPTER SIX

Eleanor Murray - 1942

Excitement bubbled inside Eleanor as her grandmother knelt on the floor beside her pinning up the hem of the beautiful new wedding dress Eleanor would be wearing in just a few short months. The satin felt as smooth and soft as a newborn baby's bottom against her skin and the whole thing sparkled like a sky full of stars. Jeff would think she was the most beautiful girl in the world when he saw her on their wedding day.

"Stand still, Eleanor. I can't get the hem straight if you keep hopping about," Gran mumbled around a mouthful of pins. She spat the pins into her hand and rocked back onto her heels. "Save your fidgeting for after I'm done. Please."

Gran started to bend back to her task when a sharp rap on the door stopped her.

"Who is it?" Eleanor called out.

"It's Jeff," came the answer even as the door burst open and, her fiancé barged into the room.

Eleanor squealed. "You can't see my dress before the wedding! Close your eyes!"

Jeff slapped a hand over his eyes but didn't retreat. "We have to talk."

"Not right this minute," Eleanor replied trying to turn him away and give him a push back through the door.

"Yes, right this minute. I have news and you'll want to know it right away."

Eleanor glanced back at her grandmother who held up two fingers.

"Wait out on the porch and I'll be out in two minutes," Eleanor told Jeff's back. She gave him one more push and shut the door. "Be quick," Eleanor told her grandmother as she moved back to her place in front of the mirror.

"Jeff?" Eleanor appeared on the porch closer to ten minutes later than the promised two wearing a dress with blue cornflowers that Jeff had told her he loved. It was the prettiest one she had, not counting the almost finished wedding dress. "What is so important you needed to speak with me so urgently?"

"I've enlisted," he replied yanking the cap off his sleek brown head, disarranging the careful cut of his hair.

Eleanor gaped at him, not sure how to respond. "Did my father put you up to it?"

"Your father? Why would you ask that?"

Because her father had called Jeff's entire family a den of cowards and ne'er-do-wells. Not to his face that she knew of, but Father might have said something similar when Jeff asked for her hand.

"W-why?" was all she could manage. The idea that she'd be newly married and maybe even starting a family and Jeff would be a million miles away shocked her into stuttering disbelief.

"Because our country needs me. It's my duty to go." He reached for her hand. "We'll just have to wait a bit for our wedding."

"Wait?!" Eleanor was horrified. "We can still be married. Then you go, if you must." She wanted to stamp her foot and be angry. Even married to a soldier off fighting a war was better than not being a wife at all. "We can have our wedding day before you go. Pastor Collins would surely understand why we needed to move the date up."

"But I leave tonight. I'm catching a ride with Vincent and Arthur. We must be at the train station in Portland first thing in the morning." He swept her into a fierce embrace. "I love you, Eleanor. We'll be married the moment I get home. I promise. And I'll write. It might take a while for letters to get here, but I will write as often as I can."

"But . . ." She pushed herself out of his embrace.

Jeff shook his head, his mouth pressed into a hard straight line. "I love you more than I can say, but there's no way I'm going to rush to the altar and then leave you behind alone and maybe with child."

"I wouldn't be alone," Eleanor argued. "I have my family and if by some wonderful chance I did have a baby growing inside of me, I'd have a piece of you here with me while you're away."

Jeff pulled her into his arms again, rocking her in a fierce embrace. "What kind of man would want to leave you to raise a child alone? That's not the kind of life for the woman I love or any child I might have. It's better if we wait. We can be married the moment I get home. Please, promise me you understand."

He didn't wait for her reply before covering her lips with his and kissing her as fiercely as he was hugging her. She clung to him, disbelief thudding in her heart, and let his mouth devour hers.

He was leaving. There would be no wedding. She wouldn't be a new bride and there would be no baby growing in her belly. A small flame of anger began to ignite.

Jeff lifted his head. "I love you, Eleanor Murray. Promise me you'll wait."

"But, Jeff . . ." He cut her protest off.

"And you still love me," he persisted, ignoring her distress.

"I love you." Her words came out barely more than a whisper.

He kissed her again, less fiercely this time. More hurried. And then he was leaping off the porch and loping toward the lane where Vincent's father's car idled.

The rear door opened, and Jeff ducked to climb inside, but stopped to touch two fingers to his heart, then hold them out toward her for a moment before he disappeared inside the car.

The Oldsmobile pulled away leaving Eleanor bereft and sobbing.

Her initial reaction was to run and hide in her room to absorb this grief. But Father was sitting with his paper and his pipe just inside the door. She'd have to pass him to get to the stairs, and she was sure he'd say something nasty, like he'd told her Jeff wasn't to be trusted.

Instead, she ran across the soft green lawn to the little lane that disappeared into the trees. She nearly tripped as she broke from the trees and scrambled down onto the rocky shore. Waves crested and broke, splashing noisily against the rocks and wetting her shoes. She didn't care about the shoes. Or even the dress she'd donned just for Jeff. The dress he'd not even seemed to notice.

It had been all about him. He'd enlisted. Eleanor should have known nothing good would come of the recruiter she'd heard spouting off in the churchyard after worship on Sunday. Jeff didn't believe in God, so he claimed. Another negative her father liked the throw at her. So, she'd been glad, for once, that Jeff had not shown up to take her to church for show. But somehow that evil man had found him.

She stumbled as she hurried over the wet rocks to another path. This one led away from the water to a secret place she and Jeff had found together. Not totally secret because other lovers had found it before them, but secret from her father.

Jeff had carved their initials, entwined with an arrow through them and a heart surrounding them. Dozens of other pairs of lovers' names or initials were similarly carved into the smooth grey bark of the massive old Beech tree. Some carvings were very old. Some, like theirs, were new.

She lurched up to the tree and reached out to touch the letters. EM & JW. Still raw and yellow. "Oh, Jeff. How could you? How could you just leave on a moment's notice and not think about me or how I feel? Why couldn't we get married before you left." The sobbing began again, mixed with a heavy dose of anger.

She'd sobbed herself out and was patting her aching eyes dry with her handkerchief when she heard her name being called.

"Eleanor?" Softly at first. "Eleanor?" Louder. More insistent." It was her friend Priscilla.

"I'm at the tree," Eleanor answered, her voice raspy with the crying. No use just staying quiet. Priscilla would just come up and find her anyway. Priscilla knew about the tree. Her name was carved into it as well. In large square letters next to her beau's name. Except her beau had graduated from medical school and wouldn't be going off to fight.

Priscilla's head, enwreathed by a neat, braided crown of jet-black hair, appeared. "Your grandmother told me about Jeff. I thought I'd find you here."

"He's gone," Eleanor blurted. "And I didn't promise." Tears began again, despite feeling like she had no tears left.

"Didn't promise what?" Priscilla asked as she seated herself on the bench someone had built around the trunk of the tree and pulled Eleanor to her side.

"He asked me to promise I'd wait for him. I couldn't find my voice. I was so shocked."

"Did you tell him you loved him?" Priscilla asked gently.

Eleanor nodded.

"Then he probably knows you will wait. Why wouldn't you?"

"Because I'm angry with him," Eleanor declared.

"Did you let him know you were angry?"

"No, but—"

"But nothing. You said you loved him. Those are the words he will carry with him until he returns."

Eleanor wiped her eyes again. Her handkerchief was soggy. She had to stop with the tears.

"But I don't understand why you are angry," Priscilla said with a frown. "Most of the young men have either already gone or will be called up soon."

"You wouldn't understand."

"Why wouldn't I understand?"

"Because Peter won't be going anywhere. He's a doctor and has already begun his internship. He gets to stay home where he won't get shot at and killed."

"Jeff might not be going where he'll get shot at either. No need to borrow trouble that might not be coming your way."

Words Eleanor had heard her grandmother say more than once. But it didn't help. Not this time. When they'd picked a wedding date, Eleanor had been sure nothing could get in the way of their love. Even after Pearl Harbor, when the draft began, Jeff had insisted he'd wait until his number was called, so they'd picked a wedding date and Eleanor had been sure nothing could get in the way.

The anger she'd felt stabs of before, reared its ugly head again. She ground her teeth and tried to breathe normally, but fury was getting the better of her.

How could Jeff do this to her?

CHAPTER SEVEN

Kenzie Ross – Present Day

Waking from a lovely dream about walking on the sundrenched beach in Maui with Garrett, I stretched languidly before opening my eyes. Then I jerked up, startled, not quite sure where I was. The smooth white ceiling I'd stared at for over twenty years had been replaced by one with dimpled plaster that needed a coat of paint. Then I noticed the beautiful satin wedding dress hanging on the closet door where I'd left it, and everything came back to me.

I was single again. Or almost. And in my new digs. In the rambling old Captain Patrick Murray House on Bailey Island, Maine. I thought of Maggie. I thought of Jaycee who might be even more enthusiastic about Maggie's gift than I was. In a handwritten letter the lawyer had given me before I left his office, Maggie's last request, not counting Duffy, had been to scatter her ashes in Garrison Cove where she'd played as a child. I almost asked Jaycee to accompany me, but somehow, it seemed like something Duffy and I needed to do. Just the two of us. Our last gift to a wonderful woman who had given both of us so much.

I slid from the bed and went to stand by the window that overlooked the sound and out over the ocean to the horizon. A cold, wet nose pushed itself into my palm. I bent to his level to give his ears a good scratch. Maggie used to tell me that scratching behind their ears released endorphins in dogs, the stuff that makes us all feel happy. I was doing my best to learn how to be a good dog mom for Duffy now that he didn't have Maggie.

"Hey, Duff. You need to go out? Or just saying good morning?"

He licked my chin in answer, his tail swishing. I took that for a yes to both and headed to my dresser to find a pair of jeans and a T-shirt.

While Duffy poked about the grassy yard beyond the porch, I went back to get the coffee started. I watched the dog's progress around the perimeter until he disappeared from sight, then went back to pour myself a mug of coffee.

The sun felt warm and welcoming on my shoulders as I stood on the porch with the sky growing brighter, sipping my coffee and waiting for Duffy to reappear.

But he didn't reappear.

"Duffy?" I called out, then waited.

No sleek black head anywhere.

Where had he gotten to? Or perhaps I should be asking what he'd gotten into that had his undivided attention. I set the mug down and went in search.

After two entire turns around the house, the discovery of a fence needing mending and a broken door on the cellar at the far side, there was still no sign of my dog. Getting worried, I called his name over and over. So much for being the best dog mom ever. Had I failed already?

Maybe he's just exploring his new neighborhood. I tried to reassure myself. It wasn't working. I forced myself to stop pacing and think.

Where would he likely go? It's not like he knew anyone around here. I glanced up to where I knew the Harpswell road where there might be traffic. Not busy like highways back in my hometown in Virginia, but people still drove fast. What if he'd been hit?

I took off running for the road, arrived out of breath and still no sign of him.

"Duffy." I called again.

Where would he go? Panic threatened. I forced myself to be calm and think.

Last time I'd seen him was just as he disappeared around the corner of the house on the west side. Then it hit me.

Garrison Cove!

Why hadn't that thought occurred to me before I ran all the way up here? Still gasping for breath, I headed back past the house and around to the path we'd used before. We'd walked down to Garrison Cove with Jaycee. Maybe he remembered the way and took himself for a swim. He did love the water.

I hurried out onto Garrison Cove Road and paused at the bottom of the hill to glance over to the wide green lawn that ended at a pebbly stretch of beach. Just in case he took a detour. No dog in sight.

Still hurrying, I didn't notice the man lying on the ground with his head under a beat up old pick-up truck until I almost tripped over his legs.

"Sorry," I muttered, still in a hurry.

In a move more fluid than I'd have believed possible, his head appeared, and he glanced up at me and grinned.

His smile took my breath away. It was the most captivating smile I'd ever seen on a man. He was probably the hottest guy I'd ever seen short of on a movie screen. But I didn't have time for civil greetings, however handsome the owner of the smile and the physique was.

"Sorry," I said again, shaking myself out of my rapt fascination. "I'm kind of in a hurry. I'm looking for my dog who ran . . ."

"You mean, this guy?" Super Stud leapt to his feet and opened the door of the truck. Duffy stuck his head out, tongue lolling, ears perked and tail thumping against the truck's cracked old upholstery.

"Duffy." I tried to sound stern, but I was too relieved to make it stick. I wrapped my arms around his neck and hugged him hard.

"I hope he wasn't bothering you," I said when I released the dog, and he hopped down onto the pavement. I almost said I was sorry a third time, but that was getting old.

"I love dogs. He was just trying to help, but I was worried he might get hit if a car came by, so I stuck him in the truck until I could figure out where he belonged."

"Well, he belongs at Murray House," I said, wishing I'd thought to grab a leash in my mad dash to track the wanderer down. "Can I give you a lift somewhere? If your truck isn't working, I mean."

"That's my truck," the man said, pointing to a polished, and obviously well-cared-for, wrecker parked in a driveway just beyond the old pick-up. "I was trying to decide if I should tow Larry's heap back to the shop or if I could fix her here."

"Oh. Well . . ." Not sure what to say next, I started to turn back toward home.

"Sam Phillips." Super Stud, held out his hand. "And you are. . .? Other than new in town?" Then he glanced at his hand, yanked it back and fumbled in his back pocket before producing an equally grimy rag.

"I'm Kenzie," I said reaching to shake his hand despite the grease.

"Any relation to the Murrays?"

"No. Just a friend. Margaret Murray Shaw was one of my college professors, and then we became friends. She left me the house in her will." I had no idea why I revealed that bit of news, but in a place this small, it wouldn't be news for long anyway.

"My condolences. I heard she passed recently." He scratched his head and looked back at the old truck. "I guess I better get this thing hooked up and take 'er back to the shop. It was nice meeting you. See you around. And you too, you rascal." He bent to ruffle Duffy's ears.

"Come on, Duffy. Time for breakfast." Reluctantly, I turned away. Sam Phillips had work to do even if I could look at him all day and not be bored.

Just before I reached the path cutting through to Murray House up on the hill, I heard my name called and turned to see Sam grinning from the driver's window of his wrecker. He held something toward me between two fingers.

I walked over to the wrecker and reached up to take his offering.

"My card. In case you ever need a tow, or a tune-up. I'm good with anything that runs and most that don't. My shop is just over the bridge on Orr's Island. Stop in some time. Bring the rascal with you."

Then he saluted and put the wrecker back in gear, continued up the hill toward the main road, and disappeared out of sight.

A part of me wished my car would refuse to start. Sooner rather than later. I laughed at that thought and headed for the house.

CHAPTER EIGHT

Sam Philips – Present Day

Sam rummaged through the layers of paper on his desk, hunting for the bill he knew was due, like tomorrow, or maybe yesterday. The one he should have paid the day it came. Once a bill was open or handed to him with a delivery, he tended to toss it on the stack in his In-basket where it more often than not, got forgotten. Thank heaven most of his creditors were as laid back as he was.

But forty-eight was too young to be forgetting things. At the rate he was going, he'd forget his own name before he hit sixty.

"Damn-it" he muttered, going through the stack again.

"Damn-it what, Boss?" His newest employee, Jack Grey, leaned into the office, both hands braced against the doorframe.

"Can't find the bill for that last delivery of oil filters."

"Ever think of getting a little more organized?" Jack came in and plopped into the only other chair in the room.

"And when is that supposed to happen? In between AAA call-outs for stranded vacationers and keeping Larry's truck running until he gives up driving?"

"It has been kinda busy lately," Jack agreed. "Good for me, since it got me this gig. Maybe you need to hire an office manager, while you're at it."

Sam sat back and stared at Jack. The kid might be onto something. "Got any suggestions?" Pretty much everyone he knew that he'd trust to take over his paperwork was already in the workforce. And folk from up Brunswick weren't all that excited about driving way down to the end of Orr's Island, especially in the winter, for a part time job. That's all it would be. Part time.

"My sister would have been great at it, but she's getting married and moving to Portland." Jack shrugged, out of ideas.

Sam began the search a third time, and this time, got lucky. "Got it." He pulled the crumpled invoice from under an empty pizza box.

Jack got up to leave.

"Did you come looking for me for a reason?" Sam set his checkbook down when it occurred to him that Jack hadn't come just to commiserate about the lack of organization on Sam's desk.

"Oh, yeah. I need next Saturday off. For my sister's wedding."

"Not a problem. Have fun." Since Sam wasn't on the guest list, he'd forgotten about the wedding. More non-residents swarming all over his island. Just what he needed.

"Maybe you should put a help wanted sign up at the General Store?" Jack suggested as he disappeared back into the shop.

That kid was a keeper. Good at thinking on his feet and not needing Sam to direct every move he made. Unlike Ed who Sam kept on only because the man was doing his best to raise two kids on his own and couldn't afford to lose his job. Ed was capable of just about anything that needed doing around the shop, but if Sam were called away on a tow, he'd come back to find Ed tipped back in a chair napping rather than looking about the shop to see what else needed doing that Sam hadn't specifically told him to do.

That thought led to thoughts about Becca. He missed her something fierce. The loss of his wife Tansey three years ago had gotten easier to bear and there were whole days now he didn't think of her until he climbed into his empty bed at night. But his baby girl had gone off to college this fall.

UNH wasn't that far away, but he'd hoped she would choose Bowdoin so he could at least see her on the weekends. Instead, she'd chosen the University of New Hampshire and had blossomed into a busy coed so quickly he doubted he'd see her before Thanksgiving.

Sam shook off his melancholy and picked up the checkbook. Then, he scoured the desk for any other unpaid invoices he might have missed and a pen to go with them.

"Headed home, Boss. Unless there's something else you need," Sam's oldest employee, Paul Garrison, announced as he hesitated outside the office door.

"Nope. See ya tomorrow."

"Right," Paul replied and disappeared the way Jack had just a few minutes earlier.

Sam stared at the usual mess of his business affairs and considered Jack's suggestion, then turned to his computer, booted up Word, and opened a new document.

HELP WANTED – Office management experience required with some accounting skills. Part time. Call . . .

Sam hesitated. Should he put the garage number or his cell? Or both? He ended up choosing the number for the garage, then hit print.

The result was kind of bland. Not very attention getting. Too bad he didn't have his daughter's graphic skills. He enlarged the Help Wanted until it filled the whole top of the page, but the rest of the ad didn't even go half-way to the center of the page.

A thought hit him, and he jumped to his feet, hurried out to the street, and pulled out his cell. He took several shots of his garage that included the new sign he'd commissioned just a month ago. Then he crossed the street and angled to get his shiny wrecker into the shot.

Back at his desk, he air-dropped all the shots onto his laptop and tried inserting them between the help wanted and the rest. But then, what if all the reader saw was the garage and wrecker? They might think he needed another mechanic and stop reading.

He rearranged the photo so office experience and accounting skills were one over the other and both above an image of the new sign over the shop door.

That ought to do it. He hit print.

Still too plain. Then he remembered the neon paper his daughter had left at the house. A quick trip to fetch that, another printout and finally he was satisfied. That bright green should grab attention and didn't dull the red of the sign too much. He printed off a dozen more. He'd figure out the money later. He knew he could afford part time help even at top dollar per hour. Especially if it got him away from the desk and out in the shop doing what he did best.

Sam climbed into his blue Ford 150, tossed the printouts on the passenger seat, and fired up the engine.

He thought about the dog he'd met that morning. Sleek, black fur. Longer than a lab. What kind of dog had it been? Maybe he should get a dog of his own to make up for the missing daughter. Well, nothing would make up for Becca, but a dog might fill the enormous empty hole in his life and house.

Or maybe he needed to find an excuse to run into the dog's owner again. She was a looker. At least a twelve on a scale of one to ten. But it was more than her looks, or the sexy figure only half hidden under an oversized t-shirt. There was something about her that intrigued him. The smile, maybe? Or the classy attitude. It was not just because she was a new face on the island. He'd spent the summer meeting new faces and been pursued by several vacationing ladies who might or might not have had anything more than a summer fling on their minds. None of them had made him regret giving them the brush off. But Kenzie Ross? She was different.

Maybe he'd take off a little early tomorrow and go for a run that just happened to pass by Murray House. If the dog was outside, that would be a great way to get himself introduced again. But that was tomorrow. Right now, he had signs to hang. From the Devil's Back Trail head to Land's End on Bailey Island. Might as well hit both islands.

He ran out of signs long before he ran out of island, so he stopped at the shop and printed more. Then back on the road. With the last of his bright green signs stapled to the last board or pole where people might notice them, Sam felt sure if there was anyone on either island looking for work, he'd be inundated with calls before quitting time tomorrow.

Then it was home to his vast empty house to fix some dinner.

A sleek black head greeted him at his back door and his heart took a leap.

"What on earth are you doing here?" He asked the dog. "Your mistress is going to be frantic with worry." The dog thumped his tail against the bare boards of Sam's back porch.

Sam had checked the collar that morning looking for a number, but there had been none. Just a Virginia license tag and a rabies tag. But now Sam knew where the dog belonged. It would have been nice to call the woman and put her mind at rest, but that couldn't be helped. This was the very opportunity he'd been pondering a way to arrange. He returned to his truck with the dog on his heels. The dog jumped up as easily as he had into Larry's old clunker.

Ten minutes later, Sam pulled up in front of Murray House, thankful to see a RAV with Virginia plates parked just ahead of him. At least she wasn't off hunting down the dog leaving him with no way to reach her.

"Come on, Dog." The dog's name came to him just as Sam's boots hit the dirt. "Time to go home, Duffy." Duffy pranced ahead of him up to the porch, clearly proud of himself. "I didn't know matchmakers came with four paws and fur," Sam muttered to the dog as he reached up to rap on the door. "But I'll take it."

The pretty woman he'd met that morning answered his knock.

She gazed at him in puzzlement. "Uh, hi!" Then she looked down and her face registered surprise. "Duffy, get yourself in here," she commanded holding the door wider.

"You might want to consider a dog trolley or putting in an electric fence if you're planning to stay long," Sam suggested from the doorstep, having not been invited in.

Kenzie was stunning, even with a frown clouding her face. "I don't understand."

"Not sure when you last saw him, but when I got home after running errands, I found him on my doorstep. On the next island up. Three miles from here."

Now horror colored her expression. "Oh my God!" she exclaimed. "I had no idea he was even outside. Someone must have let him slip out when I wasn't paying attention. How can I ever thank you for bringing him home? You, um . . . want to come in for a drink?" She glanced behind her as if she might be in the middle of something.

Sam hesitated. He wanted to get to know her better, but maybe right now was not a good time. "How about a date?" he suggested.

CHAPTER NINE

Eleanor Murray - 1942

The sun beat down with uncharacteristic heat for this time of year on Bailey Island, Maine. Eleanor set the hoe down and grabbed the corner of her apron to wipe her brow.

Jeff would have helped break ground for this new Victory Garden if he'd been here. But he wasn't. And he hadn't written either. Two whole months and not a single word. She didn't even know if he was still in the United States or already shipped out.

Her wedding dress had hung in her room, the hem still not finished for over a week after Jeff left in such a rush. Eleanor hadn't been able to bear to look at it any longer, so it had been carefully packed away in layers of tissue and the big box tucked into the back of her closet for the day Jeff finally returned. Now, every time she opened her closet the box reminded her of what hadn't happened. As if the box could talk, she kept hearing the whispered words, *He's not worthy of you,"* so Eleanor finally carried the box up to the attic. The whispers had stopped and she decided they had just been in her imagination. As if her father had manifested himself in whispers, since that was the opinion he repeated the most often when they spoke of Jeff and her aborted wedding.

Eleanor straightened her apron and reached for the hoe, picked it up and started working a new row.

"Eleanor?"

She whirled around at a familiar male voice calling her name.

Her brother's best friend, Mike Hamilton, stood halfway between her garden and the porch steps leaning on a cane. Even though his grandparents lived down the street she was surprised to see him. Mike and Eleanor's brother had gone to Canada ages ago, determined to learn how to fly and get into the war long before the United States got involved.

"Your father said I would find you out here. He suggested you might want help getting your garden started."

Eleanor dropped the hoe and flew to envelop Mike in a hug. "Mike! What happened?" Then realized he might hurt in more places than the cane would suggest and dropped her arms to stare at him in concern. "I didn't hurt you, did I?"

Mike smiled. A lovely smile that had once made her heart race a little faster, back when she had a teenager's crush on a dashing older man. If she was honest, his smile still tugged at her heart even if she no longer had a thing for her brother's best friend. He was just Mike. A good guy who could always be counted on.

"That welcome was worth everything. Even if I'd ended up on my butt. Although that would have been more than a little embarrassing. Especially when I had to ask for your help getting back to my feet."

Eleanor glanced at the cane, then back to his face. Now she saw the strain there.

"I can finish this later," she declared. She leaned the hoe against the shed. "Let's go sit on the porch and I'll get us some lemonade. You can tell me everything. Have you seen Ray lately? Is he okay? How did you get hurt?"

Mike laughed. "A glass of lemonade would be nice. And sitting on the porch is probably what my doctor would have ordered. If you're sure you are done here. Then I can answer all your questions."

Eleanor fired more questions at him as they made their way to the porch. She knew she was babbling and not giving him a chance to reply, but she was trying not to watch his labored progress. Trying not to stare, but wanting to notice if it appeared he might need help.

Out of the corner of her eye, she watched him grab the railing and pull himself up the short flight of stairs. She hurried to pull a rocker closer and urged him to sit. "I'll be right back," she told him as she hurried into the kitchen to get the promised lemonade.

A few moments later she returned, carrying a tray with two tall frosty glasses and slices of bread spread with jam.

"The lemonade isn't like we're used to since sugar so hard to come by. I used honey. I hope that's okay. And the jam is from before the rationing began." She set the tray on a small table within his reach and took a chair on the other side. "How did you get hurt?"

"My plane got shot down." Mike made a gesture with his hand, like a plane aimed at the ground and falling fast. "Actually, the plane got shot at. Our pilot was a magician who managed to get her far enough away from the Jerrys before he had to put her down. It was kind of a hard landing, though. So, I'm out of the war."

"I'm so sorry," Eleanor responded with sincerity. How hard that must have been for a man who wanted so much to be in the action. "Is Ray okay?"

"Last time I saw him." Mike smiled. "He visited me in the hospital a few times before they shipped me stateside. He's too tough and ornery to get hurt. He loves flying. Loves his job shooting at the Jerrys."

Ray would love shooting at anything, but Eleanor remembered well his determination to get to Britain as soon as possible so he could get started on the enemy. Pearl Harbor hadn't been bombed yet when Ray and Mike headed off via Canada to fly with the RAF.

"I heard Jeff is on his way to join the fighting," Mike said, clearly more comfortable now that he was sitting with his cane propped against the railing and a cool drink in hand.

"I'm . . . I'm not sure where he is," Eleanor answered honestly. "He promised to write, but so far there haven't been any letters."

"Don't hold that against him, Eleanor. There may be letters in the mail, but they all get censored before going onward. Might even be more than one on its way."

"I listen to the radio every night," Eleanor admitted. "But everything all sounds so positive. Like nothing bad is happening and Hitler is going to be defeated at any moment. I keep hoping that's true and Jeff will be home again. Maybe even in time for the wedding we had planned for June."

"Yeah, well, the news gets censored, too. The Office of War Information is very strict about what can be reported and what can't. Don't get your hopes up."

Eleanor abandoned her glass and leaned toward her brother's friend. Her friend, too. If there was news to tell, he would share it. "Tell me what is really going on. What it is like? For you and Ray, anyway. Did you get to see your parents at all?" Eleanor tried for patience as Mike downed the rest of his lemonade, his face a mask of indecision. "Everything. Tell me everything," she encouraged.

"Everything? That could take all morning."

"I've got all morning," Eleanor replied. Her victory garden could wait until tomorrow.

Mike launched into a description of the mansion he and Ray and their fellow airmen had been billeted in and the English countryside they drove through on the rare times they could borrow a car. Eleanor felt sure he glossed over the danger of flying, considering he was here only because of that danger. She'd learned enough to know she'd have been terrified if she'd been in those big unwieldy bombers with nimble little German fighters spitting machine gun bullets at her.

"I did get a chance to see my folks a few times, but they were in London, and I was out in the country."

"I saw Bertie just last week, but he didn't mention that you'd gotten hurt." Maybe the news had been kept from Mike's little brother and sister.

"He didn't know. My parents knew, of course. No keeping it from them. But they didn't want my grandparents and the kids to worry so they kept the news to themselves."

"That explains it, then." Eleanor nodded. Then she thought of Mike's little sister. "I rarely see Ruthie. I guess I should have made more of an effort to stop and visit."

"She's doing as well as can be hoped. Grams is teaching her at home since they don't know what to do with an almost blind child at the school. And Ruthie is happy. That counts for something." Mike's face took on a thoughtful expression.

"I met a man at the train station while I was waiting for my train to come home. He was completely blind and he had a dog that helped him move about. It was the most amazing thing to watch."

"A dog?"

"Yeah. A dog. Not just an ordinary dog, though. He wore a special harness with a handle for the man to grasp. I asked about it and the man said the dog had been specially trained. The dog even knew how to help the man cross a street with automobiles moving about everywhere. I was quite impressed."

"Maybe that's what Ruthie needs," Eleanor said, thinking how wonderful it would be for the little girl to move about without having to wait for her brother or her grandparents to help her.

"I don't think they train them for kids," Mike said. "But, you know, I'm going to have a lot of free time on my hands before I get to go back to work. I'm pretty good with dogs. Maybe I could teach one good enough to help Ruthie."

Mike had always been good with dogs. Eleanor remembered the tricks he taught his dogs. He'd even managed to teach Ray's impossible beagle to come when called. Something Ray had never been able to do once the dog had the scent of some animal and was off on the chase.

"Would you teach your grandmother's dog or get a new puppy? Old man Thatcher's dog had a litter and he's giving them away," Eleanor suggested. The whole idea fascinated her.

Mike glanced at his wristwatch and began to get to his feet. "I've got to get moving or Grams will be sending out a search party. She's convinced I can't get around on my own and sooner or later, I'm going to have a disastrous fall."

"I should walk you back down the hill." Eleanor jumped to her feet as well.

"Please. No. Don't let Grams convince you I'm an invalid." He reached to pull her into a brief embrace. Then grabbed his cane and headed for the stairs. "Thanks for the company and the bread and jam and the hint about Thatcher's puppies. By the way, the lemonade was lovely with honey in it. I think I like it better than when it's loaded with sugar."

Eleanor forced herself to remain at the top of the stairs while Mike made his way down the short flight and then across the unclipped lawn to the lane. She wanted to help but he clearly didn't want help. So, she waited until he turned to wave, put a smile on her face and waved back.

She watched him limp out of sight, then went to retrieve her hoe. That victory garden wasn't going to plant itself and she'd already lost half her day chatting with Mike.

"It was nice to see Mike again," Eleanor's mother said after grace had been said and their evening meal served.

Eleanor's father beamed. "Sure was. A mighty fine man, that Mike Hamilton. Good family, too. A wounded veteran . . . we need to make him feel welcome here any time."

"He saw a dog that was trained to help a blind man in New York," Eleanor said, ignoring her father's far too obvious intent to supplant Jeff in her life with a husband of his choosing.

Her father grunted as if a dog was too unremarkable to spend any time discussing, so Eleanor let it drop and dug into her potatoes. When supper was done, she hurried to clear the table and do the dishes.

For once, Eleanor did not want to sit around the radio with her parents. According to Mike, it was all sugar-coated anyway. Maybe tomorrow a letter would come from Jeff, and she'd learn more. Then she remembered what Mike had said about letters being censored. Tonight, she would write Jeff a long letter and include the promise she'd failed to put into words during his last minutes with her. Or maybe she wouldn't.

What if he was so caught up in patriotic fervor that he'd forgotten all about her?

CHAPTER TEN

Kenzie Ross - Present Day

"How about a date?" Sam Phillips asked.

Surprised at this request in answer to my question, I looked up from hugging Duffy. The man turned down an offer to come in for a drink and moved strait to asking me for a date.

Mr. Hotness had his head tipped to one side, very much like Duffy when I spoke to him. My breath caught in my throat. I wasn't ready for the dating scene. Not sure I would ever be ready to trust my heart to a man again after Garrett's defection. But Sam stood there, head tipped, waiting for my reply.

I had to admit, I'd asked an open-ended question. Not just thank you more than I can say, but how can I thank you? I'd left the thanking up to him and he'd asked for a date. Now what?

What if he was married? No way did I want to be the other woman and it seemed hard to believe that a guy as good looking as Sam would be unattached. Unless he was gay. But he had asked for a date with me so that wasn't the answer.

"We could make it something that Old Duffer here could come along, too." Sam offered when I remained speechless, trying to think of a graceful way to say no.

This suggestion sounded a little safer. As opposed to a candle lit dinner for two. My heart rate slowed a few notches. "What did you have in mind?" I asked, buying time.

Buying time for what, I wasn't certain. Time to find a tactful way to say no? Or time to find the courage to accept?

"Bet you haven't been to Fort Popham yet. Even if you aren't into history, the beach is nice, and Duffy could go with us this time of year and have a good romp on the sand as well as a swim."

That sounded harmless enough. A trip to a historic fort and a beach in October in Maine. I wouldn't even have to put a bathing suit on a body that definitely needed a little work. I was tempted to ask why he wanted a date at all. Maybe he was between relationships? I wasn't exactly between, but maybe we had something in common. The man had the patience of a saint while I dithered. One attribute in the plus column. I caved.

"Sounds like fun. When?"

"My other tow driver is off for his sister's wedding, so I've got to stay local on Saturday. Does Sunday work for you? I'm ushering at church in the morning, but we can take a picnic with us and go for a late lunch."

Sam squatted down to ruffle Duffy's fur. "I bet you like to swim. Huh?"

I stifled the snort that rose to my nose. "Like to swim? Is this a trick question?"

"Good. I'll bring a ball and a frisbee while I'm at it." He pressed his forehead to the dog's head." Sound good to you, boy?" Then he stood. "I better be going. I've got an early start tomorrow. I'll pick you up around noon on Sunday." He touched two fingers to his temple and turned away, then turning back, he pointed at Duffy. "And no more unauthorized exploration."

He was almost to his truck when I thought about my part in the projected outing. "Can I bring the picnic?" I called to his retreating back.

He turned around, hesitated a moment, then shrugged. "Sure. I'm good with anything I don't have to fix myself."

A couple minutes later, he was pulling out onto the road, and I was left wondering what possessed me. I was not ready for another relationship however engaging and hunk-worthy the guy. I needed to learn how to be my own person before I even considered a new relationship. But maybe Sam just wanted to be friends. This time the snort made its way to completion. Any guy I ever knew was not looking for friendship from a woman. Most of them didn't even believe such a thing existed.

But it was only a picnic. He wasn't asking for more . . . yet. So, I'll go just this once and then find a way to explain to him where I was coming from and where I wasn't interested in going. Hopefully, without going into all the embarrassing details.

I closed the door and fell to my knees to hug Duffy again. "What's gotten into you, running off all the time? Am I doing something wrong?" His tail thumped but that didn't answer either of my questions.

"You aren't trying to play matchmaker, I hope."

My phone began vibrating in my pocket. I stood and pulled it out to glance at the popup window and see who was calling.

Jaycee! Did she have ESP or something? She had encouraged me to get back at Garrett by finding someone new as soon as possible.

"Hey," I said after tapping to answer the call.

"What's new?"

"You've been gone for less than a day. What could be new you don't already know?" I headed for the kitchen to put the kettle on for a cup of tea.

"For starters, have you met any of the neighbors yet?"

Sam wasn't exactly a neighbor, so I skipped over that bit of news. "A lovely woman who lives down near the cove. She was swimming if you believe that. It's nearly October and the water is like ice, but there she was floating around with a pool noodle. I had goosebumps just watching her."

"You'll have to toughen up if you're going to go through with plans to move there, which I'm kind of torn about. I mean, the place is awesome, and I want you to find your new niche and all. But on the other hand, I won't get to see you any time I want. Virginia and Maine aren't exactly a short hop away from each other. How's Duffy doing?"

Unexpectedly, I found myself relating his unaccompanied explorations of our new neighborhood and meeting Sam Phillips. I stopped short of relaying the information about our 'date.'

"Ah-ha! I smell a new man in your life," Jaycee chortled.

"He's not a new man in my life."

"Well, he's not a new woman. Is he a stud?"

"Jaycee!"

"Well, is he?" she persisted.

"You're impossible, you know that, right?" I couldn't help the laughter that bubbled up. I was going to miss having Jaycee living close by as much as she professed that about me. "Yes, he's a stud. The *studliest* guy I've ever met."

"I want pictures."

I could picture Jaycee pumping the air with her fist. "I can't exactly whip out my phone and just start taking pictures of the guy. How awkward would that be?"

"You'll find a way," she said with assurance. "Description please."

"Jaycee." I sighed. She was not going to give up so I might as well give in. "He's about six feet tall, give or take. His dark hair has long bangs that keep falling into his eyes. And those eyes! Jaycee, they are the bluest eyes I've ever seen on a man. Or a woman for that matter. A smile full of very white teeth that were either perfect to begin with or saw serious orthodontia. A bit of scruff. Just enough . . ." I almost said just enough to leave evidence if there was any serious kissing, but stopped, shocked at my own thought. "He also has this habit of tipping his head to one side like my dog does. Very endearing."

"Oh, my racing heart," Jaycee squealed. "I can't wait to meet him."

"I just met him, for Pete's sake. Give it a rest. I only gave you all the details because I knew you wouldn't shut up until I did."

A heavy sigh greeted this. "Okay. So, about the house? Are you going to keep renting out parts of it to supplement income or what?"

My turn to sigh. "I don't know. I'd rather not have a stream of strangers sharing my space all the time."

"Which would only be in the summer, though."

"True," I agreed. "Which means I need to find a job if I stay here. Maybe just part time." Then I recalled the agent's suggestion. One, I think she offered reluctantly because it would mean less income for her. Or no income. "Donna, that's the agent for this place when it's renting out, had an idea. She thought maybe I could advertise for a roommate, or two."

"Just don't rent out my room. I plan to visit as often as Vance will let me."

I promised to keep *her* room available for her, and we chatted for another twenty minutes while I fixed my tea and found a comfortable chair. When she hung up without pestering me about Sam again, I settled back and sipped my tea while I studied the empty fireplace across from my chair.

I wondered if it had been used anytime recently. Or if the chimney was even reliable. If I was staying, and I was more certain with every passing day that I was, I'd want the option of a nice cozy fire come winter. Another thing I'd willingly given in to was Garrett's decision to install natural gas in the big fireplace in the home he'd inherited from his grandfather. It was pretty and did add heat to the room, but there was no crackle to it, and no scent of burning wood. It had felt fake to me, but I hadn't complained.

This was my house and this time I was determined to make my own choices.

Then my mind drifted back to the roommate idea and Jaycee's insistence on keeping her room free. I'd also need to set aside a room or rooms for Liam and Luke. They might be returning to their dad's house in Virginia most of the time they weren't staying on campus. Virginia was where they'd grown up and where their high school friends were. But I was their mom, and I hoped that meant they'd want to spend time with me sometimes. Maybe they'd even opt to look for summer jobs here in Maine. I'd been told that dozens of places were open only in the summer and relied on college kids for staffing. Perhaps the bunk room off the front landing would work for them.

Being in a whole new place removed some of the pain of my empty nest but being a mom had filled my days for over eighteen years. The void was impossible to overlook. And the ache even harder. I thought of them as I fixed breakfast for one every morning. And again, when I threw out leftovers. There had never been leftovers to toss in a house full of teenage boys. Books, jackets, discarded sneakers, and empty pizza boxes didn't litter my new space and there were never piles of damp towels or the stink of sweaty clothes in the bathroom. Strangely enough, I missed all the things I had looked forward to not having.

My phone buzzed again and this time I answered without checking the screen.

"Hi Mom." Liam's breezy voice greeted me, and I was flooded with warmth. It almost seemed like everyone important in my life had a direct line to my thoughts lately.

"Hey, Liam. How's college?"

"This is the most awesome city, Mom." He went into a lively discussion about all the new places he'd discovered on his runs through Boston but then, he got to the reason for his call. "Anyway, I'm calling because I wondered what you were doing next weekend."

"Nothing much," I replied. "Why? Do you need me to drive down for something? It's not parent's weekend or anything, right?" How could I have missed an event like that at orientation?

"Nope. I need to check out your new place. Aunt Jaycee told me all about it, and I want to see it for myself. I can catch a bus as far as Brunswick. I already checked it out. I don't have any Monday classes so it can be a long weekend."

"Send me the bus schedule and I'll pick you up."

"Will do. Gotta go. Love you, Mom."

The moment he clicked off, I remembered I was supposed to be going to Fort Popham with Sam on Sunday. Now what?

Chapter Eleven

Kenzie Ross - Present Day

I was sitting at the breakfast table staring at my phone and trying to figure out the best way to call off my date with Sam when a text popped onto the screen.

Looking forward to meeting Sam.

How on earth did Liam find out about Sam? Jaycee! It had to be her. She was the only one I'd mentioned him to, but even she didn't know about the promised picnic on Popham Beach.

I picked up the phone and started to reply, but stopped, not knowing what to tell my son. Finally, I tapped out, '*What makes you think he'll be around while you're here?*'

'*Invite him over for supper.*'

Really? Was Liam trying to fix me up, too? What about Garrett? Surely Liam owed some allegiance to his father.

'*Dad has that bimbo U deserve better.*'

It was getting scary how everyone seemed to be reading my mind lately. I had to admit, at least to myself, that part of me couldn't help feeling a certain satisfaction that my son did not approve of his father's actions or the new girlfriend.

'I'll ask,' I replied.

'ETA 7:15pm 16 Station Ave Brunswick'

He'd known my next question before I'd asked. And remarkably, had even provided the address. My son was growing up. Well, growing more mature, anyway. The twins had grown up some years earlier and both now towered over me.

'Can't wait' – I followed that with a kissy emoji.

'L8R' –Liam wasn't into emojis.

I waited to see if there was more, but when the phone remained silent for several long seconds, I decided that was all I could expect for now. Time to get to busy on my day.

Two tasks loomed. I needed to stock up on groceries and I still needed to honor one last wish for my dear friend, mentor and the woman who'd left me this place to make a fresh start.

"Hey, Duffy. Let's go for a walk. Maggie would want you along." The dog didn't need to be invited twice when the word walk was involved. He already waited at the door by the time I collected the container holding Maggie's ashes and his leash.

I tucked the pretty green urn into a tote and we set off. Maggie hadn't said where exactly, only that she wanted her ashes scattered in the sea on Bailey Island. The Giant Staircase would have been a grand place for a send-off, but given the wind today was out of the east, I opted for a less exposed site. Then I recalled the little path that cut through the spruce trees at the edge of my property and ended up on the shore. I tucked the leash into my pocket and let the dog lead the way.

Duffy trotted off as if even he was into reading my mind. I still had a lot to learn about dogs and what motivated them. Or if they could anticipate their owner's intentions.

Abruptly the trees ended, and I followed Duffy onto a small pebbly beach that curved along the edge of the shore. Perfect, I thought.

Duffy ran to the water's edge, but for once didn't immediately plunge into the waves breaking gently around his paws. Did he have a hint that we were there for something more serious than a romp in the water? He watched as I opened the container, intent in a way I'd never seen him before. Surely there was no way Maggie's scent could still cling to the remains I scooped out.

"To the best friend either of us has ever known," I told the dog as I flung a fistful of ashes out over the glistening water.

I thought of all the times this woman had been there for me, from my floundering days as a freshman in college, through becoming a supportive wife, then a good mom and finally learning to let go as my boys grew more independent. Despite never having had kids of her own, Maggie had always seemed to have wisdom to share that I'd come to rely on and now missed. I had to wonder what her advice would have been had she lived to learn of Garrett's defection.

"Wuuff," was the soft reply from Duffy. I swear, this dog could sense what I was thinking as accurately as Jaycee and Liam had last night.

It took longer than I'd anticipated, but Duffy was patient throughout, watching each new handful of ashes scatter to the breeze and fall into the sea. Once our task had been accomplished, I squatted beside the dog and wrapped my arm around him. "We were lucky to know her, right?"

He stared out over the water for a long moment, then back at me. For a few more minutes, we stayed close; I remembering Maggie over the years, Duffy with whatever doggy thoughts were going through his head. Then I stood with a sigh. I prayed this had been the farewell Maggie had imagined.

Just as I was about to turn away from the water, the approaching howl of a pair of military jets came out of nowhere, followed by the roar of the engines as they flew directly overhead and disappeared as quickly as they had come.

"How's that for a send-off, Maggie? Not everyone gets a flyover."

Duffy, head tipped as if questioning the unexpected sight, watched the line of trees for a full minute before glancing up at me. Another long minute and without even considering a swim, he headed back to the path through the trees.

Part way up the hill a smaller path branched off that I hadn't noticed on our way down. I hesitated. I had things to do, but then decided to check it out anyway.

Just twenty feet in, this new path ended in a small clearing surrounding a huge old tree. A thick bed of colorful leaves covered the ground, and they crinkled underfoot as we approached the tree. A smile tugged at my lips when I noticed all the carvings in the tree. Some with hearts wrapped around initials. Lovers from years ago, judging by the age of the carvings. I let my fingers trail over some of them. Peter loves Priscilla. HS & JM forever. Emmet and Lily. Ray and Lisa. G & D. So many couples who had declared their love for each other over the years.

Some were newer, but none really recent. Perhaps this little clearing had been forgotten? Or maybe I was intruding on private property. Duffy circled the tree, then found another spot to leave his calling card. I had other things that needed looking into today, so reluctantly, I whistled and headed back to the main path. Duffy passed me quickly to take up the lead once more, his black tail waving like a happy flag.

Back at Murray House, I waited while the dog slurped at his water dish, then called him to follow me up to my room where I offered him a chewy treat. I collected my purse and shut the door behind me to make sure my wandering companion stayed home while I was away this time. Then I headed out to my car.

I didn't mind the cost of picking up a few odds and ends at the general store on the island, which would save the twenty-five-minute drive when all I needed was a quart of milk, but with Liam coming for three days and a picnic to prepare if I didn't cancel the date with Sam, I needed to stock up.

I needed to call Sam and either cancel or ask if he was okay with having Liam along. How would he feel about that? Miffed? Maybe. I had already been planning to let him down easy over the whole idea of dating so maybe this was my way out. Most guys aren't eager to get involved with a woman who has baggage. Of course, most of my baggage wasn't as obvious as Liam who wasn't the real reason I wasn't looking for a new relationship.

As soon as I had successfully navigated the bridge onto Orr's Island, I started looking for the candy store I'd seen mentioned in the booklet of area places of interest provided by the leasing agent for visitors to Murray House. Liam had a giant sweet tooth, which, to be fair, he inherited from me. The Island Candy Company appeared on my right so abruptly, I was lucky no one was behind me when I hit the brakes. It was a cute little place with grey shingles and bright blue shutters. A small, fenced garden sat off to the left with black-eyed Susans still blooming brightly along with something that looked a little like lavender, but paler. I'd have to ask what it was. Maybe I'd plant some in my own new yard. I wanted my new place to be an overflowing cornucopia of flowers for as much of the year as possible.

Another small statement of personal resolve. Garrett had insisted on tidy, but bland, landscaping without flowers of any kind. Even this late in the year, every house I'd walked by on my daily walks with Duffy had been surrounded by colorful bushes and flowers. Some homes had little paths to the street bordered by narrow gardens with roses. Some had hydrangeas of every hue nodding their heavy heads around the foundations. I imagined forsythia and lilac in the spring, and maybe roses like the hardy ones that seemed to thrive here as well. Anything with lovely scents to share when they bloomed.

But that was a project for spring. Right now, I had to make this stop quick and then get my shopping done. As I approached the shop, I spied a notice board and stopped to peruse the various bits of paper tacked on it. A neon green page fluttered in the light breeze. The bright color and the flapping sound caught my attention.

Help wanted. Part time. Wasn't that what I'd told Jaycee I might need to look into? And it involved office management and bookkeeping. Just what I'd been doing for Havelock's Treasures for the last ten years.

I pulled my phone from my pocket and took a picture of the notice to capture the information so I could call and ask about the position later.

The rich aroma of chocolate that enveloped me as I entered the candy store was worth the stop even if I didn't purchase a single thing. I stopped to inhale, and a woman glanced up from whatever she was busy with at a table behind the counter.

"Let me know when you're ready," she said and went back to her task. She was probably used to visitors to the island taking their time studying the shop before choosing what to purchase.

In addition to candy, there was a table in the middle of the small outer area with cookies and other baked goods on display. But even more eclectic, was the collection of handcrafts and books arranged on shelves mounted on all the available wall space. Earrings made of sea-glass, notepaper designed by local artists, tote bags with Orr's Island scrawled on them and dozens of other trinkets. Also by local artists, or so I assumed, were small paintings and framed photos. Mugs, and even a small shelf of books that appeared to be mostly about the local area.

I was drawn to the books, as usual, and found two right off about Bailey Island that I knew I had to have. I tucked them under my arm and then nabbed a pair of earrings made of sea glass and headed to the candy counter.

The lady dusted her hands on her apron and came toward me.

"You actually make the chocolates right here?" I asked, gesturing to her worktable.

"We do." She smiled. "You're new to the islands?"

I told her about inheriting The Captain Patrick Murray House which provoked a hearty welcome and the hope I'd enjoy life on an island and my resident ghost.

I shook my head. "I'm not sure I believe in ghosts."

"You will if you meet her."

I began to wonder about the stories people told. Was my supposed ghost friendly or scary?

Then the candy lady glanced at the books under my arm. "Just the books and the earrings? Or . . ." she let her words trail off.

"Can't come into a candy shop and not buy chocolate," I replied and pointed to the array behind the glass counter. "How about a one-pound box. No, make that a two-pound box and surprise me with a little of everything."

As she was filling the generous box with chocolates, I wandered back to the shelves and found a mug I decided I should have. No logo or images, just a generous sized mug of royal blue tinted with lighter blue and then brown along the rim. Signed by the artist who had created it along with the year. The current year. It seemed appropriate for me to drink my coffee or tea from a mug made locally in the year I found this place.

Back in the car, I couldn't set the box aside without sampling at least one. I ended up choosing two, then placing the box behind me on the floor where I wouldn't be tempted to just keep sampling. Next it was off to the place everyone called Cook's Corner to stock up on groceries.

Then I remembered the help wanted sign. I opened my phone and brought up my photos, noted the phone number and tapped in the numbers.

"Hank's," A cheerful young voice answered. The sound of hammering in the background made me wonder what kind of place Hank's was.

"I'm calling about the help wanted ad?" I needed to stop making it sound like a question and more like I knew what I was doing. "I would like to make an appointment for an interview."

"Hang on. I'll get the boss." The phone must have been a heavy old desk model judging by the thud of what had to be the receiver hitting a solid wood surface. A moment later the same cheerful voice returned. "The boss says to stop in any time. He's here all day. You know where we are, right?"

"Sorry. I'm new around here."

He rattled off an address, hesitated and added, "just north of the candy shop on the left." Then, the phone went dead.

"Well, wasn't that handy," I muttered as I set my phone down and backed up, ready to head out.

Mr. Cheerful's added info was spot on. A long low building with a sign on the roof that read 'Hank's Garage' was less than a football field north of the candy shop. I pulled past the open bay doors and parked under the overhanging limbs of a big spruce tree on the far side. The heady scent of spruce hit me as I exited the car. Another lovely aroma that infused my new world.

As I approached the building, I noticed a glistening red tow truck. A very familiar red tow truck. The coincidence made me shake my head, and I was already wondering if the "Boss" might be Sam Phillips. I hesitated. Maybe I should just go shopping and skip this idea. Would it get awkward if I was working for the guy I planned to dump after telling him I wasn't interested in a relationship?

Another snort erupted from my nose. I didn't even have the job yet. I knew next to nothing about repairing cars. I was always just thankful my car was smart enough to tell me when it needed service, and when to take it to the dealer. But it was worth checking out. Someone once told me that every interview, even for a job you're not keen to land is a practice for the one you really want.

I headed for the pedestrian door.

CHAPTER TWELVE

Sam Phillips – Present Day

Someone kicked Sam's shoe to get his attention. "That lady that called? She's here. I took her to your office."

"Thanks," Sam replied wheeling out from under the car he'd been working on. He hoped the state of that office wouldn't scare the woman off before he even got to meet her. He went to the big sink at the side of the shop and lathered up his hands. Even the stiff brush wouldn't get all the embedded grease out, but it wasn't like he'd be holding hands with her. He dried them off on a clean shop rag and headed for his jumbled office.

This can't be the woman about the help wanted ad, Sam thought when he strode in and saw Kenzie Ross standing by the single dingy window, gazing out at the street.

"Hey, Kenzie," he said crossing to the business side of his desk. "Old Duffer give you the slip again? Need help tracking him down?"

Kenzie wheeled around at the sound of his voice. She grinned and shook her head. She had the nicest smile, he suddenly realized. Of course, he'd noticed how pretty she was before, but that 100-watt smile was something else. His heart did a strange little jig.

"No. The escape artist is home alone, in my bedroom where guests can't let him out by mistake." She gazed at his cluttered desk, then around the equally cluttered office before returning her gaze to his. "I came about the ad someone put up at the candy shop."

"I hope this craziness didn't change your mind," he offered, bending to sweep a pile of car parts catalogues off a chair so she could be seated. "Have a seat and tell me what kind of experience you have with organizing chaos."

She perched on the edge of the chair like the dirt on it might soil her sleek grey slacks. It probably would. Maybe he should just offer up the cleaning bill and be done with it.

"I've been an office manager most of my working career. All small offices, though. Nothing big or formal. I've pulled things together for a boat builder who had no office staff before he hired me. I'm guessing you haven't had anyone whose only job was keeping the office organized?" She perked one eyebrow up with that query. Even that was cute.

"Not for a long time. I've been pretty much it and I suck at . . . sorry about the language. I'm not very good at this sort of thing. My mom used to keep order for my dad, but they are both gone now."

"I'm sorry for your loss," she said.

"Been gone awhile," he muttered back. "So, are you up for a challenge? Have any experience with bookkeeping? By the way, you'd be allowed to bring Duffy to work with you. The guys would love having him around."

As would he.

"My last job, one that recently uprooted itself and moved to Dallas, which is partly how I ended up here in Maine and looking for employment, involved keeping their books. I was in charge of inventory and billing as well."

"Perfect. When can you start?"

"I, uh, don't suppose there are any benefits." She frowned.

"Not many," Sam reluctantly saw the chance of her wanting the job slipping away. "I do offer a Simple IRA plan. You open the IRA and I contribute a match to your deposits. But we aren't big enough for a health plan. You'd get all your car maintenance for free, though."

Her smile flashed again. "That would be helpful. What about salary?"

Sam fished around in the clutter of his desk for the scrap of paper he'd done the math on to see how much he could afford. "I was thinking part time when I put up the ad, but since then have begun to wonder if it would be more hours than half time, or perhaps even full time eventually. So, I thought maybe thirty-five an hour to start and if, once you get busy here, it turns out full time, then seventy-five K a year?" How much might she have been earning where she came from? Was his offer an insult?

But she nodded her head. "Sounds perfect." She stood. Interview over. And he hadn't once mentioned their date, if you could call it that, for the following Sunday.

"I'll get a cleaning crew in over the weekend so you'll feel more comfortable in here, and you can start on Monday?"

"Monday," she said agreeably as she moved toward the door. Then she turned back. "About Sunday . . ."

Sam's stomach sank. She was going to squash that hope even before it got started. But he waited for her to finish before blurting out something he'd later regret.

"My son called from college. I haven't seen him since I dropped him off in August and he wants to come up for the weekend. I forgot all about our picnic to Popham when I told him I'd pick him up at the bus station downtown on Friday. It's kind of an imposition, but would you mind awfully if he came along?"

She fidgeted with the pleated fold of her slacks. Good to know he wasn't the only nervous one in the room.

"Not a problem. I look forward to meeting him. What time will he need to be back at the bus station?" This might be the shortest, most chaperoned date in his life.

"Monday morning," she replied, looking relieved.

"It's a deal. Popham Beach on Sunday. Then you can start work here after dropping him off at the bus." Sam held out his hand. She took it, totally ignoring the grime.

He watched her walk across the lot. A walk as captivating as the smile. Her ride was a fun, bright blue Rav4, with roof racks. He wondered if she ever carried anything on them.

Where had she said she came from? Or maybe she hadn't said. He couldn't recall. But those racks would be good for skis up here in Maine. If she didn't already know how to ski, he could teach her.

But Damn! He was getting ahead of himself.

Already his first attempt at a date had been turned into a family affair. Too bad Becca wasn't home for the weekend.

Maybe he'd lost his touch over the years. He hadn't dated since Tansey died, and they'd been high school sweethearts married less than a month after his discharge from the Marines. He was totally out of practice.

Kenzie had been hesitant when he'd first asked for a date. That had been ballsy to start with, and he'd been as surprised as she appeared that he'd asked. But she'd agreed. There was hope.

CHAPTER THIRTEEN

Eleanor Murray – 1943

Turning over her garden this year was far easier than the first time. It was early still, but she had plans to have peas ready to eat by the 4th of July which her mother assured her was a traditional goal. Despite the March chill, Eleanor began to feel hot in the thick pullover that had been Jeff's and she stopped to pull it off. Her father would have been angry if he caught her wearing such a garment, but he was away. Eleanor liked it because wearing it made Jeff feel closer.

"Hey, Eleanor. Need any help?" It was Mike Hamilton. If she hadn't been engaged to Jeff, her high school crush might have risen from the ashes in the months since he'd been discharged and come home to Bailey Island. Her father was all for just such a match, but she'd promised Jeff. At least in her heart, she had promised to wait for him. But Mike was a good man, and she enjoyed his company.

She mopped her brow with the sleeve of her flannel shirt and considered the man still waiting for her reply. The cane was a thing of the past now, his stride confident. She wondered why he hadn't found a woman to pursue. He was a handsome man that half the girls on the island would be happy to go out with if only he showed an interest. But he hadn't so far as she knew.

As soon as he'd been physically up to it, he had been hired to do detailed carpentry work for a local contractor. In his free time, he seemed mostly focused on training up the pup he'd gotten from Mr. Thatcher to serve as a guide dog for his little sister. Once the idea of giving his baby sister some independence was in his mind, he hadn't let go of the possibility.

Eleanor suddenly realized she had been staring and Mike was giving her a quizzical look. Doing her best to ignore the bangs that fell so attractively across his forehead, now that the short military clip had grown out, she asked the first question that came to her mind. "How come you're not at work today?"

"Finished up the work at Widow Toothaker's yesterday. We don't start on the new barracks for the Harbor Defense station until Monday. Which leaves me with a few free hours to help you."

A year ago, the first observation tower had been built in response to the sighting of a German Submarine off the coast. Those towers and the buildings to house the men stationed here were important to the defense of the country. Eleanor knew Mike chafed at the turn of luck that had put him out of the fighting early on, so he must be excited about this new job.

"Maybe you should be turning over your own victory garden." She leaned on her hoe. "I bet your grandmother would love to have fresh vegetables and cucumbers to pickle."

"I beat you to it. Got the ground turned over last weekend and Gram's planting seedlings in a little hothouse thing I made for her. Have you heard from Jeff lately?"

Eleanor sighed. She didn't like to admit that she hadn't. His first letter home had been mailed before he even left the states but that one hadn't arrived on Bailey Island, Maine until six months later. It had been brief and disappointing. Another had arrived almost a year to the day after he'd left and had been mailed from Ireland. That one had been all about how wonderful the Irish people were to the American soldiers. And even more discouraging was his description of the pretty red-headed daughter of the family he'd been billeted with at the time. She jealously wondered if he'd told Bridget about his fiancé waiting for him back home.

Maybe a letter would come today, Eleanor had promised herself on waking that morning. But so far, the postman hadn't been by.

"Ruthie wanted me to invite you to her birthday party," Mike said, pulling Eleanor from her resentful thoughts.

That brightened her mood. "I'd love to. When is it?"

"Saturday. Gram said to ask you to stay for dinner, too. I'll walk you home afterward if it's all right with your parents."

Eleanor's father would approve anything that might sway Eleanor from her allegiance to Jeff in favor of Mike. "I'm sure they will be fine if I stay. And I'd enjoy spending time with your family."

And she would. Bert was one of the funniest kids she knew and Ruthie was always smiling despite her disability. Mike's grandmother, who had insisted, since Eleanor was just a child, to be called Grams, was a warm, loving woman, the kind Eleanor wished her own grandmother had been. Her mother's mother had been gone since Eleanor was a baby so she never knew her, and her father's mother was such a strict disciplinarian with no tolerance for children that she'd been a difficult woman to love at all.

"With that settled, can I help you with the garden, now?"

Before she could answer, her mother called from the porch.

"Eleanor? Did you forget it's Victory Knitting Circle today?"

Eleanor groaned. At this rate her garden would never be ready to plant. But warm socks and scarves were important for their men fighting in Europe.

"Coming, Mama." She turned back to Mike. "Thanks for the offer, but as you can see, I've apparently other things I need to be doing for now."

"Better be getting cleaned up then," Mike said making shooing motions to the house and reaching for the hoe. "I'll put this away for you."

"Thanks." With one last wave she headed for the house.

Eleanor was sure she was the youngest woman sitting around the room at the First Parish Church. Most of the women her age had moved in with relatives in Brunswick, Bath or even as far away as Portland or Boston, and taken factory jobs left vacant by the men who went off to war. Eleanor wasn't so fortunate. Her only relatives not on Bailey Island were all the way down in New York.

Even Priscilla had moved away. Married to her Peter, who had landed a residency in Boston, she'd left just before Christmas. Priscilla wrote glowingly of her new city. She loved everything about it, even the machine shop where she'd learned how to run a drill press. The loss of her closest friend left Eleanor stuck sitting with a gaggle of women who talked about things from long before her time while everyone knit socks and scarves as their way to help with the war effort.

Eleanor heard far more about the Great War in these knitting circles than she'd learned in school. And most of the women were convinced the current war was nothing like the last.

She held up the sock she was fashioning and made a correction to turn the heel. Then went back to ignoring the chatter all around her and thinking about Jeff. She wondered if he had been given a warm pair of socks to wear. Perhaps she should knit a pair just for him and mail them off.

Finally, the endless afternoon drew to a close, and the women bundled up their work. All the completed pairs of socks were turned over to the Red Cross lady who was in charge of passing the goods along.

Eleanor's mother stopped to chat with friends outside. Like they hadn't been talking non-stop for the last three hours. But thankfully, their chatter gave Eleanor a chance to escape and hurry home.

Her heart lifted when she noted the mail truck stopped halfway to her home. Maybe. Just maybe. She hurried faster, determined that if there was a letter from her sweetheart, she'd collect it and retreat to her room before her father got back from Brunswick.

She flew up the long slopping lawn to her home, flung open the door and hurried to the table in the hall where mail was always left, if they had any that day.

A single very thin envelope sat square in the middle of the table. Who might have collected it and set it there? Her name was printed large in handwriting she didn't recognize.

She dashed up the stairs and down the hall, shut her bedroom door behind her and flung herself on her bed.

She studied the unfamiliar hand for a long moment, refusing to admit the dread tugging at her heart. Then she slid her finger under the sealed flap and opened it.

She'd seen the thin airmail paper that folded into its own envelope before. Jeff's letter from Ireland had been like that. But this didn't bear an Irish stamp. Instead, the word V-mail was printed across its front and the letter bore a stamp with a big V on it.

Curious, Eleanor finally turned to the letter itself. *My dear Eleanor,* it began, still not in Jeff's handwriting. But no one else called her My Dear Eleanor.

What a wonder this new style of mail is. They handed out these forms for us to compose our letters home on. I am told that they reduce all the letters onto some kind of magical film that will hold hundreds of letters. Then the films are sent home via aeroplane so that our thoughts will get to our loved ones much faster. Someone in the states will read the letters off the magic film and transfer them to paper again. I should feel embarrassed that someone will read my words to you, but I am not. I am just happy that I am finally able to keep my promise to write in a more timely way.

I cannot tell you where I am at present, but so far we have not seen any action. They tell me it will grow warmer soon. I pray they are right about that. You cannot begin to imagine what it is like to sleep rolled up inside a dirty poncho with nothing more than a thin wool blanket to keep me warm in a tent crowded with equally chilled soldiers. Makes me wish I was back in Ireland with Bridget's family. At least there I was warm.

I am running out of room so must end this letter.

Yours, Jeff

Yours! What happened to Love? Jeff must be afraid to say love because someone else would read the letter before transcribing it for her. Was the only reason he wished to be back in Ireland with Bridget and her family was for the warmth? He was so eager to be in the action.

Eleanor closed her eyes and clutched the letter to her bosom, wishing it could make Jeff feel closer. But his words had been so different. It had to be the new way of communicating. She would knit those socks and send them off as soon as possible so he would know she was thinking of him and perhaps his next letter would be more affectionate.

Chapter Fourteen

Kenzie Ross – Present Day

Three days wasn't going to be enough. I'd only picked Liam up twenty-four hours ago and it seemed like we'd gabbed almost non-stop but still hadn't caught up to the last time we'd been together. Which struck me as odd considering that before I drove him to Suffolk in August, he'd been out with friends most of the time and even when he'd been at home, we had both been busy with other things.

Only a week after he and his brother had gone off to college, I'd been in the grocery store listening to two mothers going on about how glad they were that school was back in session and the kids out of their hair. I'd wanted to grab them both and give them a good shake. Please, I'd wanted to beg them, don't wish these days away because you'll never get them back.

I guess we all need to learn the hard way. Or maybe it's just the nature of life. Kids grow up and leave home, but before that happens both they and you are so busy with the everyday stuff of life that you don't notice the weeks speeding by and the opportunities to be in the moment with each other slipping away.

Until they are gone, and you realize how much you miss the busy, day-to-day small stuff.

Whatever the reason, I was determined not to hurry through even a moment of this unexpected visit. Liam had been as drawn to the shadowy, cobwebbed attic as I'd been, but his big find had been a trunk of old jigsaw puzzles.

"These must be worth a mint," Liam exclaimed lifting each new puzzle from the trunk he'd shouldered down two flights of stairs to the big living area with the fireplace.

"How do you know they are worth a mint?" I asked.

"My new roommate is something of an expert on puzzles. At least, that's what he claims. His uncle is in the business. These are made by Par, and Skip tells me they are worth buckets."

"If they are antiques, should we still be putting them together?" I asked as he dumped the pieces onto the card table he'd set up under one window.

Liam shrugged. "Puzzles are made to be put together. Besides, would you sell them?"

He had a point.

Duffy came over to sniff at the old box top when Liam dropped it on a chair.

"You want to help?" Liam asked the dog as he scratched Duffy's ears.

Liam had been as excited to meet Duffy as he'd been to check out Murray House. On his first evening, Liam had taken Duffy to the cove to retrieve tennis balls from the water, and this morning he'd taken the dog along when he went for his daily run. My boys had missed out on the companionship of a dog growing up, I realized. Another loss because I'd caved to Garrett's decree. I smiled at the sight of Liam now, one hand still on the dog's head as he hunted for edge pieces. Tomorrow, we would all be headed to Popham. I just hoped that trip would be as fun as today had been.

Relaxing in a bright red canvas beach chair Sam had provided, I watched Sam and Liam toss a frisbee back and forth. At the start, Duffy had done his best to snatch the frisbee out of the air before it got to its intended target, but he'd finally grown tired of that game and come to settle beside me.

Watching Sam and Liam made me both a little sad, and happy at the same time. I might not be ready for a romantic relationship, but Sam was turning out to be a very pleasant friend to spend time with, and it made me happy that Liam liked him, too.

But I was sad as I reflected on the fact that Liam and Luke had never experienced this kind of free time sport with Garrett. It was the sort of thing sons and fathers should enjoy together, but Garrett had always been too busy with work, or too bored by little boy activities when they were younger. That had turned into two teens that were too busy with their own things to find time to spend with their father.

Garrett had only himself to blame. But watching Liam hoot and holler with glee when he had Sam diving into the sand to make a catch or Liam snatching a sailing disc from the air that Sam had done his best to make uncatchable, made me realize it wasn't just the companionship of a dog that my boys had missed.

Worrying about how today would work out had been a waste of my emotional energy. They'd hit it off almost from the moment they shook hands, chatting about the Red Sox's failure to make the playoffs, followed by the chance of the Patriots pulling their season together in the weeks still left to play. I enjoyed both sports, sort of, but I didn't know all the players, their weaknesses and promise, so I was mostly silent on our drive north while they argued all the finer points.

The old Fort at Popham had been as fun to explore as Sam had promised. I found it hard to imagine that anyone ever believed a fort would be needed to protect Maine's capital against a Confederate invasion, but perhaps the folk in power in Washington at the time had a better appreciation for Lee and his abilities than depicted in history books. Eventually, even Liam had tired of exploring the fort's many nooks and crannies and we'd retreated to the beach where Duffy had headed straight into the water.

I let a hand drift down to Duffy's now half dry fur. He briefly lifted his head to glance at me, then returned to his nap.

"Hey, Duff," Liam said plopping himself down next to the dog and wrapping an arm about Duffy's neck. "You guarding the picnic? Or did you eat it all up on us?"

Duffy's tail thumped on the sand as he came instantly back to life to greet his new two-legged brother.

"Get your appetite worked up yet?" I asked, ruffling Liam's hair in a way he'd have shirked off just a few months earlier, but now seemed willing to tolerate.

"Famished," he replied dragging the hamper over and lifting the lid just enough to peek inside. "Nothing for you, you beggar," he told the dog. "Oh, wait. I lie. Mom packed a snack for you, too." With that, he flipped the lid open and withdrew a plastic dog dish and a baggie filled with kibble.

"Do we get kibble, too?" Sam asked joining Liam on the blanket.

Liam made a show of studying the contents, then one by one lifted out the containers I'd filled with fried chicken, slabs of watermelon, and brownies. Laying them out on the blanket and giving the dog the command to leave it, he tossed a bag of taco chips into the mix. "Drinks are in there," he told Sam, pointing at the cooler holding down the corner on Sam's side of the blanket.

Chatter was minimal as we all dug in and enjoyed the feast along with the increasingly colorful sky.

"We're on the wrong side of the peninsula to see the sunset," Sam observed when I commented on the changing sky.

"Well, it's pretty anyway," I said.

"Not as pretty as my view," Sam replied.

Liam gave Sam a swift glance, then wagged his eyebrows at me.

I Ignored both and bent my head to take another bite of chicken.

Once back at Murray House, sated with sun and play, Liam decided we needed to relax in front of a fire. Thankfully, I'd been able to reach the agent who had confirmed that the chimney had been cleaned and the fireplace safe to operate. The little printed sign above it stating the opposite had been put in place so renters with no idea how to build or tend a fire safely wouldn't end up burning down the historic old house. With that news, my son had snagged my car keys and took a quick trip up to the general store to purchase a bundle of firewood.

Now he flicked a lighter and touched the flame to his careful construction. The tiny flames licked their way through the kindling and began to spread. After that well laid start, the first of the seasoned logs caught and Liam rocked back on his heels. "Am I good, or am I good?"

"You are better than good." It was so nice to have him home, even for just a few days and even if it wasn't the home he'd grown up in. "I'm glad you had the idea and made me call Donna. I thought about it last week, but never followed up."

Liam eased back to lean against the ottoman, elbows on his knees as the fire grew. Once satisfied that the fire was going well, he closed the mesh curtain protecting the rest of the room from sparks that might escape and smolder on the carpet or old wood floor. Then he came to sit on the couch with me.

"You better find a place to get a whole load delivered, cause I'll be back and I love being able to have a real fire in the fireplace." Apparently, Garrett's gas insert into the fireplace in his old family home hadn't been popular with his sons either. "I'd stack it for you, if I was here," Liam went on, "but I bet Sam would do it." He turned to wink at me.

"Just what makes you think Sam wants to stack firewood for Murray House? He's got his own place to keep supplied and cared for. And a garage that seems to be busy and in demand."

Liam grinned. "I saw the way he looked at you. Maybe you didn't notice, but if that's the case, you're blind."

I didn't know how to answer that. I had seen Sam looking at me with a gleam that seemed to go beyond friendship. I just wasn't ready to admit it. Or perhaps it was that I wasn't ready to let myself care. Added to that was the oddly disconcerting issue of my son not only noticing but commenting on it.

"Look, Mom. You deserve to have someone as nice as Sam care about you. Dad's an ass. Sorry, I know he's my father and I love him, but he's still an ass and the way he treated you was just not right." Liam shocked me with this insight.

"It takes two to make a marriage work," I replied. "Maybe I was too busy with everything else and didn't give your father the time or consideration he deserved."

"Bullshit," Liam spat. "You might have been busy with me and Luke, but we're your sons. And Dad's. Half the time you were making up for what he wasn't doing that other fathers do. When did he ever attend any of Luke's basketball games? Or my track meets? Did he ever go to a school affair? If he did, I was too young to remember it. And stuff like with Sam today? Dad never came out to the yard to toss around a football. You know what not going to any of your kids' things tells the kid?" Liam lifted his brows and waited for me to comment.

"I don't know, Liam. What does it tell the kid?" I honestly had never given the issue much thought as I navigated through the ups and downs of raising two active boys with little input from my work-obsessed husband.

"It's not about a parent liking the sport, or marching bands or the plays their kids are in. It's about caring about the kid. Or at least not caring about us kids as much as he did about his job. If a parent doesn't care enough to go and cheer them on, then the message the kid gets is that their mother or father doesn't care about them." He said this with gritted teeth and drawn brows. "I know Dad loves us in his own way, but that way didn't translate itself to us growing up. He didn't even make time to visit our choices of college and have input into our decisions. So, don't tell me what you do or don't deserve. You were a great mom. You're still a great mom and you deserve someone like Sam."

Astonished at Liam's bald assessment of his father's failings, I couldn't think of an appropriate reply. While I was still processing, Liam launched himself my way and pulled me into a bear hug, rocking me back and forth for several long minutes before setting me free. Then he went back to the fireplace to add another log before speaking again.

"Luke and I talked about it. We know it hasn't been that long since you separated. And we know this, being here, in this state, in this house . . . it's a whole new life for you. New job even. Yeah, I heard about that, too. I just don't want you to wish away what might happen between you and Sam because you think it's too soon. Or any other stupid reason."

I was still being blown away by my son's wisdom. Only eighteen and yet he had a better grasp of what I might be going through than I'd stopped to consider myself. I'd just been surviving until this moment. Trying to make lemonade from the lemons I'd been dealt. But perhaps I should stop thinking of them as lemons and start calling them blessings.

Beginning with my old boss freeing me from the only remaining commitment that would have kept me tied to my old life in Virginia. Then there was the legacy Maggie had left for me in this wonderful old house that fit my spirit better than Garrett's ever had.

Duffy wandered in from the kitchen, sniffed at Liam's hands, then plopped down, set his muzzle on Liam's feet and faced the fire.

Even Duffy, my new furry companion. Ironically, the blessing that had introduced me to Sam in the first place.

"Promise me, Mom." Liam wore a stern look of determination. "Promise me you won't shut any doors you'll wish you'd walked through later."

"I promise," I said softly. Realizing the biggest blessings of all were my own boys. They would always be my babies, but they had grown into young men that had somehow become my champions and grown wiser than I could have ever imagined.

Chapter Fifteen

Kenzie Ross – Present Day

On Liam's last day, I found him out on the lawn staring up at the roof.

"What are you looking at?" I asked as I joined him. I craned my head back to look up, wondering if I'd see some enormous bird perched on my roof or maybe it had been another flight of aircraft that had caught Liam's attention.

"Why is there a fence on the roof?" my son asked pointing to the elaborate white fence that enclosed the widows walk.

I hadn't been up there, but the agent had explained about it during our first tour of the house. "It's called a widow's walk," I informed Liam. Then I repeated Jaycee's recital from the book she'd purchased about the history of the island.

"Back in the days of the tall ships, when a ship went out to sea, no one was really sure when it would return until the sails became visible on the horizon. No one is really sure why widow's walk, but some surmise that wives who waited for their sea-going husbands, waited in vain and became widows. You want to go up there?"

Liam was already headed for the house with Duffy on his heels. "Where are the stairs? In the attic?"

I hurried after the two. "It's a hatch that opens in the upstairs hall. At least that's what I was told. I haven't even explored all the attic has to offer yet so haven't tried the hatch."

Liam scrambled up the stairs and by the time I arrived, he had a fold-down set of ladder-stairs opened into the hall by my bedroom door and was already halfway up them. Even Duffy seemed eager to check out the new territory and had braved the odd new contraption with his nose glued to Liam's leg.

The sound of something heavy scraping against wood was followed by a flood of sunlight streaming in from what had to be the door to the widow's walk. Liam's legs disappeared and Duffy followed, leaving me to pull myself together and climb up after them. Heights were not one of my favorite things and I usually avoided ladders whenever possible.

My bravery was rewarded when I stuck my head above the opening and got my first glimpse of the view. Liam stood in the center of a surprisingly spacious deck that had obviously been kept in good repair, one hand on his hip, the other shading his eyes.

"Awesome!" He dragged the word out as he turned slowly to take in the full three-sixty view.

I joined him, equally amazed. "How far out into the ocean do you supposed you can see?"

He shrugged. "Miles. I bet. And those old ships had really tall masts and big square sails. You'd be able to see them first before the ship appeared. Maybe even hours or a day before the ship arrived at the harbor."

While Liam and I continued to take in the extraordinary view, Duffy sniffed along the perimeter of the fence that surrounded the decked area.

Liam moved to where the dog seemed to have found a particularly interesting scent and squatted beside him. "What ya smelling, Boy? Some lady from a hundred years ago?"

I snickered. This place has been kept in good repair. Any scent from a hundred years ago has been washed away a long time. Or painted over. But even as I said the words, the fur on Duffy's neck began to lift. He didn't growl like he usually did when his ruff lifted, but he cocked his head as if he was listening to something we couldn't hear.

"He's communing with your ghost," Liam said with a laugh.

"There are no ghosts," I repeated the opinion I'd shared with Jaycee.

"Believe what you want, Mom. But I'm not so sure. Besides, wouldn't it be fun if a ghost did live here? I wonder who it might be?"

"According to the tales people have been repeating for years that your Aunt Jaycee read in a book, her name is Anna Rose Murray, and she's been watching for her husband's ship, her namesake, the Anna Rose, to return since sometime in the early eighteen hundreds."

"That shit slaps," Liam said adding a hearty slap to his knee before standing up again.

I wasn't going to call him on his language. I'd heard worse. And if he wanted to believe there was a ghostly presence in my house he was welcome to it.

He did another slow turn, taking in the view, then looked at his watch. "Guess we should get going or I'll miss my bus."

I followed him over to the open hatch and waited while he held Duffy's collar so the dog could descend without falling. As I descended, I looked back at the hatch. "How do you close this?"

Liam let me step off the stairs before he climbed halfway back up. I watched while reached for a big brass handle and carefully lowered the heavy door.

"Latches with these," he said as he slid the bolts home on both sides of the hatch. "Just pull down on the handle while you close them. There's some kind of weather stripping that keeps the rain out, but you have to tug on the door before the latches work."

"Good to know." I wondered how often I might have a desire to go up there. I certainly didn't want any of my tenants doing so and risking a fall for which I'd be liable. Maybe I needed to add a lock. At least the ceiling hatch was on my side of the house.

Liam scurried off to grab his gear and I went to collect my purse and car keys. I'd enjoyed every minute of his visit and all too soon he'd be gone back to Suffolk.

Once he'd learned that Liam's return bus to Boston wasn't until four in the afternoon, Sam had amended my start day to Tuesday. He'd added that dress was casual to downright informal.

So, here I was. First thing Tuesday morning, dressed in Jeans with Duffy still damp from his morning swim, staring at the open bay doors of Hank's Garage. I sucked in a lungful of air and let it out slowly, taking a moment before plunging headlong into my new job.

A young man crossing the bay looked up, saw me and waved. Then he called out to Sam. A moment later, Sam appeared.

"What are you waiting for? I hope it isn't that you're reconsidering?"

"No," I stalled, not answering his question. "I was wondering why it's Hank's Garage and not Sam's." I got myself in gear and headed in. Duffy was less formal, first trotting, then galloping towards Sam, his tail a happy flag.

"Hank was my dad," Sam said glancing up at a sign that appeared to have had a recent coat of paint. The rest of the garage was a peeling color that might once have been blue. Or maybe grey. "Didn't seem right to change the name after he retired. It was still his garage. I just ran it. And then he was gone, and I didn't want to change it."

"Does that extend to not painting it now and then?"

Sam laughed. "No. I just haven't had time. Or let's say I haven't made the time."

"I'm good at painting stuff. Not pictures, but furniture, houses, rooms. That kind of thing and I enjoy it. Maybe once I get your office whipped into shape, I'll paint the outside." I astonished myself with this bold offer, but it was too late to take it back now.

Sam just nodded. "That would be great, but you're assuming that my office isn't going to take you months to undo the tangle I've created from my mom's careful work. Ready to get started?"

With that, my first day on the job at Hank's began. After Sam introduced me to the basics, he left me to it and disappeared back into his shop with Duffy on his heels.

I didn't have time to feel like my dog had changed allegiance, though, because the dog stopped just outside the door, then turned and came back to sit by my feet and look up at me. I thought about the old dog bed Maggie had installed next to her desk. Maybe that's what Duffy was remembering as well.

"We'll go buy you a dog bed for this office since you'll be coming with me every day." I told the dog as if he understood my every word. He thumped his tail as if he agreed. "How about for now, I go get your old blanket from the car?" Another thump.

I trotted out to my RAV with Duffy on my heels, grabbed the old, paint-stained blanket I'd spread across the back seat to keep the upholstery from getting ruined, and returned to my new office.

Not sure where to start, I sank into an ancient wooden desk chair that had seen a lot of rough use and studied the cluttered space. Duffy curled up on the blanket and closed his eyes. At least he knew where to begin, but sitting in the remarkably comfortable chair wasn't going to get anything accomplished. I sighed and got to work.

"Wow!"

I looked up to find Sam on the threshold.

"Wow, what?" I asked. Hoping he was just commenting the cleanliness I'd managed to achieve and not the fact that I'd rearranged everything.

"Looks amazing," he muttered moving into the room, absently patting Duffy's head when the dog got up to greet him. "Mom would approve."

I sagged with relief.

"But you should have called for one of us to help move stuff. Those file cabinets weigh a ton. Never mind the desk."

"I cheated," I admitted with a grin. "I borrowed that little lift thingy in the corner outside the door."

"Still," he said taking another turn around the reorganized office.

I'd decided to move things for two reasons. The first was that I liked having the desk where I could see out the window as well as into the shop. Also, the new setup left more open space, which made the place feel less cluttered.

"I still have to organize the files and I hope you won't mind if I get a few things from Staples for the desk."

He hauled out his wallet, extracted a credit card and handed it to me. "Get whatever you need." Then he nodded at the blanket Duffy had patiently spent most of his day curled up on. "Get him a proper bed while you're at it. This cement floor gets cold in winter, and it's always hard."

"Thanks," I said, taking the card.

"Ed's headed up to the Gurnet to get us some sandwiches for lunch. I know this was supposed to be part time, but if you're going to be here much longer, he can bring something back for you, as well."

I considered the time, then asked for a lobster roll. It would be a while before I'd had my fill of fresh Maine lobster. Then, it was back to work. I finally knocked off around three, deciding I needed more than a few pencil stubs and a stapler that only worked if you smashed it with a closed fist before I tackled the filing cabinets. The trip uptown for office supplies and Duffy's new office couch took up the rest of my afternoon and it was something of a relief to pull up to Captain Patrick Murray's beautiful old house with time to relax a bit before having to decide what to fix myself for supper.

Then I noticed the familiar car with Virginia plates parked in the space I'd claimed as my own and Jaycee sitting on the bottom step of my porch grinning at me.

"What are you doing here?" I spilled out of the car and hurried to hug her.

"Vance had a little business trip, and I decided I wasn't eager to rattle around my big old house alone. I hope you kept my room free like I told you to."

"The last of the fall leaf-peepers are gone. You have your pick of any room in the place," I told her as she followed me across the porch.

"Leaf-peepers?" she asked as I unlocked the door.

"That's what the locals the bus-loads of retired folk who come north to see the changing foliage."

Jaycee laughed as she parked her suitcase by the stairs. "Be back in a flash." And she disappeared back out the door. A moment later she returned with a box, it's lid folded shut.

"I brought you a present. Call it a housewarming gift." She pointed toward the kitchen island.

I dropped my purse on the counter and accepted the box. It was heavier than I'd anticipated, and I nearly dropped it, but Jaycee shot out a hand to help guide it onto the counter next to my purse.

"Open it," she commanded. "I'm ready for some of it now."

I pried the folded lid open. Nestled in a sea of foam peanuts were three items wrapped in white paper and a bag of chewy dog treats.

Duffy, having given Jaycee a thorough sniffing, came over to inspect the box. I took the treats out, opened the bag and gave him one. He carried it over to his bed by the fireplace and flopped down with his prize.

Then I carefully withdrew the next item and unwound the paper.

"Oh, Jaycee. You didn't have to," I gushed. "But I love it."

A gracefully shaped vase was hand-painted with tall tapering clusters of florets on long stems. Some pink, some purple, some white and several shades in between.

"They're called lupine," Jaycee informed me. They grow wild and cultivated and the lady who sold me the vase said they blossom everywhere in the spring."

"Now I can't wait for spring," I said turning the vase around to see all sides. "I wonder if there are any out in my yard?" I'd have to ask around. Maybe Evelyn knew.

"You can put any kind of flowers in the vase, but from what the woman told me lupine itself would be too tall for anything short of an umbrella stand. Grows like this tall." Jaycee held her palm out about chest high. Then she gave my shoulder a nudge. "Open the other ones."

I set the vase on the table and reached for another wrapped package, this one square. It turned out to be a set of stemless wine glasses with the word LOVE etched on the side. Except the O was the outline of the state of Maine. Good choice. I was falling very quickly for my new state.

"And the next," Jaycee urged, removing the box of wine glasses from my hands.

A burble of laughter greeted the last unveiling. Jaycee's favorite brand of grenache wine.

With that, she reached into the box and handed me the wine bottle opener I'd missed. "About time. I thought you were never getting home, and I'd have to sit out on your veranda in the dark drinking the whole dang bottle by myself."

Chapter Sixteen

Eleanor Murray – 1943

Eleanor sat on the floor watching Ruthie and her friends, wishing she lived in this household rather than her own. The Hamilton home was only half the size of the Captain Patrick Murray House and everyone shared a bedroom, but the love and warmth made up for the cramped quarters. Eleanor knew her parents loved her and her brother Ray, but they never showed it. Even her mother was rare with expressions of caring.

Mike's father and mother were currently living in England, and had been there for almost three years, working at a busy hospital in London. Ed Hamilton was a doctor and Beverly a nurse. Both had answered what they felt was a calling, coming to serve in a capital torn apart by nightly bombings and more injuries than the London medical staff could keep up with. In their absence, Mike's grandparents had come down from Augusta to care for the house and the two youngest of Mike's siblings.

One might never guess there was a war on once one stepped across the Hamilton threshold. Somehow, despite rationing and often empty shelves at the store, Grams Hamilton had created a party to mark Ruthie's birthday that outclassed any Eleanor had ever had. There had been home-churned ice cream and a four-layer cake. Both miracles in times like these. But it was more than the food. It was the love so freely shared, the uninhibited laughter, and the welcome shown to all the young guests and Eleanor herself. No wonder her brother Ray had preferred spending his growing up years here instead of at home.

"It's so soft," Ruthie marveled brushing her latest gift across her cheek.

"Guess. Guess. You have to guess," her young friends insisted.

Unfazed by her inability to see well, Ruthie ran her fingers over the length of the knitted scarf. "That's too easy. It's a scarf. And I love it."

"Don't you want to know what color it is?" one girl asked.

"That would be nice," Ruthie replied. "But it's going to keep me warm in winter whatever color it is."

"Guess. Guess," the chorus began again.

"Pink?"

"Guess again."

"Hmm." Ruthie squinted at her scarf. "Yellow?"

"How did she do that?" another girl marveled.

"I can see a little," Ruthie explained.

"Bet you can't guess this one," another guest declared handing Ruthie a lumpy package wrapped in newsprint.

Eleanor smiled as Ruthie tore the paper off the teddy bear Eleanor had fashioned from an old fur muff and some felt she'd found in her grandmother's sewing trunk.

"Ooooooh!" all the girls marveled in unison.

Ruthie ran her hands over the body, down each arm and leg, then touched the face that had two bright shoe button eyes. "It's a teddy bear. A teddy all my own." She pressed it into a hug, a grin splitting her face.

Mike glanced at Eleanor and smiled almost as big as his sister. "Perfect," he mouthed the word.

"Hey, Rascal," Ruthie called to her dog. "We'll have company in bed at night, now."

The dog, a mongrel mix of Lab and who knew what else, had been patiently curled at Ruthie's side. He sniffed the new friend and appeared to nod as if he approved.

"That's the last one except for mine," Mike said placing a box across his sister's knees.

Everyone hovered in anticipation as Ruthie carefully sat the bear next to Rascal, untied the ribbon, and lifted the lid. Another round of Oooooooohs followed as Ruthie ran her fingers over the fabric of a pretty dress with a lace collar.

"What color, Mike? What color is it?"

"It matches your eyes, Pipkin," Mike replied using his pet name for his baby sister.

"Then it's blue. Can I try it on?" Ruthie asked scrambling to her feet.

"Of course," Grams answered. "But hurry so your friends can see it before they have to leave."

Eleanor watched in amazement as Rascal, already on his feet the moment his little mistress stood, nudged Ruthie's thigh, guiding her through the seated girls and toward a bedroom door.

"Can I help you, Ruthie?" Eleanor asked getting to her feet as well. She knew Ruthie usually dressed herself, but this was a new dress. One she wasn't familiar with, and she might not even know the buttons ran up the front instead of the back.

Ruthie nodded and Eleanor followed. It was harder to get the dress on the girl than Eleanor would have thought, given how Ruthie hopped from one foot to the other in her excitement. But eventually the dress was on and Eleanor guided Ruthie's hands to the buttons and helped her get the first one started. Once started, her own hands itched to help, but she kept them folded in front of her and let Ruthie do the task for herself. She knew the girl thrived on achieving things on her own.

"I did it!" Ruthie crowed when the last button was done. "All by myself! Out, Rascal," she commanded and the dog moved to guide her back to the main room again.

After everyone had marveled at the lovely new dress and told Ruthie how beautiful she was, they began to gather up their coats as their parents would be waiting outside to walk them home. Grams wrapped a piece of cake for each girl to take with her and soon Ruthie was standing in the doorway, her faithful dog at her side, calling out thanks and farewells.

"How did you manage a new dress way out here on Bailey Island?" Eleanor asked Mike in the lull before supper would be served.

"Mother left a few dresses behind. I just found a lady eager to earn a dollar fashioning one for Pipkin out of the material." He winked at Eleanor. "I'd have asked you, but you were busy knitting socks for soldiers. And an extra couple of pairs for Jeff."

A pained expression flashed across Mike's face, but disappeared so quickly, Eleanor wondered if she had imagined it. "Well, I think it's pretty and so thoughtful to have the buttons on the front so she can do them up herself."

"Your gift was pretty special too. I'm just amazed you came up with something so quickly. We only invited you two days ago."

Eleanor wondered if she should tell him the teddy bear had been sitting on her own bed for the last two months – ever since she'd found that old muff in the attic and decided to make a teddy out of it – or if she should just let him think she was a miracle worker. But before she had a chance to say anything Grams announced that supper was ready and everyone jostled for a seat at the table, with Rascal guiding Ruthie to her chair.

Supper was a tasty mix of leftovers and happy chatter. Eleanor enjoyed every moment. Tomorrow it would be back to the stiff formality that reigned at Murray House while her father dominated the conversation.

"Do come back again, Eleanor," Ruthie begged when Eleanor bent to give her one last birthday hug.

"I would love to come again," Eleanor responded. "You just be sure to invite me. Come summer, I just might bring you a big fat tomato from my garden."

Grams gave Eleanor a hug and echoed Ruthie's invitation. Mike waited with Eleanor's coat, ready to help her slip her arms into it before stepping out into the chilly spring air. Mike's grandfather, who spoke rarely, also came to give her a hug and a wink before Mike opened the door to usher her out into the night.

Mike offered his arm and, with only a slight hesitation, Eleanor looped her hand through it. Then they were off up the hill.

"I can't believe how many stars there are," Eleanor said to cover her sudden awareness of how close they were and how good he smelled.

Mike chuckled. "There are always a zillion stars in the sky, Eleanor. What makes tonight so special?"

Walking with Mike was what made the night special, but that was a thought Eleanor shouldn't have. She was an engaged woman, waiting for her fiancé to come home from the war. She had no business being attracted to another man.

"So, are you going to tell me about that bear?" Mike asked.

Thankful for the diversion, Eleanor told him about finding the motheaten muff in the attic and deciding to turn it into a teddy bear a couple months ago. "He's been on my bed since then, but when you invited me to Ruthie's party, I just knew where that wee bear was really meant to be."

"She's going to love it. She already does. Thank you for sharing it with her."

They reached the top of the hill and turned toward Murray House Lane. Eleanor felt totally out of breath and told herself it was the hill that made her feel that way. Not Mike's closeness, or his approval.

"Do we need another birthday as an excuse to invite you to dinner again?" Mike asked as they approached the wall along the front of Eleanor's home.

"Oh, I hope not. I had a lovely time," Eleanor replied pulling her hand from Mike's arm and moving toward the steps. "You needn't walk me all the way to the door," she said when he moved to follow her.

"Of course, I do. Grams would be appalled if I did not. I doubt your father would approve either."

Of course her father would not approve, but for a far different reason. Father would dearly like to have her tumble out of love with Jeff and into love with Mike. So, anything that might help that happen would meet with his approval. But she was already half in love with Mike.

More than just the schoolgirl crush she'd had when she was four-teen. More than just liking her brother's best friend because he was such a nice guy. She needed to stay faithful to Jeff. She hurried across the lawn and up the stairs to the porch, but Mike kept pace, so she turned once she had her hand on the knob.

"Thank you for walking me home. And thank you for the invita-tion. I had a lovely time." Before Mike could reply, or she could say anything else, she turned the knob and pushed the door open. "Good night, Mike." She stepped into the dimly lit hall.

"Good night, Eleanor. Sleep tight and don't let the bedbugs bite." Even in the gloom of the porch, Eleanor could see the white of his teeth as he smiled.

"We don't have bedbugs." She laughed, the anxious, guilty feeling fleeing. Then she closed the door and hurried up the stairs, not wishing to speak to her parents.

CHAPTER SEVENTEEN

Kenzie Ross – Present Day

Life settled into a rhythm after Jaycee's surprise visit that had included several more bottles of grenache and more ribbing about Sam. Jaycee had lobbied for an introduction that I'd tried to avoid, but given I had to work in the morning, she'd just followed me to work and camped out in the office until Sam popped his head in between jobs. I was never going to hear the end of it now. She'd been as taken with his charm as I was.

"If I wasn't a happily married woman, I'd be all over that guy," Jaycee said later while we lounged on my new porch enjoying the sunset, wrapped in blankets against the growing chill.

I'd argued that I wasn't ready for a new relationship, but she'd dismissed that excuse as nonsense.

"It's not like you're committing to anything. Have some fun, woman. You deserve it." Her words, so much an echo of my son's, hit home.

The last of the scheduled renters had come and gone until the following spring and the house was all mine. And way too big. During one of those evening sunset watches, Jaycee had come up with an idea for that as well. I just needed to decide if it could work out, or if I even wanted to try.

"Instead of summer renters and an empty house the rest of the year," Jaycee had said setting her wine glass down and jumping to her feet. She'd flung an arm out and turned to take in the house itself. "Or roommates you might or might not get along with and would still have to share your public spaces with. What if you could get someone in to renovate the back half of this place and create a couple small apartments? I bet it could be done. You could keep the great room for yourself or maybe share it. You'd have to think about that. But then you could rent small apartments to year-round residents. It would boost your income, and you wouldn't rattle around alone for nine or ten months of the year."

Ever since that night, I'd come home from work and wandered through the rooms, both my own and the rental spaces and considered her plan. I wasn't sure about making the big living room a space for everyone. I liked it just the way it was and didn't know if I wanted to share it as I'd had to with the last of the fall renters. I wanted to be able to enjoy a fire in the fireplace or the freedom to curl up in a comfy chair to read in my jammies in the evenings. I did need to find an old table somewhere, maybe on one of those online sale sites, or at an actual physical flea market, to replace the card table Liam had found for jigsaw puzzles. So many possibilities that I didn't know if I wanted to share.

Maybe I'd ask the boys what they thought when they came for Thanksgiving.

Torn about their new-found independence, I'd offered to pick them up, but they insisted they knew their way around by bus and could thumb their way down the peninsula once they got to Brunswick. They'd finally given in and agreed to having me pick them up at the bus station instead of the proposed thumbing option. As a mom, it's hard to let go of the concept that your kids need you. That they'd chosen to spend the holiday with me rather than their dad, meant more than I could put into words.

Working at a small family-owned company had been my forte in Virginia, so I didn't miss the hustle of working for a big company, and my new job was more interesting than I'd thought it would be. Sam's three employees were very different, and each, in his own way, added to the fun of working at Hank's.

I'd stopped bringing a lunch after the second day on the job because Ed always stopped to ask what I wanted from whatever purveyor of lunch fare he had chosen to visit that day. I'd stopped asking for a lobster roll and instead, just told Ed to surprise me. He knew all the places and their specialties better than I did and so far, I hadn't been disappointed.

Ed was clearly a devoted dad and most of the stories he shared were about his kids' latest escapades or achievements. Jack had a sense of humor that had me in stitches every time he took a break and showed up to pour himself a cup of coffee. Paul was quiet, but a fount of information about the islands, their history, and the residents both past and present.

I'd begun to meet more of those island inhabitants sooner than would have been possible had I found a job up in Brunswick. Half the time I felt like I knew them before I actually met them due to Paul's gossip. Some were as old and colorful as the owner of the ancient truck

Sam had been under when I almost tripped over him. A few were as new to the islands as I was. Everyone was friendly.

My new life wouldn't be complete without a weekly stop at the Island Candy Store and that lady was fast becoming a friend, too. Although she warned me that the shop would be closing in December and not reopening until April. Which would help with my Lenten fast, I'd miss my regular fix of her divine chocolate creations.

Working with Sam wasn't as awkward as I'd feared. It was a little frustrating at times given how totally disorganized he seemed to be everywhere outside of the garage floor itself. But he was an easy guy to please and only grumbled when he couldn't find something due to my organization of his previous haphazard system. I had my doubts that it was my reorganizing that should be blamed though, given Jack's comments.

Jack had poked fun at Sam the last time he'd cursed when he couldn't find something, reminding him that he would lose his own dick if it weren't attached. The humor might have been a little cruder than I was used to, but everyone had laughed, and Sam's irritation had evaporated.

Sam had even sprung for a new coffee maker when I complained that the old percolator he and his mechanics were used to turned out a brew that tasted the way I imagined the oil they drained from cars would. The credit card he'd handed me my first day on the job now resided permanently in my purse with the carte blanche that I was to get anything I thought the office needed and didn't need his permission first.

One evening, as I walked down to the water for Duffy's daily swim, I found an upholstered easy chair sitting out by the road with a sign declaring it was "free." I plopped into it and discovered it was a lot more comfortable than I'd have guessed given the faded old chintz that covered the thing. I could buy a cover that could be removed to toss in the wash and it would be a lot better in my new office space than the rickety folding chair that Sam or one of his guys currently used when they came in for a break.

I patted my pockets looking for a pen to write "Taken" over the word free. But since when did I carry random pens in my pockets? While I stood there trying to decide on the likelihood of the chair still being there if ran back up the hill to get my RAV 4, a slender, blonde woman stepped out on the stoop of the house.

"If you want it, I'll make sure no one takes it before you come back," she said as she bustled down the path toward me.

"I do want it. That would be great," I replied. "It's really comfy. Why are you tossing it?"

"My aunt went into a nursing home and we inherited her almost new living room set. Can't fit everything. My son claimed the couch for his den in the basement, but he couldn't squeeze the chair in too. So, it's out here begging for a new owner. You're new here? I've seen you going by with the dog. Good looking pooch. Hey, Boy." She squatted and extended a hand for Duffy to sniff.

Duffy sniffed more than her hand, but she patiently waited for him to check her out. "I've got a few of my own. He's probably sniffing their scent." Then she stood and extended her hand to me. "I'm Dawn."

Kenzie," I replied, taking the offered hand. "Kenzie Ross. I'm the new owner of The Captain Patrick Murray House."

Her face folded in sympathy. "I heard about Maggie Shaw's accident. We hadn't seen her in some years, but we stayed in touch. So sad."

A big white pickup pulled into the driveway and a man climbed out and headed our way.

"My husband, George," the woman told me. Then after giving her husband a peck on the cheek, "This is Kenzie. She moved into Maggie Shaw's place."

"Nice to meet you," George touched the brim of his hat. "You claiming the chair?"

"I thought it would be great in the office where I work," I replied.

His brows rose. "That old thing? In an office?"

"It's not your usual office. I work at Hank's, organizing his office, and right now all that anyone can sit in besides the desk chair is a folding thing that threatens to collapse any time anyone sitting in it so much as sneezes."

"So, Sam's got someone organizing his chaos?" George laughed. "Tell you what. I'll drop it off there tomorrow on my way to work. That work for you?"

Relief flooded me. "Not only would that work, but it saves me from having to fold down all my seats and hoping it will fit in the back of my RAV 4."

"Done, deal." George grabbed the chair and hoisted it over his shoulder like it weighed nothing and carried to his truck.

"He'll toss a tarp over it for the night," Dawn said. "I'm glad it's going to find a new home where it will get appreciated."

"I'll owe you both," I replied. "It was nice to meet you finally. I think we've met your dogs. Or a couple of them anyway."

We chatted about her dogs and she imparted a few tidbits about the neighborhood while Duffy checked out the truck and then returned to sit gazing up at me with a hopeful expression.

"Looks like he's ready to go," Dawn said. "And I've got supper to fix for my boys. It was nice to meet you." She turned to head back up the walk while I offered one last farewell and started for the cove with Duffy leading the way.

What surprised me most was that I didn't miss my old home nearly as much as I'd thought I would the day I packed the last of my things into the car after dusting and cleaning every familiar nook and cranny in Garrett's house. I hadn't cleaned the house for the new girlfriend, I had assured myself. Or even to remove all the dog hair for Garrett. But to erase any hint of myself. I'd even removed all the family photos. If Garrett wanted copies, let him come begging. The bulk of the artwork had been either things he'd chosen or already on the walls when we first moved in so parting with them hadn't been a wrench.

The only piece I'd kept was one we'd bought from the photographer himself on a long-ago trip to Hawaii. It featured the silhouettes of palm trees backlit by the sun rising in all its glory over a breathtaking azure sea. It was a small print, and I doubted Garrett would even notice it was missing. But if he did, I didn't care. It was a promise to myself that someday I was going back to Hawaii, even if I had to go alone. I looked forward to enjoying the laid-back, sunny warmth and all the island charm that had so captivated me the first time.

If Bill and Sarah had moved their company to Hawaii, I'd have gone with them in a heartbeat. But Dallas wasn't Hawaii, and now I had this beautiful old house in Maine, instead. And two boys in college just a few hours' drive away. There was a lot to be said for that.

Standing at my bedroom window, gazing out at the sun setting on my new view of the Atlantic Ocean, I remembered the Hawaii print and realized it was still in one of the boxes I'd chosen to bring with me when I came north, rather than in the storage unit in Virginia.

I hustled down the stairs to the kitchen and then to the oversized closet I'd stashed those boxes in. I really needed to unpack them and put things away. At the time it had seemed best to leave stuff I didn't need right off in the boxes while renters were still coming and going.

I'd gone through the three biggest boxes before I recalled having wrapped the picture in brown paper with cardboard to protect the image. Where?

I began hauling the piles of boxes aside and finally located the wrapped print. Yay! A sigh of relief. Now to figure out which box I'd stowed my meager set of tools and something to hang the print on. I got lucky on the second box I tried. Now armed with a hammer, a picture hanger, and my print, I started to trek back up to my bedroom but then had a second thought.

The living room currently had several lovely old paintings decorating its walls, most of them originals. Had any of the artists been in this room? Or were the paintings purchased elsewhere and brought here? A question likely never to have an answer, unless the ghost people kept informing me lived in my home appeared and shared what she knew.

Someone knocked on my front door. Jaycee again? I hurried to open it.

"Sam!"

I hadn't expected to find him on my doorstep. Hadn't expected Duffy to be standing next to him either. "Did he run away again?"

"Nope. He was sitting out on your front lawn when I drove by and decided to stop. Hope I'm not interrupting anything," Sam said, stepping past me when I opened the door wider and gestured an invitation. Duffy followed him in.

I still held the Hawaii print in one hand. I held it up. "No. Not really. I remembered I had this photo and wanted to hang it somewhere." I held the image up for him to see.

"Stunning," he said with a sharp intake of breath. "Did you take this?"

"I'm not that talented," I admitted. "I bought it from the man who did take it. In Hawaii," I added. "A place I promised myself I would return to some day. Some day hasn't happened yet, but I love the image and decided I wanted to hang it where I could enjoy it and the idea of a return visit."

Sam turned slowly on his heel surveying the walls and their current artwork. "It's small, but I think it would be great over the fireplace."

I looked at the fireplace myself. "It won't be dwarfed there?" It would look great against the dark fieldstone of chimney.

He took the picture from me and walked over to the fireplace, then held it up against the currently bare stone.

I studied the result. And liked it. "Yeah. Good idea. How did you know I needed you to stop in and suggest it?"

"I had no idea. I wasn't planning to stop, but I did want to ask you something."

Sam set the picture on the mantle leaning against the chimney. "By the way, that hammer isn't going to do it. Not with the stone. But I think I have something in the truck that will. Hang on."

With that he went to the door and disappeared.

What on earth was he planning to ask me? Not another date. I wasn't ready for a date. Not a serious boy-girl date, anyway. I could hear Jaycee in my head scolding me for being a dumb cluck. *A hunk asks you out. You like him. You're not attached. Say yes for Pete's sake!*

"But he didn't ask me out," *I replied to her imaginary rebuke.*

"I was going to. Sort of, anyway."

I sucked in a surprised gasp. Holy crap! Sam had heard my out loud reply to Jaycee.

"That's why I stopped. I saw the poster for a Mo Briggs fundraiser and thought you might like to go. He's a local musician and everyone loves his music."

I had zero idea who Mo Briggs was, but Jaycee's advice rang again in my head. "Mo Briggs?" I faltered uncertainly.

"Everyone who can squeeze into Library Hall will be there, and I know where to get tickets," he cajoled with another heart-stopping smile. That smile was going to be my undoing.

"Sounds like fun," I finally managed to get out.

Another safe date, I told myself. Attending a community fund-raiser didn't make Sam and me an item.

"Excellent. Now where do you want this exactly?"

He tucked something small and white between his teeth and returned to the mantle. He picked my Hawaii photo up and held it against the granite again. "Here? Or a little higher maybe?" he said around the thing in his mouth, He moved the picture up a few inches.

When I still didn't answer because my brain was still processing the non-date I'd agreed to, he gestured to me. "You come hold it."

We switched places and I held it about where he had while he retreated to the center of the room to consider. "Maybe about halfway in between."

I lowered it a couple inches.

"Perfect." Sam strode back to my side. The white thing in his hand turned out to be one of those Command things you can stick on walls and hang things on. He eyeballed the width of the mantle, peeled the backing off and stuck the mount in place. Then he took the picture from my hand and hung it.

We both retreated to the center of the room to admire it.

"That's one place I've never been. Looks as beautiful as everyone claims," Sam mused as we admired the palm trees, the sunset, and the beautiful blue water of the Pacific Ocean.

"Well, I better be going," Sam finally broke the reverie. "Tonight is bingo night at the old folks place up town, and my Aunt Phe will be disappointed if I don't show up."

"Thanks for the help," I said as I followed him to the door.

"My pleasure," he responded. He stepped off the porch. "Thank you for agreeing to go to hear Mo Briggs with me."

I watched him climb into his truck before I closed the door, locked it and paused for another study of my picture before heading to the kitchen. "Well, Duffy? I guess you're thinking it's time for your dinner. Huh?"

With the dog fed and the kettle on for a cup of tea, I sat at the counter to wait, and saw for the umpteenth time, the envelope I'd done my best to ignore.

"Time to face forward and stop holding onto the past," I told Duffy who chomped away as if I hadn't said anything.

I fidgeted with the fat envelope that had been propped here since the last guest had gone, unopened, because I knew what was in it.

My head knew my marriage was over. Garrett and I had cut pretty much every tie, divvying up the investment and savings accounts, and dropping a healthy amount into new accounts to see the boys through school. Garrett took my name off his 401k and I removed his from my Roth account. We were over and done.

So, why was I holding out signing the papers to end it all officially?

I didn't love him anymore. That was one thing I'd learned in the months since we'd parted. And I'd gotten over the infidelity which had been more shock than hurt if I were being honest. I just hadn't realized it at the time.

I got up and turned the kettle off. Then I fetched one of Jaycee's fun wine glasses from the shelf, filled it from a bottle of my own favorite Riesling, and resumed my seat.

I stared at the envelope. Took a sip of wine. Stared some more. It was time.

"It's time!" I announced loudly to the room at large.

Duffy, having finished his dinner and flopped onto his kitchen mat for a nap, lifted his head and gazed up at me.

"Sorry, didn't mean to disturb you." I told him in a more moderate tone.

He got to his feet and wandered over to me, placing his chin on my thigh. I ruffled the soft fur behind his ears, thankful for the zillionth time that Maggie had rescued this amazing animal and then left him to me.

I leaned down and kissed him on the top of his head. "It's time," I said in a far softer tone. "You're my man now. At least when the boys aren't here. Then you'll have to share."

He wagged his tail as if he understood every word I said. Intelligent dog.

I unfolded the little knife I kept on the counter to open packages and slit the envelope.

Chapter Eighteen

Kenzie Ross – Current Day

"So, who's this Mo Briggs I keep hearing about?" I asked my two new friends who had joined me on the beach this morning. The day was sunny and warm and Evelyn, Dawn and I sat on a folded old quilt with our arms wrapped around our drawn-up knees while Duffy poked along the shore sniffing out evidence of previous critters and possible treats.

I had yet to meet either of Evelyn's offspring, but since the day of the chair, I'd met both of Dawn's sons. Hunter was a high school senior with his sights set on joining the Air Force and learning to fly planes. Trey was legally George Hamilton the third and had grown up being called Little George. Usually the biggest kid in his class, he'd gotten taunted with that appellation, so his mom had settled on Trey and it stuck. He'd been hauling lobsters from a dinghy with an outboard motor throughout high school and now, four years since graduating, already had his own handsome forty-foot boat.

Dawn, I had also learned, worked at the Super Walmart up town most of the year but preferred cleaning rental cottages in the summer when college kids came home to work at the big store. Dawn and Evelyn knew everyone, so I figured they'd be the ones to fill me on Mo Briggs.

"Home boy who hit the big time," Dawn answered at the same time Evelyn started to speak.

I looked at Dawn, then at Evelyn waiting for one or the other to go on. Duffy brought me a stick and I threw it as far down the beach as I could. He scampered after it.

"Mo grew up here," Evelyn added. "He can play anything with strings."

"Someday I'm going to one of his regular concerts," Dawn announced with a nod. "You know. Like the ones he holds in football stadiums with hundreds in attendance."

"How is that better than right here at the Bailey Island Library Hall?" Evelyn leaned out to look past me at Dawn seated on my other side. "Here you get to shake hands with Mo and all his musicians. That big stadium, you're lucky if you can even see him from any seat I could afford."

Dawn shrugged. "I like big concerts. I like the energy."

"Neither of you have told me who he is yet," I reminded them.

"Everyone knows him," Evelyn offered. "But Dawn knows him better, so I'll let her tell you."

Dawn proceeded to fill me in on a boy named Maurice Briggs who could sing like an angel and play, as Evelyn put it, anything with strings. "He makes your heart weep when he does something classical or romantic on the fiddle. I guess it's called a violin if it's that kind of music, though. But he's just as good at Bluegrass on a fiddle. He plays oldies and contemporary stuff on his guitar. Sometimes he throws in a little banjo to be different. Have you got a ticket? They sell out fast."

"If the weather holds, they'll leave the doors open and anyone can come sit on the lawn outside and listen for free," Evelyn offered.

"Sam asked me to go. I assume he has tickets," I replied.

Dawn and Evelyn shared a knowing nod.

"It's not like you think," I protested. "It's not a date or anything. I thought it was a fund-raiser for that kid who got seriously injured in a motorcycle accident and is learning to walk again."

"It's always about raising money for some cause or another," Dawn agreed. Mo, as he calls himself now, says he's paying it back to the community who stood by him when he started out. He comes back every year to do a concert for the community and he pays all the expenses, too."

"Sounds like one of the good guys," I said. Anyone who made it to the national stage but remembered their roots and went out of their way to do things for others was a good guy in my opinion.

"He never knew his father. Maurice senior was a lobsterman who got tangled in a pot line and pulled overboard and drowned when Mo was, I don't know, two or maybe three. His mother did her best to make ends meet but she didn't have much education and couldn't get much of a job. Then she just up and disappeared." Dawn pulled her shoulders up to her ears and shook her head.

"Mo just soldiered on. He was in junior high then and it wasn't until he failed to show up for school one day that anyone knew he was living on his own. The community rallied around him. With his mom gone, a neighbor family took him in. Another guy in business sold the house and settled the estate, then invested what was left for Mo's future. Actually, I think the guy ponied up some of the money himself. But then Mo met his sweetheart, who happened to be a musician and introduced him to music and half a dozen instruments. The rest, as they say, is history."

The following week, I was trying to decide what to wear to this benefit concert with the great Mo Briggs when my phone rang.

"Hi Jaycee. I can't talk long. I'm getting ready for a local concert."

"What kind of concert," Jaycee asked, instantly interested.

I repeated what Dawn and Evelyn had shared with me. "It's 'come dressed for a hoe-down'. At least that's what I was told."

"You have a cowboy hat?"

"When would I have acquired a cowboy hat?" I laughed, trying to picture myself wearing one.

"Well, then, what are you wearing? And who are you going with? I hope it's that handsome hunk I met at the garage."

"I'm going with Sam, but it's not a date, Jaycee," I said as I slipped into a cream-colored linen blouse.

Her peel of laughter echoed all the way from Virginia. "Keep telling yourself that. But seriously. What are you wearing. Might I suggest that lovely cashmere sweater that brings out the blue of your eyes?"

After a few more suggestions she ended the call to let me finish dressing and be ready on time. Despite myself, I pulled the blue sweater over my head and decided she was right.

It was hoedown, whatever that meant, but I got the gist of casual, so I added a pair of jeans and skipped the layers of jewelry that Garrett had always insisted on.

If the gleam in Sam's eye was anything to go by, Jaycee had been right about the sweater. To my surprise, he pulled a hand from behind his back and plopped a cowboy style hat on my head. Almost the same blue as my sweater.

"Whose hat is this?" I was a little suspicious. Not being familiar with the whole cowboy thing, I wasn't sure if it denoted anything special when a man put his hat on a woman.

"Yours now," he saluted me, touching a finger to the brim of the black hat tilted rakishly over his brow. Then he offered me his arm.

Another gallantry I was not familiar with, but I took it with only a few butterflies batting their way about my stomach.

Library Hall was an elegant old building sitting on a slight rise overlooking Mackerel Cove. Light poured from the windows and dozens of beach chairs were parked all over the lawn outside. The weather was perfect for a night like this, and I was thankful I'd thought to leave the blouse on beneath the sweater in case I got too warm. A hall filled with people tended to heat up, even on a brisk night in November in Maine.

Sam led me inside where chairs had been lined up six deep around the walls leaving a small area of the glistening wood floor bare in the center of the hall. At the far end, a handsome man dressed all in black, tuned a guitar, his face shaded by the brim of his hat. Three additional musicians were doing the same behind him. The great Mo Briggs and his back up, I had to assume.

Sam found us excellent seats in the second row just to the right of Briggs and his entourage, and we'd barely gotten settled before the music began.

Mo Briggs was every bit as good as Dawn and Evelyn had claimed, and I enjoyed every minute of his eclectic selection of music. He switched, as I'd been told, from one instrument to the other as the music changed. He had moved to a mix of old and new music, all slow and dreamy when couples began to filter onto that small patch of floor to dance.

I grew more and more aware of Sam, his arm touching mine as the music drifted from one romantic number to another. What did it say about my confused state of mind that one minute I prayed Sam would ask me to dance and the next feared he would do just that.

In the end, he didn't ask. He just got to his feet, took my hand, and drew me onto the floor with a smile that had my heart in my throat.

Then his hand was at the small of my back. When he tipped his head to rest his cheek atop my now bare head, the beating of my heart nearly drowned out the sound of the sweet guitar playing so close it almost felt like Mo was playing just for us.

When Mo began to play Eric Clapton's *Wonderful Tonight*, Sam's hand left the chaste location on my back and circled me, pulling me close.

This was not where we were going, I reminded myself as my body disobeyed the thought and melted into his. We drifted on this sea of romance and warmth until the last notes of the song died away and we stopped moving. The lights flickered, then dimmed. Vaguely, I was aware of the musicians setting their instruments down, but Sam and I just stood, very still, in a moving mass of people.

I finally lifted my head, preparing to step away and back into reality.

Sam's mouth, so close now I could feel the faintest hint of his breath on my cheek, closed the gap and he kissed me.

Chapter Nineteen

Eleanor Murray - 1944

January 1944

My Dear Eleanor,

It feels like an age since I last held you in my arms and kissed your sweet lips. It gives me great hope and encouragement, to know you will be waiting for me when this awful war is over. I received the socks you knit for me and much appreciate the thought.

My unit has been sent back to England to recuperate now that the campaign in North Africa has ended. So many of the men I fought alongside did not make it. Many were returned to the States if they were injured. Some didn't make it that far and I am saddened by the losses of so many good friends. Those who survived thought we might continue onward to Italy, but for some reason that didn't happen and now I am wandering about this bleak English countryside, not sure where or when I will see action again. I would have been happier had we been sent back to Ireland which is much greener and lassies more welcoming.

I have lost touch with Vincent and fear he may have been among the wounded, but I am not certain. Arthur is here in England with me, although he has been transferred to a different unit for reasons he apparently can't reveal. Have you heard anything from your brother? Last I knew he was flying out of an airfield somewhere here in England, but I have not run into him.

I fear something big might be in the works, but all is hush hush and I cannot tell you much. I don't even know that much myself, but it just feels like something intense is in the works. Pray for me. I need every good thought and prayer you can offer up in my name, and I promise I will return to you as soon as I am able.

Thank you again for the toasty warm socks,

Jeff

Eleanor rolled onto her back and started reading Jeff's letter again. When she had finished, she kissed his name. The handwriting was not his, and his lips had never touched this paper, but he had been thinking of kissing her when he began the letter. She couldn't help wondering what he'd written that the censors had blacked out. Mike had warned her that much was kept from the American public, even things their sons and husbands might have mentioned in their letters home.

"Please bring him home safe, God," she whispered into the dimming light of a late winter evening.

"Are you nearly ready yet?" Eleanor's mother called from across the hall.

"Almost," Eleanor answered, rolling off her bed and shoving Jeff's letter under her pillow.

She'd almost forgotten the March Fling, as the big affair at Library Hall was called. It happened every year and had continued despite the war. She had always looked forward to it before. But that was when she had danced with Jeff.

Tonight, she prayed no one would ask her to dance. It wasn't likely with so many girls and so few young men, but it could happen. Except for Mike. He would surely be at the March Fling and he might ask her to dance. She was torn about that. She knew she would enjoy dancing with him, but she was afraid of her own heart when he was about.

She hurried to her closet and took the only nice dress she had left off the hanger. Tossing it across her bed, she shrugged out of the work clothes she had been wearing all day. A quick wash with cold water from the pitcher on her dresser.

She almost gasped at the cold but managed to stifle the sound even as goose bumps reared on her arms. Only one pair of nylons left that had no runs in them. She debated saving them for when Jeff came home. No telling when it would be possible to get a new pair of nylons again. Then she tucked that new pair under her unmentionables and started pulling on the older pair. There was only one run in one stocking and just the tiniest start of a run in the other. She applied a dab of fingernail polish to keep it from getting worse. Maybe no one would notice in the evening light.

She rushed to the mirror and ran a fresh layer of lipstick over her lips. Bright red. It was supposed to be patriotic. A sign of solidarity with the soldiers. She pressed her lips together and nodded. A quick comb of her bangs and she patted any wayward strands of hair behind her ears before fluffing out her curls with her fingers.

"Eleanor?" Her mother's voice came from the foot of the stairs now.

She had to hurry. She pulled the dress over her hair and tugged it into place. Thankfully, this dress buttoned up the front. A lot of tiny buttons, but at least she could do it herself instead of getting her mother to help, which would only betray that she hadn't been as ready as she'd claimed.

Grabbing the stylish little clutch purse Aunt Emily had sent her, Eleanor tucked a hankie and her lipstick into it and hurried to join her mother waiting impatiently at the foot of the stairs.

Her father had left an hour earlier to help open the hall and make sure all was ready for the evening. A good thing since he wouldn't get a chance to inspect her and take note of the old nylons.

"Mike is waiting for us in his father's car," Eleanor's mother announced as they stepped onto the porch and drew the door shut behind them.

Eleanor's heart fluttered uncomfortably. She replayed Jeff's letter in her head, doing her best to banish the unwanted feelings.

The classy black Studebaker idled at the end of the walk, its headlights wearing their dimming shades, half covering the full headlamp lest any German planes overhead see the light and anything it might illuminate. Not that anyone had seen any German planes during the day or at night on this side of the Atlantic.

Mike jumped out and held the front door for Eleanor's mother. Then he opened the rear door for Eleanor. She climbed in, gathered her skirts about her, and waited for Mike to close the door. His grandfather was driving. Which meant Mike would be sitting in back with her. She scooched herself as close to the door as she could.

Considering how much light escaped from the open doors of the Hall, the whole thing with the car headlights seemed senseless. Most of the windows had been covered with heavy drapes, but even there, bits of light leaked out onto the still brown earth.

At least the last of the snow had gone. Her lovely heels, also a gift from Aunt Emily, would not be ruined. Mike hastened to get out and open doors when they arrived, but common courtesy meant helping Eleanor's mother from the car first. Eleanor opened her own door and climbed out, pulling her cape close. Not trusting herself, she started up the walk to the hall, leaving Mike to offer his arm to her mother. Every time she'd been in Mike's company lately, her feelings for him had become harder to ignore. What was wrong with her? Would her heart have behaved differently if she'd actually made that promise to Jeff verbally? What if she'd become a married woman instead of being left behind still unattached while Jeff went off to fight?

As soon as the woman at the coat check had taken her cape, Eleanor hurried to find her friend. Sissy was part of a larger group of chattering young women on the far side of the hall. Eleanor headed their way, determined to remain faithful to Jeff no matter what.

The evening was almost over. Eleanor had enjoyed herself far more than she should have with her Jeff freezing and alone with just other soldiers to keep him company in England. Mike had claimed her hand to do the swing which was all the rage and he'd been good at it. Better than she was. Later, she'd done a Charleston with Sissy's brother Alfred. She'd even tried a jitterbug with two of her friends. Now the evening was almost over and soon it would be time to head home.

"You promised me another dance," Mike said, appearing out of the crowd.

She had. Of course, she'd hoped it would be another swing instead the waltz currently being played.

With a deep steadying breath, she put her hand in Mike's and allowed him to lead her into the melee of dancers. Without a lot of room to spare when he pulled her into his arms, it was closer than she should allow. Closer than Jeff would have thought proper.

Close enough to smell Mike's cologne. Not the Old Spice her father used. Or Aqua Velva which Jeff preferred, but something more exotic. It made her think of Cary Grant. Some rebellious part of her enjoyed the feel of Mike's arm about her waist and his scent in her nostrils. With a guilty start she tried to put a little space between them.

"Let me enjoy the illusion," Mike whispered, his head almost touching hers.

"The-the illusion?" She tipped her head up to ask.

"That you might be my girl," he replied, and before she could grasp his intent, he lowered his head to hers.

Mike kissed her as she'd never been kissed before. She should pull away. She should run away. She parted her lips and let him in.

CHAPTER TWENTY

Kenzie Ross – Present Day

It was just a kiss. People kiss all the time. It doesn't mean they are in a serious relationship.

I kept telling myself that.

In the breathless minutes after Sam and I were jostled by the crowd exiting the hall and stepped out of each other's embrace. In the equally breathless moments that I couldn't drag my gaze from his. During the walk back to Murray House when meaningless small talk seemed to have dried up. I kept telling myself it was just a kiss.

Except that it wasn't just any kiss.

Sam had been as gallant walking me up to my door and waiting until I let myself in before returning to his truck as he'd been when he'd put that blue cowboy hat on my head and offered his arm to lead me out.

I stepped into the house but failed to flip on any lights as I sagged against the closed door, still strangely breathless.

Duffy greeted me with his usual enthusiasm, but I was distracted by the thudding of my heart. He plopped on his butt gazing up at me in the semi-dark, head tilted as if asking a question. The same tilt that Sam adopted when waiting for a reaction, my reeling brain reminded me.

I finally gave myself a good shake and squatted down to wrap my arms around my main man. "Hey, Duffy. Did you miss me?"

His tail thumped the floor, and he licked my face.

"I guess that's a yes?"

More licks. Then he got up and trotted to the door, clearly asking to go out. He had his shit together even if I didn't.

Okay, then. Life back to normal. I set the blue hat on the back of the closest chair and let my dog out.

As I watched him sniffing his way along the perimeter, leaving his mark here and there, I started to repeat my mantra, *It was just a kiss.*

Who was I kidding? Sam kissed like no one ever. Super Stud was as over-the-top in the kissing department as he was in looks and affability. So far, the only flaw I could tag the man with was his hopeless disorganization, but since that had landed me the job I knew I needed, I could hardly hold it against him.

Duffy returned to house, found his way to the kitchen and after a short slurp at his water bowl, headed toward the stairs. He knew it was time for bed, but I wasn't sure I'd be able to sleep at all. I could turn the TV on and watch some late-night re-runs. I could make a snack. But I didn't feel like either. I followed my dog and headed for the stairs.

On second thought, I turned back for a moment. Took my phone out of my pocket, turned off the ringer and set it on the counter. With my luck, Jaycee would call to see how my night went and I had no idea how to deflect her super intuition.

When I woke, sun poured in the window and Duffy lay like a sphinx at the foot of the bed staring at me.

Amazing. I hadn't expected to sleep a wink. But I'd slept the sleep of the dead, judging by the brightness of the sun. I glanced at the side table where my phone usually rested in its charging cradle, but then remembered where I'd left it.

Duffy continued to give me the eye. Clearly, he thought it was time to get up. Time for a morning walk. Maybe even a swim. And more than time for breakfast. If he hadn't come into my life, there's no telling how much longer I might have been out.

I swung my legs over the side of the bed and Duffy jumped to the floor. He was eager for the day to get under way.

I was eager to get out for a brisk run and power away the dregs of sleep. Maybe even get a grip on the breathless feeling that hit me the instant I remembered Sam's kiss.

Donning the first thing I came across and grabbing my sneakers, I headed for the kitchen. A few minutes later, Duffy and I were jogging down the road toward Garrison Cove. It was fortunate that the Mo Briggs affair had been on a Sunday because that meant the road was deserted. Kids off to school, everyone else off to work. I had the road to myself.

It was also fortunate that I didn't currently work full time and had Mondays off. Otherwise, I'd have been embarrassingly late for work. And I had no idea how I was going to relate to Sam the next time I did show up for work.

Pretend it never happened? I blush too easily, so that avenue was out. What if Sam decided once wasn't enough?

We reached the cove while my mind still ran on about Sam with no solutions in sight. I headed along the beach toward the bridge. Duffy gazed longingly at the water, but dutifully followed along. Thankfully that amazing bridge with its narrow lanes, also had a sturdy rail keeping the pedestrian sidewalk safely separate. We crossed the road and headed out over the bridge, turned at the far end and headed back. As soon as we returned, Duff's forbearance ran out, and he plunged in for a swim. I sat down on the pebbly beach to watch just as my phone vibrated in my pocket.

"How'd it go?" Jaycee's cheerful voice greeted me.

"It was just a kiss," I blurted the first thing that came into my head. Oh My God! Did I just say that out loud?

"Just a kiss, huh?" A long sexy whistle followed.

I had.

"Super Stud, right?"

"Sam. His name is Sam," I told her, wishing my impromptu announcement undone.

"Sam the Studmuffin. I really, *really* like this guy."

"I'm never going to let you come up again if you insist on calling him Studmuffin."

"I promise to call him Sam to his face," Jaycee said, with more than a bit of a chuckle in her voice. "So, tell me all about it. Every single, luscious detail or I won't hang up."

"I can hang up on you," I reminded her.

"And I'll just keep calling back until you come clean."

"Mo Briggs was fantastic. I can't figure out why I've never heard of him before."

"So, the music was great. But cut to the chase."

Jaycee was a force to be reconned with, so I caved and did as she requested, starting with the sky-blue cowboy hat that now hung on the post of that old mirror in my room, the arm he'd offered while we walked, the dance that got more intimate as the music got more dreamy, and finally the kiss that was so much more than just a kiss.

The next morning, still not sure how to react if Sam said or did anything that remotely touched on what had happened between us two nights ago, I launched into a request about something else before he had a chance to even say good morning.

"I've been thinking about renovating Murray House," I said the moment Sam showed up in what I now considered my office.

He glanced at me briefly, then turned away to drop a K-cup into the single serve coffee maker I'd installed. He shoved a mug with the image of Calvin and Hobbes under the dispenser before replying.

"Renovate, how?"

"Into three, maybe four independent apartments. The place is way more than I need or want and my friend thought maybe I could divide it up. Rent out what I'm not using," I explained. I prayed the breathlessness I felt did not color my words.

Sam did that head tipping thing and I reached for my own coffee to distract myself.

"Could work," he said after a beat. "Summer rentals like before you came, or annual?"

"Year-round. Like people who live there, instead of folks who come for a week and then are gone. I'd like to get to know the people living in my space."

"That could work. Not a lot of options down here on the island for apartment rental. My cousin was trying to find a place last spring and there wasn't anything. She gave up and lives up in Bath. For now, anyway."

The coffee maker gurgled to a finish. Sam turned to grab the mug, then dropped into the stuffed chair George had delivered as promised and I'd covered with a hunting plaid that wouldn't show dirt. "Haley would love living at The Captain Patrick Murray House."

Maybe Jaycee was onto something if I could find renters that quickly. "Do you know any contractors you'd recommend for this kind of thing?"

"Contractor or lone handyman? A lot of the men who have smaller boats and don't fish deep water, haul their boats and take on carpenter or handy-man jobs for the winter. I could give you several names. But off the top of my head there's a kid named Marcus Muralles. He isn't a fisherman, though. He moved back here after getting out of the Army and took over a job on another old house that needed a lot of work. Guy that hired him can't say enough good things about him or his work."

"Sounds like the kind of man I need to talk to. You have his number?" Excitement stirred in me as thoughts of actually making it happen percolated in my head.

"I don't, but I can get it for you. Hang on." He set his mug down and pulled out his phone. A moment later he was talking to someone, asking for Muralles' number.

I pushed a pad of paper across the desk and added a pen. Sam snagged the pen and scribbled a number, thanked whoever he was talking to and hung up.

"Davis says get in touch sooner rather than later, because this guy is going to be in hot demand."

"Hey, Boss!" Jack leaned in the door, one hand clinging to the doorframe. "A lady asking to see you out in the yard. She came in with the tow truck." Then Jack was gone.

Sam set his mug down and stood, then followed Jack, stopping just long enough to wink at me before disappearing into the shop.

A wink doesn't mean anything more than a kiss, I told myself, trying to ignore the fact my heartbeat had spiked in reaction. I was so not ready for a relationship. I'd fallen in love with Garrett so long ago and trusted him without question. Now, nothing seemed permanent, and I wasn't ready to trust my heart or my sense of self-worth again. Maybe I never would.

CHAPTER TWENTY-ONE

Eleanor Murray – 1944

Tears leaked from Eleanor's eyes and ran down her face into her pillow. She'd been unfaithful to Jeff. It wouldn't have been so awful if it had just been Mike kissing her, but she'd kissed him back.

Despite her determination not to let her feelings for Mike grow stronger than they already were, the kiss had sent shivers all the way down those nylons with runs in them to the toes of Aunt Emily's stylish high heels.

Jeff would be so hurt if he ever found out.

People had seen Mike kissing her. Those that hadn't left the hall, anyway. Eleanor tried to remember who had been still milling around, wondering if any of them were the sort to report her indiscretion to her father, or worse, to write to Jeff.

Maybe she should write to Jeff first and confess. But was that fair to him? To find out how unfaithful she had been behind his back. Should she just wait until he returned and confess to his face? And pray no one told him before she could?

Sleep finally came, but it was filled with a mish-mash of dreams. She woke feeling completely unrested and riddled with guilt. She dressed to work in her garden and headed for the kitchen.

Her father sat at the table reading his morning paper. He shook it as she entered, turned a page, shook it again and kept reading.

Eleanor walked to the stove to see if there were still any eggs left in the fry pan.

"I expected better of you, Eleanor," her father said to her back.

She whirled and faced him. "You expect a lot from me that I don't understand anymore."

The paper went down, and his brows rose. "What is it you don't understand?"

Before she could lose her nerve, Eleanor launched into an answer. "Before this awful war, you called Jeff and his entire family a passel of ne'er-do-wells that never amounted to anything. You even suggested they were cowards because Jeff's father didn't go off to become a soldier in the Great War. Now Jeff is over there fighting and still you disapprove. You didn't disapprove of Mike or my brother when they left to join up before this country was even in the war. So, I don't understand how you can disapprove of Jeff."

She shut her mouth before she could say something her father couldn't forgive. Her chest heaved with emotion, but she kept her lips buttoned against further comment.

"Neither Raymond nor Michael were engaged to be married when they left. They didn't leave their intended at the altar."

"Jeff didn't leave me at the altar either. He came to tell me—"

"Near as makes no difference," her father cut her off. "He volunteered when he had no need to."

"He just asked me to wait," Eleanor said, hating the pleading tone that had crept into her voice.

"And I suppose kissing Michael Hamilton in the middle of Library Hall for all the world to see was waiting? You are shameless."

Eleanor wasn't hungry anymore, and she had no answer for the latest of her father's salvos. She turned and fled back to her room.

After her father had departed for work, and her mother to the church office where she volunteered three days a week, Eleanor came out of hiding and went to her garden. The ground had thawed at last, and she could finish getting everything ready to plant.

Sissy's father had given her six old storm windows from a house that was being renovated and she had created six miniature greenhouses with them. Now she'd be able to start her vegetables far earlier, lifting the windows during the day and shutting them over the boxes when evening came to keep the young plants from freezing at night.

By late afternoon, the work was done, and her back was aching. Since father still hadn't returned from work, she set about filling the kettles and planning a nice long soak.

"A letter came for you today," Eleanor's mother said as Eleanor headed for the stairs.

"Jeff," Eleanor exclaimed as she flew through the kitchen to the table by the front door where mail was always left. It had been less than a day since she'd had the last letter from Jeff. How had another come so soon? The guilt gnawing at her insides all day grew more intense. How could she have been so faithless?

It wasn't Jeff's handwriting, but that didn't surprise her considering the new way of posting letters from soldiers fighting in Europe. The fact that the envelope seemed heavier than the last one did make her pause, but not for long before she snatched up the ivory letter opener and slid its slender blade beneath the flap. Then she had another thought. No way did she want her father walking in the front door to catch her mooning over Jeff's letter.

Even her room wouldn't be the sanctuary of privacy it usually was because once the water for her bath was hot, her mother would call her to come get the buckets, or worse carry them up herself. Eleanor hurried up to the widow's walk atop the roof where she'd have only the seagulls to share her letter with.

Pushing the hatch to the widow's walk open, Eleanor emerged into the late afternoon sun and crossed to the railing. Sighing with anticipation, she pulled the letter from the envelope and unfolded it.

Dear Eleanor, the letter began. Eleanor's heart fell. It was not from Jeff. Not unless she'd ceased to be his My Dear Eleanor. She hurried on.

I received your lovely thank you letter for the shoes and purse. I am so glad they were to your liking. As I read your note, I sensed a hint of regret about having turned down my previous offer to come to stay with me in the city. Perhaps I am mistaken in thinking you are envious of your friends who have relatives in cities where they have found employment to help with the war effort. If I am not mistaken, I am renewing my invitation for you to come to me and stay as long as you wish. We can shop together where you would be able to choose your own shoes, or purse. Perhaps even find a new dress or two. Fabric is not always easy to come by, but it is available here in the city and I have a sewing machine so you would be able to fashion a garment of your own if you preferred. There are many opportunities for employment as well, thus you would be able to pursue finding a wartime job if you wished. Do consider it. I would love to have you. Especially now that Trudy has married and moved to Maryland, and it is just me, rattling around in all this space alone. Your parents might not wish to part with you with Raymond gone, but they still have each other, so I am hoping they would grant their permission. I have enclosed a cheque to cover the cost of train fare to New York. Should this not be possible, consider it an early gift for your birthday and buy yourself something special.

I hope to hear from you soon,

Your loving Aunt Emily

Eleanor rested her elbows on the railing and read the letter again more slowly.

If she accepted Aunt Emily's invitation, she would be spared having to cope with her father's disapproval. Even better, she wouldn't have to find ways to avoid Mike Hamilton and a repeat of her faithless behavior. She would have to leave her garden to her mother's care, which was a problem. Her mother had never seemed all that anxious to engage in the activity of growing things, even as a patriotic war effort.

Would Jeff know where to find her if he came home before a letter from her could reach him?

How can you be sure Jeff will come looking for you at all?

Eleanor jerked around at the sound of the unfamiliar voice, but no one was there. Had it been her imagination? Maybe it was a premonition that he was going to die in this war and she was waiting on a ghost. Perhaps he had already died but the news had just not caught up to her yet.

He's alive, my child. But your father might be right about some things.

It was her mind. She was talking to herself. Trying to reassure herself. Except for that last part. Her father wasn't right about Jeff. Jeff loved her. He'd be looking for her as soon as he stepped back onto American soil.

She read her aunt's letter a third time, ignoring the imagined voices.

There seemed to be no end in sight for the war. There would be plenty of time for her to write and let Jeff know where she would be if she decided to go to New York.

Eagerness began to grow in her breast. How exciting it would be to live in the city even for just a short time? She had never been to her aunt's apartment before, but her mother had been and her stories had sounded like a fairy tale. In a building as tall as a castle, her aunt's apartment was high on the seventh floor overlooking Central Park. A park her mother claimed was bigger than all of Bailey Island.

Eleanor returned to the hatch, climbed halfway down the steep stairs, and lowered the hatch back into place. Then she returned to her room to find the kettles already sitting by the empty tub.

As she removed her dusty garments and filled the tub, she continued to mull over Aunt Emily's invitation. If Eleanor accepted it, she would be able to go shopping in all the grand stores her mother had marveled over. She could find a war job as Aunt Emily suggested. And she would be closer to wherever Jeff landed on his return. They would be reunited that much sooner.

Yes, she decided. Yes. This time she was going to accept Aunt Emily's invitation. Her mother would understand even if Father didn't.

A pang of regret shot through her, darkening the moment of anticipation. She would miss spending time with the Hamiltons. But wasn't that one of her biggest reasons for going? To take herself away from temptation? Jeff was counting on her to be waiting for his return. He would not understand how she could fall in love with another man.

Still warm from the bath and wearing a clean dress, she descended to the kitchen with the letter in hand. "Mother? My letter was from Aunt Emily."

"I know, dear. She wrote to me as well. What do you think about her offer?" Her mother set the rolling pin she'd been using down and waited for Eleanor's reply.

"I think it would be nice."

Her mother nodded and picked up the rolling pin again. She made several passes over the pie crust she was preparing, then stopped and looked at Eleanor. "I thought you would be more excited than this. Do you not wish to spend some time in the city with my sister?"

"I am just worried that Father won't let me go," Eleanor replied honestly. It would be just like him to deny her the opportunity. He'd give some excuse like she couldn't be trusted to behave herself, but his real reason was that he hoped she would forget about Jeff entirely if Mike was constantly thrown into her presence.

"Aunt Emily must be lonely and I'm sure would enjoy your company," her mother answered, echoing her aunt's comment. "I will deal with your father."

CHAPTER TWENTY-TWO

Kenzie Ross – Present Day

Marcus Moralles touched the tip of his pencil to his tongue before scribbling a few lines in the little spiral notebook he'd taken from his rear pocket along with a tape measure.

I followed him as he went from room to room measuring every angle and nook, scribbling some more, then measuring again and adding more notes. Duffy accompanied us, sitting like a well-behaved gentleman every time we stopped in a new location.

"Well? What do you think?" I asked when we returned to the main floor.

"Exciting project, Ma'am. I'll have to work up some quotes, but I think it's very doable. With a lot of possibilities that I'd like to suggest once I sort things out in my head." He'd been ma'am-ing me since he walked in the door. He was making me feel older than I wanted to admit to.

"As long as I can afford them, I'm all ears. Do you think you could dispense with the ma'am?"

"Yes, Ma'am. I mean Mrs. Ross. Sorry, it's kind of a habit the military drilled into me and before that it was my Georgia Grandmother who brought me up."

"How expensive is it likely to get?"

It wasn't that I didn't have some resources but selling the investments Garrett and I had split meant selling at a gain, for which I'd have to pay taxes. I wondered vaguely what the chances of getting a mortgage to cover renovations would be with my job being just part time. But no need to buy trouble before it happened, as my grandmother would have said.

Moralles wagged his head. "Depends on a number of things. Got anywhere we can set down and talk, Ma'am?"

Clearly dropping the ma'am wasn't going to happen any time soon. Best I just get used to it. On second thought, it was better than Mrs. Ross. Since I wasn't actually Mrs. Ross anymore and Ms. Ross didn't sound any better.

"Would you like a cup of coffee while we talk?" I asked.

"Yes, Ma'am."

I shrugged and led the way to the kitchen where I dropped a k-cup into the coffee maker. Then I gestured to island and the stools arranged along two sides.

By the time the coffeemaker finished gurgling and I slid the steaming mug onto the counter along with a sugar bowl and a carton of coffee creamer, Moralles had produced a legal sized pad of paper and was sketching a layout of the ground floor. I started a second cup of coffee and when that was done, I joined the young ex-soldier-turned-contractor, sitting catty-corner so I could watch him draw.

"You said you wanted to keep the main living area as is. Correct, Ma'am?"

"That's correct., and my name is Kenzie." Maybe he'd start skipping the honorific once he got into the meat of his ideas. "That would be my area along with the kitchen, the master suite upstairs and the two rooms across the hall. Is there a way to create separate entries for each apartment. For privacy and convenience. There wouldn't need to be any renovations to this whole half of the house, Mr. Moralles."

"If I try hard to lose the Ma'am, maybe you can call me Marcus," the kid grinned at me, engagingly.

"It's a deal, Marcus. So lay the ideas on me and we'll see where we go from here."

Marcus sketched madly and talked almost as fast as he scribbled. He admitted there was no way to get a reasonably accurate estimate until I decided exactly what I wanted and chose materials, but he gave me a ballpark figure for two options. One with two apartments in addition to my own and one for three.

"The upside of two apartments and leaving the living room and kitchen intact, allows us to leave the laundry room, mud room and connected storage as it is," Marcus said running his pencil over lines already drawn on the pad. "If we go with three, then we'd have to rearrange some of that, maybe just leave the laundry and set the mud-room aside for access to a third apartment. And the apartments would have to be one bedroom each, which is limiting. If we go with just two, then one of them can be a two-bedroom apartment."

"What about the sixth bedroom?" I asked.

"We need to use that to create a living room for one of the other apartments."

I closed my eyes, envisioning the upstairs we'd just toured. One of the rental suites already had a cute little kitchenette and living area big enough for a couple without kids, so I could see his point.

"Okay. Then suppose we go for two. What then?"

By the time Marcus left with one last "Night Ma'am," my mind was reeling with possibilities. He'd been right about the two over three and I went with that. He promised to come up with a quote for his work, and a rough estimate for plumbing and electrical work that would have to be done by licensed workers. I needed to visit either Lowes or Home Depot to choose cabinets, but he promised to drop off a catalog for me to go through to get some ideas.

"What do you think, Duffy? You ready for men with hammers and saws to invade your space?"

Duffy wagged his tail and looked at his dish.

I looked at my watch and gasped. I'd no idea how long we'd spent discussing plans.

"Eat first," I told the dog as I picked his dish up and began preparing his dinner. Then we'll walk to the cove, but there will be no swimming. Got it?"

The following week Marcus called and asked if he could stop by with blueprints and estimates. Armed with the actual blueprints and some skillful hand drawn sketches, his enthusiasm was hard to resist. He created a mental picture with his words I could almost envision completed.

Before the meeting was half over, I told him he was hired, and we got down to specifics. As I'd noticed on my first sight of Murray House, but not really thought much about, the roof was clearly new, and most of the old windows had been replaced with triple-paned heat-saving models. The outside had been kept in good repair. That, at least, was not going to be a problem, and none of the suggestions Marcus outlined seemed terribly extreme. I was happy with my new plans and the man I'd hired to make them happen.

On his way out, he suggested I might want to call his girlfriend. She was near the end of her apartment lease in Bath and not happy about renewing. He thought she would love renting from me once the job was completed and she'd be fine with living here amid renovations in the meantime if it meant she didn't have to sign a new lease where she was. She worked from home and all she really needed was a place to sleep and the internet.

"It's not like we're gutting the place," he said as we stood on the porch where he'd paused on his way to his truck. "We're just installing a couple new walls, some plumbing, replacing the narrow old staircase in back and adding a few doors to close off your space."

"I'll think about it," I replied. Marcus had let slip that his girlfriend was Sam's cousin but that didn't mean she was as easy to get along with as Sam. Or that having her living in my home wouldn't complicate the relationship I was trying not to have with Sam.

Marcus shared Haley Ames' contact information then waved as he headed off across the lawn.

Now all I had to do was make a few more decisions.

I had to figure out how to pay for it. Which might include giving up the job I'd come to look forward to at Hank's Garage and head up to the city for something full time.

Or I could take out a mortgage for the renovations. But that might require a full-time job as well. I still had most of the severance package Bill Havelock had given me, but I was living on that and with Christmas coming, would need to spend some of it on my boys.

Last option was selling some of the investments Garrett and I had put away over the years. Usually, it's a good thing when investments increase in value, but selling them means taking a tax hit. Maybe it was time to find a new broker in this neck of the woods instead of relying on phone calls and email from the brokerage in Virginia and get some advice face to face.

Another question to address. Did I want to have a roommate right away? A woman I'd not yet met. Even if I liked her, until the renovations were complete, we'd be sharing some spaces, like the kitchen and dining area.

The fact that I was in a dither over which way to go with this, I reluctantly had to admit to myself, was because until just few short months ago, I'd let Garrett make all our decisions. I think the last independent decision I'd made was my choice of college. Where, ironically, I'd met Garrett in the first place.

The end of our marriage, the loss of my employment, those decisions had been taken out of my hands. The boys had made their college decisions with minimal input from me. Even my decision to move to this new place in Maine I couldn't claim as entirely my own. Garrett had requested that I leave the dwelling I'd called home for the last twenty years and Maggie had chosen to leave the Captain Patrick Murray House to me. I'd needed a place to go, and the easiest path had brought me here.

What did that say about me?

I couldn't even claim the idea to renovate Murray House was entirely my decision. Well, it was my decision to go ahead with it, but Jaycee had suggested it. My sons had thought it sounded like a good idea, too. And Marcus' enthusiasm was impossible not to get caught up in.

So, I did what I always did.

I called Jaycee.

"Fantastic!" Jaycee said when I finished describing the project. "As long as that room across the hall is still mine."

"Both those two rooms across from mine will remain as they are now, so you're good to go."

"Awesome," Jaycee said. "You like this Marcus guy? Have you checked his credentials?"

"If you mean references, yes. Nothing but high praise from everyone he's done a job for. He'll be getting a licensed plumber for that part of the job. Ditto electricians. That solve your doubts?"

"I'm proud of you, Kenzie."

"For what?" I asked, confused about what I'd done to earn it.

"For taking my random idea and running with it. I just tossed it out there because you were worried about wasting all that space and finding a way to pay for it. But you found a guy to come up with plans and hired him. All by yourself."

"Well, I still haven't figured out how to pay for it."

"You will," she replied with confidence. "Now tell me how things are going with Sam."

"Nothing's going with Sam," I protested, even as my mind drifted to the wink he'd sent my way at work the day he'd given me Marcus' phone number, or the fact he'd taken me to lunch two days ago, leaving his shop in the hands of Paul and Jack.

"Last time we talked he knocked your socks off with a kiss. No way am I believing that hasn't changed anything between you two."

I sighed. The mind reader hadn't lost her touch.

Chapter Twenty-Three

Sam Philips – Present Day

"We need to talk," Kenzie announced when Sam poked his head into the garage office just before quitting time.

"Oh?" He stepped all the way into the office. A totally different place than it had been before he'd hired her to take over his mess. Clean, comfortable, coffee that didn't taste like sludge. She'd even found an old easy chair left out on someone's lawn with a 'take-me-I'm-free' sign on it. After installing a new slipcover that wouldn't show dirt, it had become his favorite hangout when he wasn't working on someone's car.

But the look on her face at the moment wasn't the kind of expression that boded well.

"Something wrong?" The Kenzie he'd gotten to know was always cheerful and upbeat. But clearly something was troubling her today.

"I'm reading help-wanted ads," she said folding a copy of the Times Record and setting it aside.

A lance through his gut. "I thought you enjoyed working here."

He'd been under the impression she liked her job keeping Hank's Garage running smoothly. Sure, he'd often been frustrated when he couldn't find something and probably wasn't very gracious about it, but that didn't seem like an excuse to quit. And he'd gotten used to seeing her here. Never mind he'd gotten used to not having to think about office shit.

"I do." Her shoulders slumped. "But things have changed and—"

He cut her off. "And I've been pestering you to go out on a real date? Is that what this is about? Just say the word, and I'll back off."

Not that he wanted to. He liked her. Like her a lot more than he'd have believed possible just a few months earlier. He'd even begun to imagine what being in a relationship with her might be like. That was a thought none of the women he'd spent any time with since his wife died had triggered.

"It's not that," Kenzie said, her shoulders rising and falling again.

"Then I don't get why you want to leave Hank's?" Or me, his gut wanted to add. He sank into the comfortable old chair.

"I need a full-time job, but—"

"Work full time for me," he blurted before she could go on.

"Sam . . ." her tone was soft and regretful. "Much as you might want me to stay, as much as I'd like to stay, there's just not enough to keep me busy here full time. And I need the income."

"It's about money?" He swallowed his surprise. "You're worth your weight in gold here." He was probably arguing in vain if she'd already made up her mind, or even started on interviews. "I'll give you a raise. And I'll find more work for you if you just need to work more hours. How do you feel about detailing?" He threw that out there because it was something people had asked about, but he and his crew just hadn't had time to add such a service. You didn't have to be a mechanic to detail a car.

"Detailing? What's that?" A frown decorated her pretty face.

"Basically, it's cleaning cars. A bottom-line detailing package includes washing the car, the windows, giving it a wax job and vacuuming it inside. But it can expand to include washing tires, trim, hubcaps, interior everything, including upholstery. It's a lucrative business that folks have asked about, but we're busy just keeping up with repairs and general maintenance. If you're interested, we can clean up that unused bay and set you up to give it a try. We can advertise. You can keep all the proceeds above costs."

He shut his mouth because it sounded like he was begging even in his own ears.

Her brow rose giving him hope. "Garrett used to pay to have his car cleaned like that, but he never told me how much he paid. What does it pay, anyway?"

Aha! A spark of interest. Time to fan the flame. "A good job? A Hundred. A really great job maybe twice that or more. And tips."

Kenzie surged halfway out of her chair, her eyes wide. "You're kidding me. Right?"

"Google it," Sam said. "I'm not kidding."

She stared at him for a long minute, then fell back in her chair and swung around to the new computer she'd insisted his office needed. Her fingers danced over the keys. Her head jerked toward the screen, then she swung back around to him. "Holy Crap! I had no idea."

"So, you'll toss that newspaper and give it a try?"

She sagged back in her chair, but it was clear her mind was whirring at top speed.

"Think any harder and I'll be smelling smoke," he joked, or tried to. He was desperate to keep her working for him, not in some stuffy office up town, with some other guy who might seem like a better catch than a mechanic.

"How many detailing jobs would there likely be in a week? Or a Month?"

Thank God! At least she was considering it.

"Won't know until we try." He didn't want to make any promises, but he was pretty sure the idea would pay off for both of them. Bring more business to the shop and augment her income. "If it's not getting too personal, has something changed that you need more income? Anything I can help with?"

She frowned. "I don't want a loan, if that's what you're implying."

"I wasn't implying anything. I just wanted to help if I could."

"Marcus came by with plans for renovations. Eventually having two apartments I can rent out will provide all the income I need, but the big expense is upfront. I considered selling some of my stocks but the broker I discussed that with said the tax consequence would be even steeper than I had imagined."

She tapped the newspaper but didn't pick it up again. "I talked to a guy at the bank about a loan, but my income doesn't meet with their requirements. He said when I had a full-time job, I could reapply.

"It's not like I want to go to work up in Brunswick or Bath. I like being down here on the islands and not having a commute. But I really like Marcus' ideas and I want to get started sooner rather than later."

"What if I was your backer?" Sam didn't trust the stock market, so all his savings, what he hadn't put aside for Becca, was in CDs. And they weren't paying shit right now.

Kenzie stared at him for a long time. He began to squirm in that comfortable chair she'd installed, afraid he'd totally offended her.

"Unlike you," he decided to explain. "I don't have money in the stock market. Mine is all in savings and CDs, which with the current interest rate, isn't paying me all that much. If I floated you a building loan, I'd charge you less than the bank and I'd still earn more than I'm making now."

She shook her head. "That's a generous offer, Sam. I appreciate it and your faith in me, but—"

He stood up. "Tell you what. I don't want you to feel pressured. You don't need to answer right now. Think about it. We can talk more tomorrow. Or the next day. Or even next week. But I'm serious. Hank's doesn't want to lose you and setting up a detailing shop would just enhance my business. We can have a professional draw up the paperwork if you want to do the loan thing and aren't comfortable with a handshake. But think about it before you say no."

He moved to the door then turned back. "I like you, Kenzie. I'd like to keep you around."

Before he could do something he couldn't take back, he left the office. Something like blowing her a kiss or just sending a wink her way. Both of which he'd like to do more of.

CHAPTER TWENTY-FOUR

Kenzie Ross – Present Day

I thought about Sam's offer, both of them while I was walking Duffy. While I poked about my big old house, fixing meals and eating them. Even when my attention should have been on something else, like the book I'd picked up to read, or the program I'd tuned into on the television.

I was reluctant, for once, to call Jaycee. She would have been up-front with me about her opinions, both for and against. But this time I wanted the decision to be my own.

Once I realized why I hadn't called Jaycee, I understood what was bothering me about Sam's offer.

Not the detailing part, but the loan part. I'd been a stay-at-home mom until my boys were in high school and only then began to add an income to the family coffers. Even that paycheck, as generous as it had been for the work I was doing, hadn't come close to Garrett's. Which meant I'd never been financially independent.

I wanted to be that now. Maggie's gift of this house had given me a leg up. Bill and Sara's severance package had given me time to get a grasp of my economic affairs. Turning down my attorney's suggestion to go after alimony had been more about emotionally distancing myself from Garrett but had also severed my dependence on his income even though I'd not considered that aspect of it at the time.

Accepting Sam's loan offer would undo all the progress I'd made toward supporting myself. I'd just be relying on a different man to keep my boat afloat.

I still had most of my severance cache. I could use some of that to get things started, and after I'd had a chance to try the detailing thing, I'd have a better idea how much it would add to my income. At the broker's suggestion, I'd stopped having dividends reinvest and instead dump into cash I could just transfer to my checking account. Even though the banker had been reluctant to include them in consideration for a bank loan, they weren't insignificant.

Sitting down at my computer with this decision made, I brought up the Amazon site and proceeded to order two books on the subject: The Art of Detailing and The Profitable Auto Detail Shop.

Pleased that I'd conquered this resolve, I called to Duffy.

He lifted his head off his fluffy bed in front of the fireplace and looked at me.

"Wanna go for a walk?"

His head tipped, his eyes seeming to light with agreement. Then he scrambled to his feet and hurried to my side.

"All right, then," I said giving his ears a scratch and getting to my feet.

"Did you know your mom is going to become an auto detailer?" I asked as I reached for his leash and opened the door.

He wagged his tail and preceded me out onto the porch.

He might not be big on conversation, but he was a good listener, and he sure knew how to make me feel good. How had I existed all these years without a dog to keep me company and agree with every word I said?

By the end of the week, I'd not only received both books from Amazon, but had read all of one and most of the second. I also had a start on a list of things we'd need to order to get the work done once we had a customer signed up.

I found Sam under the hood of a cherry red Chevy Malibu. "I decided I'd give it a try."

Sam straightened, clocking his head on the hood. "Ouch!"

"Sorry. I didn't mean to startle you."

"De nada," he said, rubbing his crown and disrupting his hair until it stood on end. Now he resembled Duffy after he'd gone swimming and shaken vigorously. The two new males in my life had a lot in common despite being totally different species. At least in quirky, adorable behavior. Sam also listened attentively, but unlike my dog, he frequently had a comment to add.

"Give what a try?" Sam said with one last rub to his head.

"The detailing thing." I held up the two books, one of which had a dozen little markers tabbing pages I'd wanted quick reference to.

His smile was instant and wide. "I was hoping you'd opt in for that. Business was slow today, so I set Ed to cleaning out that extra bay in case you said yes." He raised his voice. "Hey. Ed."

"Yes, boss?" Ed appeared wiping his hands on a shop rag.

"Show the lady her new digs." Sam tapped the books I clutched to my chest. "Put together a list of things you think you'll need. We can go over it later and maybe there'll be stuff I can add you haven't thought of. Might be some we already have on hand."

Sam ducked his head back under the hood, and I joined Ed. We headed off to see where I'd be plying my new trade.

Late in the afternoon on the Tuesday before Thanksgiving, I stood in the center of my new work domain. On a day when there had been only two cars in the shop for work, Jack had pried the tops off the paint I'd purchased and given the old bay a whole new look.

A coat of pale blue paint made the place look twice the size and much brighter. I'd explained, parroting what I'd read in my book on the subject, that folk who bring their cars in for a detail job would expect the place it happened to be as impeccable and shiny as they wanted their cars to look. I still shared the shelves along the far wall with the rest of the shop. Boxes of oil and air filters had been returned to the freshly painted shelves along with other things I had no clue about.

The floor had been scrubbed and bleached almost to its original gray, and new bulbs had been installed in the overhead light fixtures. The whole place glowed.

I couldn't wait to get started.

Sam had informed me just that morning, that my first appointment had been set for the Monday after the holiday. He didn't mention who my customer was, just that we had our first detailing patron.

"You're totally transforming this place," Jack said spinning on one heel to take in the whole. "First the office actually looks like an office instead of a dump. Now this space looks clean enough to do surgery in."

"I hope that's a good thing," I replied giving him a glance.

He grinned. "Just don't go trying to clean us up. If we are too clean, it might give customers the wrong impression about our ability to fix their car problems."

I scanned his greasy overalls and grinned back. "Deal. You have any plans for dinner on Thursday? If not, you're welcome at Murray House." I'd already invited Sam and his daughter, whom I'd not yet met, but what was one more place at the table when I had a twenty-two-pound bird thawing in my refrigerator?

"Headed to my girlfriend's. Her dad's kind of a bore, but her mom's a killer cook."

"Have a good day then. See you on Monday."

Jack saluted and left me to admire my detailing bay one more time before heading home myself. Sam had taken off earlier to pick Becca up at the University of New Hampshire. Hank's was officially closed for the rest of the week unless someone needed a tow. Then Sam was on call.

My boys were due into the bus station up town later this evening, and I was looking forward to having them with me. Liam had been up to check Murray House out, but Luke had yet to see my new home and I was excited about showing it off.

Garrett had called to complain about the boys coming to me rather than home to the house where they'd grown up. I'd tried to calm the waters by reminding him they only had a couple days off and I was close enough to get to without spending half their time traveling. Reluctantly, I'd promised to encourage them to spend at least half their winter break in Virginia.

Not that I thought they'd need much encouragement. They both had almost a month off and I expected they would be eager to reconnect with friends from high school. Luke might or might not still have a girlfriend to be with. They'd parted with promises to keep their relationship going, and given the ease of texting, I expected they'd stayed connected and shared everything about their new experiences despite her being on the west coast.

Liam's girl had signed up for a year of study abroad and wouldn't be home again until May. They had parted amicably but with no promises.

I hoped both of my boys would spend some of their winter break with me, but I wasn't holding them to it. I was going to make the most of their Thanksgiving visit, then dive into the renovations to Murray House, my new detailing gig and maybe even letting myself see where a relationship with Sam might go.

I wasn't giving up my independence, and it wasn't like I was making a life commitment. But it was time to stop pretending that I was immune to his charm. Or that I didn't enjoy spending time with him. I'd given up telling myself it was just a kiss because as soon as I'd admitted I wanted more of them, that mantra no longer worked. I hadn't asked for a dog either and just look how that had worked out.

CHAPTER TWENTY-FIVE

Eleanor Murray – 1944 – New York City

Eleanor Murray stepped down from the hissing locomotive and was bumped and prodded along with all the other passengers headed toward the main arrival concourse of the Grand Central Terminal. When she emerged with a tapestry carryall over one shoulder and a battered, leather-bound suitcase gripped tight in her other hand, she ignored the jostling of the milling crowds, and gaped at vastness of the station in awe.

Her trip had been both exhausting and exciting. The voices in her head that had haunted her up on the widow's walk had not returned, giving her confidence that the decision she'd made to come to New York was the right one. The whole idea of traveling so far from her home was exciting enough, but she'd also had a chance to see a little of the city of Boston when she'd had to get off the Maine Central line and wait for the train going to New York.

Even Portland had felt like a bustling metropolis, but Boston had been a world away from her quiet little island at the northern reaches of Casco Bay. Now here she was in the place folks called the city that never sleeps and even Boston faded in contrast.

Grand Central, all by itself, was an eye-opener. It felt like she'd walked a mile between stepping from the train onto the platform and arriving in the main concourse. A concourse so vast all of Bailey Island would have fit inside it with room to spare.

Awed, she gazed up at a giant mural depicting servicemen from all the branches and the words, *"That government by the people shall not perish from the earth."* She'd definitely come to the right place. A place she might find a bigger niche in the war effort than her paltry Victory Garden.

An enormous clock loomed above the ticket counter. Behind that rose a long balcony, beneath a blue painted ceiling so high Eleanor imagined birds soaring from one bright window to the next.

As beautiful and amazing as Grand Central was, Eleanor was more than a little intimidated. Rooted to the spot, she prayed Aunt Emily would find her, because she had no idea where to go next.

But after waiting for some time with no sight of her aunt, Eleanor took a deep breath, lifted her suitcase, and headed toward a wide set of stone steps leading up to enormous arching doors she hoped led out to the street. Maybe there she would find the nerve to hail a taxicab and give the driver her aunt's address.

"Oh, here you are, at last!" Aunt Emily descended the stone stairs in a rush and enveloped Eleanor in a welcoming hug.

"This place is so magnificent," Eleanor declared when her aunt finally released her and stepped back.

"It is quite the place, is it not? I understand it's in a class of its own, as train stations go, but then, I've never seen Chicago or the west coast. I've only ever been to Washington DC. Perhaps we shall go there one day. But for now, is this all the luggage you have?" Emily took the battered suitcase from her hand.

"It's all I cared to bring to the city," Eleanor replied. "You said we might shop and I feared most of what I own would not be at all up to snuff here." If the rest of the city was anything like this impressive train station, Eleanor was doubly glad she'd left her country clothes at home.

"Yes, yes, we will definitely shop," Emily gushed as she took Eleanor's arm and urged her toward the stairs. "You must be exhausted. All those hours on the train. Did you have a decent meal, at least?"

Not quite sure what her aunt considered decent, Eleanor thought the meal in the dining car had been one of the most elegant she'd ever eaten. "I am a little tired, but I did have dinner."

"Well, then, let's get you home for a nice cuppa and a chance to put your feet up."

Grand Central Terminal was as impressive outside as it had been inside, but Aunt Emily didn't give Eleanor time to admire much of the surrounding city as she bustled her into a long black car with luxurious seats driven by a man in a uniform who appeared to know where they were going without being told. Eleanor gazed in awe at the teeming traffic as her aunt chattered on during the ride.

Far fewer cars and a lot less bustle greeted her as she climbed from the car opposite what her aunt told her was Central Park. A vast green space carved out of the busy city. Eleanor prayed she would have an opportunity to explore this park that seemed, from what she could glimpse of it, bigger than her whole island and the island next to it back home. Everything in New York City seemed bigger than home.

But with that brief glimpse, she was hustled up the wide granite steps of one of the tallest buildings Eleanor had ever even seen, never mind been inside. Her next revelation was the elevator.

Would she ever stop running into things she'd never seen or done?

One thing she'd either forgotten, or never knew, about her aunt who'd made only rare visits to Bailey Island, was how much she loved to talk. There was a constant barrage of questions Eleanor was never given time to answer mixed with comments about everything from the proper tip for the bellman to possible options for employment if Eleanor still wished to find a war job. Awed into speechlessness, Eleanor was happy to let her aunt go on while she just soaked up as much of the new ambiance as she could.

They paused only briefly in a living room that looked like it belonged on a movie set before bustling down the hall where Aunt Emily ushered her into an elegant bed chamber.

The word bedroom wasn't even close to adequate to describe this new space. High ceilings painted pale lavender contrasted with the bold gold and purple wallpaper and gold drapes that ran all the way to the floor from matching wood valances. A bed twice the size of her bed at home was covered with an elegant comforter and a dozen fancy little pillows. A small divan sat at its foot, also piled with decorative satiny pillows.

Luxury was the order of the day and something Eleanor planned to enjoy every moment of for as long as she was here. However plebeian that might be, she would stick to her determination to find a war job, but coming home at the end of the day would be an indulgence to be savoured.

"Just leave your things. My woman will unpack for you and put them all away. I have a lovely little afternoon repast planned," Aunt Emily said as she parked the battered little suitcase on a wooden stand beside an elegant mahogany dresser. "Yes, yes, I know you said you've already eaten, but Alice will be hurt if you don't at least sample her meat pie and scones.

Long before her usual bedtime, Eleanor's eyelids were drooping, and Aunt Emily urged her to lie down and rest. Tomorrow would be time enough to discuss what to do first now that Eleanor had finally come for a visit. From the chatter during their 'repast" that had been more than elegant to a country girl like Eleanor, it seemed as if Aunt Emily had her days planned well into the next month. Places she wanted to show Eleanor, places Eleanor might wish to explore on her own, shops they simply must visit, and of course, a trip to the top of the Empire State Building.

Vaguely and with some reluctance, Aunt Emily revealed that women were now being employed at the Brooklyn Navy Yard to take on jobs left behind by men going off to war. They were essential positions the country needed filled. If Emily was still of a mind to pursue war work, that's where she should apply. Training, Aunt Emily had assured Eleanor, was included with the temporary hiring, thus Eleanor's lack of experience would not be a deterrent.

Finally left on her own, Eleanor found her nightdress tucked neatly in a drawer next to her underwear. A quick trip to the bathroom, another luxurious amenity fit with an enormous tub, what looked like gold faucets and a toilet that was more like a throne than a mere necessity, and then she climbed up the little stair-stool and onto the bed and stretched out. Every joint and muscle in her reveled in the luxury and comfort and she was way too tired to worry about the shabby nightdress she wore.

Eleanor closed her tired eyes with one last thought coursing through her. Coming to New York might have been the best decision she could have made considering Mike's kiss and her deplorable desire for him to do it again despite her promises to Jeff, but it was also turning out to be a most fantastic adventure.

It was nearly a month before Eleanor was finally allowed to visit the Brooklyn Navy Yard seeking employment. She had not been allowed to find her way via the subway system, but instead, had been delivered by her aunt's driver in the same black car of Eleanor's first ride through the city.

Everything in New York was vast, and this ship building place was no exception. Even Bath Iron Works which Eleanor knew was building and launching a new warship every seventeen days could not compare to the Brooklyn yard in size or the number of people bustling about.

She wondered if she might get lost finding her job every morning if she was hired on but didn't have time to worry about that aspect before her name was called. She was ushered into an office where a harassed looking man shuffled papers around his desk before looking up to acknowledge her presence.

"You want war work?"

Eleanor nodded.

"I don't suppose you've ever seen the inside of a machine shop?"

Eleanor shook her head. Her tongue seemed to have become glued to the top of her mouth.

"You mind wearing overalls and getting dirty?"

"N-no." Eleanor finally managed to speak. "I just want to do what I can to help the war effort, and I was told this is the place where things get done."

The man nodded and handed her a piece of paper. "Fill that out and I'll have someone come show you around."

The application didn't ask for much more than her current address, age, place of birth and contact information. She filled it out and handed it to the equally harassed looking secretary outside the man's office and was then directed to wait in a plain wooden chair.

The wait lasted long enough for Eleanor to begin to have doubts. Aunt Emily had assured her that she need not lift a finger while she lived here in the city. But Eleanor was determined to do her part, so she waited.

And waited.

And waited.

After what felt like hours, a man wearing dirty coveralls poked his head in the door and cleared his throat before asking if she was Miss Murray. When she stood, he crooked a finger in her direction and disappeared. She had to hustle to keep up.

He walked with a limp, but that infirmity didn't seem to slow him down any. Before she had time to consider much else, he showed her into a room filled with rows of giant machines connected to overhead wheels by slapping leather belts. The noise was deafening, and he had to raise his voice to a shout to make himself heard.

"Tomorrow you will report here at eight o'clock sharp and we will see if you are trainable. You will ask for Mr. Hubbard. He will be your instructor."

Then the young man handed her a folded garment. He glanced at her shoes. "Get yourself a pair of work boots."

Then he turned and left her standing just inside the workshop door.

Eleanor wasn't sure if she'd been dismissed or not. While waiting to see if the man would return, she watched a woman not much older than herself working one of the gigantic machines just a short distance away.

She inched closer to see what the woman was doing.

The big machine had a long fat rod clamped in its jaws and the thing was spinning. Driven, apparently, by those belts that whirred and slapped. Meanwhile, the woman held a slender piece of metal in both hands, propped on wood pedestal with a notch in the top and mounted on rails that ran the length of the machine. Slowly, the woman advanced the thing in her hands toward the spinning rod and with a soft sound, a spiral began to appear in the rod's surface. She watched fascinated by the deepening groove and the ease of the cutting.

Abruptly the woman pulled back, put a hand on a lever and the spinning stopped. She peered at her work, released it from the metal jaws and dropped it into a basket at her side. Then she installed a fresh rod, and the process began again.

Eleanor had no idea what the rod was meant to become, but if this was the kind of work she'd be doing, she was confident she could learn how. Her certainty returned, even if the man who'd brought her here and instructed her to buy some work boots didn't. She could do this.

She turned and let herself out, clutching the coarse gray fabric bundle to her chest.

Chapter Twenty-Six

Mike Hamilton - 1944

Mike finished tightening the last screw into the leather harness he'd created for Rascal. He'd had to fashion the guiding harness based entirely on memory. He'd watched the seeing eye guide dog in New York in amazement, fascinated by how the dog always seemed to know what to do next to help his blind master navigate the crowded train station. Even stairs had posed barely a hesitation before the man lifted his foot and placed it on the first step, then ascended just like the rest of the teeming throng of people.

In all that attention to the amazing dog, Mike hadn't really thought much about the harness it wore. He only remembered that it had a sturdy leather handle the man could grasp as he followed the dog's direction.

Mike held his hand made creation up to inspect it. He'd measured Rascal several times during the process to make sure it would fit him securely and the handle would always stay in the proper position. Now it just remained to test it out with Ruthie and Rascal. He set the screwdriver down and headed out to find his sister.

She was gliding back and forth on the swing he'd hung on Gram's porch. That had been another task to distract him from missing Eleanor after her abrupt departure from Bailey Island. Gram had wished for a porch swing for months, maybe years, but his grandfather had just pretended not to hear.

Scrounging up enough lumber to create the two-man seat, then attaching it to the porch roof using pot warp he'd begged off a lobster fisherman, had been both a labor of love for a woman he owed so much to and a diversion from the woman he loved and missed.

He'd always loved Eleanor Murray. Her being his best friend's little sister had put him in her company often, but the four years that separated them in age had felt like a chasm he couldn't breach back before he'd left for England.

When Ray told him of her engagement, he'd been crushed. He'd missed his chance to declare himself and she'd found someone else. That she'd promised herself to a man like Jeff Winslow just made it worse. To give him his due, Jeff had still been a teenager when Mike last saw him, and maybe he'd straightened himself out. But what if he hadn't? What if he turned out just as nasty or unreliable as his old man. Everyone knew Curt Winslow was a mean drunk who regularly beat his wife and cheated on her frequently.

If only Mike had told Eleanor how he felt before he'd left. Maybe she'd have been waiting for him to return, instead of Jeff. But that was water over the dam. Mike couldn't go back and change the past. He had tried to be a decent loser and just watch out for Ray's kid sister on his return from the war. But loving her was harder to turn off than he'd anticipated.

He'd held her too close when he'd finally had an excuse to hold her at all. But even that wasn't his worst offense. He'd given in to the overwhelming desire to kiss her. Lost in the sweet sensation of her lips beneath his, it had taken a bit before he realized she was returning his kiss.

Rather than shove him away in anger or alarm, she'd opened her mouth and let him in. And then he'd really been lost. Taking total advantage of her innocent acquiescence, he'd turned what started out fairly chaste into a declaration of desire that had shocked him in its intensity.

Apparently, it had shocked her as well. She'd not said anything to him, either that night or the next time he'd been in her company, but in less than a week she'd been on a train to New York. Running away from him, he was sure.

His heart was in tatters, and it was entirely his own fault. To be fair to himself, his heart had been broken the day he'd learned of her engagement, but it clearly hadn't recovered by the time he'd returned, a wounded man, and found her wearing her brother's overalls and turning sod for a garden.

So many ifs. If he hadn't been so stupid about not declaring himself years before. If she hadn't gotten engaged to Jeff Winslow. If Mike hadn't been injured and needed to recover before finding employment, thus keeping him on the island close enough to keep finding excuses to see her. If he hadn't kissed her.

Rascal jumped down from the swing, disturbing Ruthie's gentle rocking and Mike's unhappy thoughts on the pitfalls of his own life.

"Is that you, Mike? Want to swing with me?"

"I've got something better. At least I hope it will be better." He held up the harness he'd fashioned then remembered she couldn't see it so moved to her side. "Give me your hands."

She held her hands out, palms up. He settled the harness into them. Her face puckered in a frown. "What is it?"

"It will be easier to just show you. Wait a minute."

Mike reclaimed the harness and told the dog to sit. Then he slipped it over the dog's head and buckled it into place.

"We should probably go down onto the grass," he told Ruthie, reaching to take her hand. She jumped to her feet and let him lead her down the steps and onto the lawn with Rascal at her heels. The dog had taken on the responsibility of being her guide like he'd been born and bred to it.

Once on flat, grassy lawn, Mike positioned the dog at Ruthie's left side. He took her hand and placed it on the strap that served as a handle on Rascal's new harness. She drew back, not sure what he was doing.

"No, keep your hand on the strap, Ruthie," Mike instructed. "It's attached to Rascal. So long as you are holding it, he can take you anywhere you tell him you want to go. We'll have to teach him some more commands and probably a whole bunch of new words for places you might want to be or things you might want to fetch. But he's a smart learner. He'll be able to help you go everywhere eventually. Wait here a minute."

Mike left her clinging to the new harness and walked about twenty feet away. Then he called to her. "Tell Rascal to go to Mike."

"Why?" Ruthie asked.

"Just tell him and see what happens."

Ruthie took a breath and then spoke in comical seriousness. "Go to Mike, Rascal."

The dog glanced at her just briefly, then stepped out gently as if he knew instinctively that he needed to go slowly until the girl learned to trust him.

Mike watched them approach with a sense of satisfaction that blossomed in his chest almost as fiercely as his love for Ruthie or Eleanor.

When they arrived in front of him, the dog stopped moving and looked at the girl.

"Are we there yet?" Ruthie asked.

Mike fell to his knees and wrapped her in a celebratory hug. "Yes, you are. And Rascal brought you."

Ruthie hopped happily from foot to foot. "I can go anywhere now. All by myself."

"Yes you can," Mike told her, letting her free of the hug that inhibited her gleeful hopping. He patted the dog's head. "Good boy, Rascal. Now let's see what other new places we can teach him to go."

Chapter Twenty-Seven

Kenzie Ross – Present day

The first time I had a meal at this old trestle table, I felt like it belonged in a mess hall and would seat a whole platoon. Admittedly, a bit of exaggeration, but it just seemed so enormous when it was just me eating alone that I'd taken to eating at the island in the kitchen most of the time. But today, there were thirteen of us, if you didn't count Duffy who kept a close watch for any tidbit that might escape and land on the floor. I was thankful for every inch of the big table.

Liam and Luke had arrived on the last bus into town the night before just as they'd promised. Sam, his daughter Becca, and my new friends Dawn and George with their boys, Trey and Hunter had all joined us. I had also invited Sam's mechanics when I learned that Paul was planning to eat a TV dinner alone and since Ed had two young kids, Davy and Trisha, that he was raising on his own, it just seemed right to add them to my growing guest list.

The chatter was high-spirited, and everyone seemed to be enjoying themselves. And I was feeling happier and more in tune with my life than I had in a long time. Perhaps you need to lose something you thought was important to be fully grateful for what you have. Thanksgiving was a good time for me to be realizing this vision, so I offered up big thank-you to the man upstairs.

"Hey, Mom," Liam grabbed my attention. "Guess what? Becca wants to be a veterinarian. Is that awesome or what?"

"That explains why Duffy has been parked at her feet since she arrived. He knows a dog person when he sees one."

"I love cats too," Becca added. But I saw her hand moving beneath the table and I guessed Duffy's head was in her lap. The beggar.

"Becca saw the Budweiser Clydesdales get all groomed and hitched up at a county fair this fall." Liam's voice was filled with awe and a hint of envy.

Becca began describing the process which sounded formidable.

"And the funniest part was the dog," she ended her description. "I have no idea how those horses managed not to step on him because he was running around under their feet the whole time."

"Why is it funny if a dog gets stepped on?" Ed's youngest boy asked with a frown.

"Not funny, really," Becca admitted. "I just thought it was kind of amazing the little dog didn't get stepped on."

"What kinda dog was it?" Davy asked.

"On TV it's always a golden puppy," his sister Trisha, informed him.

"There's a golden puppy in the ads on TV, but when I saw the real Clydesdales, the dog was like the ones in the movie 101 Dalmatians. White with black spots. And he was too small to jump all the way up to the wagon so when they were ready to go, someone had to lift him up." Becca explained.

Davy and Trisha began pelting Becca with questions about the horses and the dog and I tuned into a conversation about the upcoming football game and who everyone thought would win. I didn't have any favorites, so I just listened, enjoying the hum of conversation around the table.

I was relishing the day more than I recall any holiday in recent memory, but I didn't want to dwell on how much Garrett's strictures and my own constant caving to whatever he decreed might have played in my past. I just wanted to savor this day and the friendships and company it brought. And, of course, precious time with my boys.

Later, the dishwasher hummed, and I was just finishing the last of the pots when two arms snaked around my middle and gave me a hug. "You should have waited, Mom. I'd have done those for you." Luke let me go and ducked around to grab the dishtowel off my shoulder.

"Go sit down and let me finish at least."

"Isn't there another game?" I asked as he tackled drying the roasting pan.

"There's always another game on Thanksgiving. One thing you can count on. Sam's building a fire in the fireplace and Ed just took his kids home, so things are calming down."

I reached up, pulled his head down, and planted a kiss on his cheek. "It's good to have you home."

"You already told me. Now go." He snapped the towel in my direction.

I went.

Sam's fire was well underway. My remaining guests were in various states of relaxation, some bordering on, or outright napping. Becca, Liam, Hunter and Trey were playing cards, and despite their ages and supposed sophistication, it sounded like Crazy Eights. I was pleased that they all got along so well.

"Come sit with me," Sam invited, patting the pillows he'd arranged in front of the fireplace.

I glanced over at the game table and wondered what my boys would think of their mom snuggling with a man who was not their father. Then I remembered Liam's words to me on his first visit to Maine. *You deserve better.*

I did deserve better. I settled myself in the nest of pillows Sam had arranged and let myself enjoy the lovely warm feeling of his arm around my shoulders and the fire crackling before me.

Life was good.

The following morning, Trey came to collect the twins for a promised fishing expedition, and now the house was quiet again.

Sam had echoed what Marcus had told me about Haley Ames. Her lease uptown was up on December first, and she was eager to find somewhere down on the island. Since she worked from home, there was no need to be closer to town and she preferred the island.

I'd reminded Sam that I didn't have separate apartments yet, but he said she'd be happy with a bedroom, use of the kitchen, space for a desk and internet access. Exactly what Marcus had suggested and all of which I could give her. Reassuring myself that I'd like her as much as I liked Sam, a call had been made and she was due any minute now so I could meet her and discuss the possibilities.

Thankfully for the twins fishing outing, the rain had held off, but it was cloudy and glowering, so I didn't walk Duffy to the cove for a swim as I'd gotten into the habit doing of since we'd first arrived on Bailey Island. Easy going canine that he was, he'd done his thing in the unkempt area behind the house and come back in to park himself in front of the fireplace.

Having enjoyed the fire yesterday, I had started one myself today to take the chill off. I was just getting ready to join Duffy when a knock sounded at the front door. Had to be Haley. Everyone else I knew tended to just walk in.

"Well," I said to myself as I headed for the door, "Let's hope I like this lady because deciding she can't stay won't go over well with two of the men currently in my life."

"Hi. I'm Haley Ames," the pretty young woman said in a happy voice the moment I opened the door. She looked so much like Sam with the same dark hair and blue eyes they could have been siblings rather than just cousins.

"And I'm Kenzie Ross. Come on in." I gestured to the big room with the fire burning brightly at the other end.

"I love this room," Haley said dragging out the love to four syllables. She stopped square in the middle and turned slowly around to take it all in. That seemed like everyone's first reaction to the main living area of the old house. It was a great room before that became a thing. I'd done the same the first time I'd walked in while my agent waited patiently to show me the rest of the place.

Relief flooded through me. I liked Haley immediately. Both for her cheerful greeting and her appreciation of my home. With such a positive feeling about her, I decided to go with my gut.

"Good thing. If you plan to move in right away, because this is where you'll get to spend most of your time outside of your bedroom."

"Yeah, Marcus told me about the construction stuff going on."

"Not going on yet, but the work is supposed to get started on Monday. I asked Marcus to wait until after Thanksgiving or the place would be dust and noise already. But let me show you around."

"I hope the idea of me moving in right away is still on the table, because I can tell you already, I can't wait. I love this house. I've never been inside before, but I've always loved it from the outside," Haley gushed.

"There's plenty of room if you want to set up your workspace down here. Some of the bedrooms are generous, too. You can have your choice. Come on upstairs and let me introduce you to the options."

A half hour later we figuratively shook on the deal. She liked the smaller of the two bedrooms on the west side because it had a view of the ocean. It already had a connecting door to the bathroom and the other bedroom on that side would eventually become her living space. She was thrilled. We agreed on a rental fee, and I had my first tenant.

"You know," she said as we stood at the door. "Once Marcus finishes doing his thing, your great room would make a wonderful place for people to hang out. Like sort of a money-maker."

She already knew I was worried about money? Who blabbed? Or was this just another facet of living in a small place I needed to get comfortable with. Everyone knowing my business – sometimes before I did.

Wondering what she had in mind, I started to ask, but she hurried on before I got a word out.

"Like a tea house. Except I can't imagine a tea house here on Bailey Island. Most everyone guzzles coffee like they wouldn't survive without it. And I wasn't thinking of a breakfast place, either. There's one of those right over the bridge. By the way, if you haven't been there yet, they make the most awesome scones. Be sure to check it out. But this," She gestured once again to the room behind us, "could be more like an afternoon place. With coffee or tea and something yummy like cookies, or maybe cheese and crackers. Most of the year, you could have a fire in the fireplace like today. All those books are just begging for someone to come settle in and read them. You know what I mean?"

It was my turn to slowly scan the room with fresh eyes. Maybe she had an idea worth exploring. But that would be down the road. "Sounds like an idea we can talk more about later." The woman's enthusiasm was hard to dismiss, but I'd have to give up a lot of personal privacy to turn my main room into a public place. Even just for a few hours in the afternoons.

Haley shoved her hand my way. "I am so glad we met. I have five days left to vacate or sign the new lease at my old place. Which means I'll be here sometime next week or earlier."

"Just give me a call and I'll be sure to be here. And I'll have a set of keys for you."

"Ok. Well, Bye. For now." She said, with a grin. Then she turned and ran down the steps to her little red Mini Cooper waiting in the parking area. I sure hoped Marcus planned to help her move because if she owned anything more than what would fit in a carry on, it would take a lot of trips in that little car. I could have offered, but even my RAV 4 wouldn't fit that much. Definitely not furniture. I should have asked her about furniture given the bedroom she'd claimed was already furnished.

Now I would have to decide what to do with the furniture currently occupying the rooms to be renovated sooner rather than later. Of course, I was going to have to move that stuff anyway to make room for the work crew. I wondered how far away the nearest storage unit was. Or maybe renting one of those pods would be easier.

Before I had a chance to dwell on that question, my phone buzzed.

CHAPTER TWENTY-EIGHT

Eleanor Murray – New York - 1944

Eleanor had gotten used to the hum and clatter of the machine shop that had seemed so noisy the day she'd interviewed for a job. They had started her out on a drill press, drilling holes in large plates that she was told went into the creation of machine-gun mounts. That had been a mind-numbing task. Thankfully, when several new lathes had been added to the shop, she'd been diligent enough at drilling holes to be transitioned to the bigger, more interesting piece of equipment.

She'd gotten good at turning out a variety of parts on the big lathe, all of which would eventually go into outfitting new ships. She had no idea what those parts did or where they would get installed, but she was inordinately proud of her effort to help America win the war, both in Europe and the Pacific.

She and Aunt Emily listened to the radio every night, hanging on every word, censored or otherwise, of the voices reporting on the progress of the war. Aunt Emily especially liked Franklin Roosevelt's Fireside Chats. Eleanor enjoyed them as well, more so now that she didn't have to listen to her father's constant and often negative comments. Lawton Murray was not a fan of Roosevelt and he never held back any criticism.

Eleanor wasn't sure which party she was drawn to, but it just seemed the opposite of patriotic to be bad-mouthing their president at a time like this. She wondered what Jeff thought, but he never said in any of his ever briefer and less frequent letters.

If he'd written any letters that had arrived in Maine after she left, her father had not forwarded them. This didn't surprise her, but she had been swift to send a letter off to Jeff with her new address, and his first letter to her here in New York had finally come earlier that week.

Which was a good thing, she told herself. Missing Jeff had become a close contest to missing Mike. She had no business missing Mike. He was just a friend. Jeff was her fiancé.

Jeff had sounded homesick. Maybe she should find a way to send him another package. Could he use more socks? If not, then what should she send?

Now that she had joined a local USO group, she helped to pack things that went to soldiers in general. Things like tins of meat or jam, cigarettes, and chocolate. It was useless to send baked goods because they would be stale long before they arrived. But now that she was in New York, perhaps she could find something Jeff would like.

Her mind had drifted while she went about the job of running the lathe, making the same cuts on the same piece for several days now. Suddenly she became aware of someone at her elbow.

"How is it going Miss Murray?" Her supervisor asked as Eleanor grabbed the clutch and let the lathe spin.

"Okay, Sir." She responded nodding her head toward the nearly full box of parts.

He picked a piece at random from the box and inspected it. He pulled a micrometer from his pocket and measured the piece. Finally, he nodded. "Keep up the good work."

Then he was gone, off to inspect the next station and that woman's work.

He was a kind man and had endless patience teaching so many untrained women their tasks. Eleanor could have gotten a supervisor like the grouchy boss her new friend, Maria had in the next section of the shop. She was thankful she'd been assigned to this man.

She went back to turning the current piece and was just removing it from the chuck when the whistle blew.

Quitting time.

Her back ached from standing all day. She was thankful to take off her apron and hang it on the machine.

She was also thankful for Aunt Emily's distain of public transportation. Eleanor had planned to ride the subway to work like everyone else. Or most everyone else. But Aunt Emily had refused to hear of it. Instead, she had instructed her driver to bring Eleanor to work each morning and be waiting outside the Brooklyn Navy Yard gates every day at quitting time. Eleanor could walk briskly to the gate, find her aunt's now familiar black Studebaker, and sink gratefully into the lush upholstery for her ride back up town to Central Park and her aunt's equally comfortable apartment.

"I'm home," Eleanor called out after letting herself in and bending to remove her dusty work boots in the tiled front hall so they wouldn't leave footprints on the carpet.

"Another letter from your beau," Aunt Emily called back from somewhere out of sight.

Eleanor hurried over to the little table with a mosaic inlay top.

Jeff's letter was the only thing setting on it, so she snatched it up and headed to her bedroom to read and savor in private.

My Dear Eleanor,

Imagine my surprise to find another letter from you already. I just had to reciprocate. It appears that life in the big city agrees with you, but I do hope that doesn't mean you won't be happy with me back on Bailey Island because I confess, I am most homesick for our lovely island.

Your work at the Navy Yard must bring you much satisfaction as well. I know how you chaffed at being so far from anywhere you could make a meaningful difference in the war effort. Your dedication is commendable, but it is just one of the many things to admire about you.

I was most privileged to hear General Eisenhower speak recently. He talks of a new push in the works to roust the Jerries from France and win this war. We have no idea what is being planned, but I do hope it will bring me home soon.

Jeff

Eleanor let the letter drop to her lap. Jeff used to end his letters with SWAK. He used to mention missing her specifically, but this letter only suggested he missed Maine. Had distance erased the love he'd once professed for her or was he just growing more circumspect because others would be reading his words as they transcribed the Victory Mail?

She read the letter a second time, but this reading planted another seed of unease. What if whatever had been blacked out by the censors had been about plans that would end up putting Jeff in the sights of German guns?

She slid off the bed and down to her knees beside it. Burying her face in his letter, her hands clutched together, she prayed for his safety.

"Eleanor?" Aunt Emily called from the parlor. "The news is coming on. Do you not wish to hear it?"

Eleanor scrambled to her feet and hurried out. She definitely needed to hear the news tonight. If Jeff couldn't share what was coming, the reporter likely wouldn't either, but that didn't mean she wanted to miss hearing whatever he did have to say. Even if everything worth knowing was censored out as Mike claimed.

"On April nineteenth, German troops and police entered a Warsaw ghetto with the intention of deporting its surviving inhabitants," the radio voice was reporting as Eleanor sank onto the ottoman in front of Aunt Emily's polished mahogany radio cabinet. *"The ghetto fighters put up a much stronger resistance than had been expected and they held out for nearly a month. Sadly, the revolt has ended, and the starved and humiliated Jews saw their homes go up in flames. But it does go to show that a spirited and determined effort can make a difference. These men and women held out against the Germans for far longer than some independent countries have."*

The man's voice was replaced by another who had news from the Pacific to impart. Eleanor should care about the Pacific, but she couldn't make herself be as concerned about Marines defending islands on the other side of the globe as she was about soldiers in Europe. Jeff was in Europe so far as she knew.

Jeff who thought Bridget was a sweet Irish colleen. Jeff who no longer sealed his letters with a kiss. Jeff who missed Maine, but not her? Maybe she should care more about those Marines. Maybe the voice that has spoken to her in the widow's walk at home was wiser than she. But the voice had been in her own head. Had it not? What did that say about her?

She'd promised to wait and be faithful. If Jeff had changed his mind and no longer loved her, then she would deal with that once he was back home. She would keep her promise, even if it meant doing her best not to think of Mike. Or the kiss that had changed everything between them.

She turned her mind back to the plight of the Jewish people who had defied the German soldiers to keep their homes yet lost everything despite their courage and endurance.

When the broadcast was over, a whole minute passed before the introductory sounds of *Fibber McGee and Molly* began. Aunt Emily switched the radio off and announced that dinner was waiting for them in the dining room.

Usually, Eleanor enjoyed the antics of *Fibber McGee and Molly* and would have wanted to put supper off until that show was over. But tonight, her mind was full of conflicting emotions. Desperation over what Jeff's words might mean for her. Sorrow for the Jews in Europe. Even worry over the Marines defending islands in the Pacific. And if she was honest, missing Mike.

Following Aunt Emily to the dining room, Eleanor offered up another heartfelt prayer for all those whose homes and businesses had been lost, all thanks to the ego of a nasty little man who wanted to rule the whole world, and the American lives lost on the other side of the world because of another greedy emperor.

"How did your tasks go today?" Aunt Emily asked as her maid brought hot serving dishes to the table.

Eleanor loved her aunt, but how she could ask such an everyday question after the news they'd just heard baffled her.

"Where do you suppose those people went?" She asked after accepting a plate of what appeared to be some kind of meat in a sauce with green beans and who knew what else. Even Aunt Emily had to live with the rationing, despite her wealth.

"What people, Dear?" Aunt Emily asked as she whisked her napkin into her lap.

"The people whose homes were all burned down by the German soldiers." Suddenly, Eleanor didn't feel even the least bit hungry.

"They will likely be taken to camps for the duration of the war," Aunt Emily replied as if she was discussing the disposition of furniture that was moved out of a house while it was being painted. "Now eat up. Cook has gone to pains to make the canned meat tasty, and you need your strength for another day of work tomorrow."

Eleanor filled her fork and brought it to her mouth, but in her current mood, even cook's efforts were in vain. Nothing would likely taste good again until this war was over, and Jeff was home, and all those poor displaced Jewish people were free again.

CHAPTER TWENTY-NINE

Kenzie Ross – Present Day

Duffy and I came in through the mud room off the kitchen since he'd been in swimming, and he was soaking wet. I found the towel I left by the back door and wiped him as dry as a towel can manage with a long-haired water dog.

"Kenzie!" Haley appeared just as Duffy shook, spattering the remaining water clinging to his fur all over Haley. She ignored the unplanned shower. "Marcus needs to talk to you. We've got a problem."

We've got a problem? Haley hadn't wasted any time appropriating a vested interest in my remodeling project. Yesterday, the cost of plywood had gone up. The day before the dumpster they'd delivered had cost twice what I'd been told to expect. God forbid today there was another unbudgeted expense.

"Any idea what it's about?"

"Something about asbestos?" Haley said leading the way back through the kitchen. "Marcus is upstairs."

Haley returned to her desk tucked in an out of the way nook with a single tall window on the far side of the great room. I headed for the stairs.

I found my handyman on the phone in the middle of what would one day be Haley's living room. I waited until he was done, then stepped into view.

"Oh. Kenzie. I'm glad you're here. We ran into a problem I wasn't expecting."

"More money?" I hazarded a guess, based on his grim expression.

"Definitely more money. Unless you opt to skip the professionals. Which I wouldn't advise given the possibility of exposure and the danger of contracting mesothelioma."

Good God! I'd heard ads on TV from law firms promising to get top dollar settlements for the stuff. "Please say no one is suing me," I begged.

"Nope. Just that we found asbestos where we didn't expect to find it. This house is so old most of the insulation is just layers of old newspaper, but somewhere along the line someone must have decided to add asbestos insulation. Back when that was all the rage and before we knew what the stuff could cause."

"How much?" my reeling brain wanted to know.

Marcus shrugged. "Not exactly sure. I just got off the phone with a company that does contained removal. They are sending a guy down tomorrow to give us a quote."

I groaned. My budget had been tight to start with, but with the dumpster and the plywood already claiming some of the buffer, I was beginning to worry that I might have bitten off more than I could chew.

"There is some good news, though," Marcus added encouragingly. "This side of the house apparently wasn't updated when the northeast addition was put on. I have no idea about the downstairs but since we aren't pulling any walls out down there, we can leave that alone. To be honest, I doubt the downstairs has anything more than newsprint either. The upstairs push out in the northeast corner was added long after the original construction. It's the only part of the house that was built when asbestos was being used."

"How can you tell?" Dollar bills on fire flitted through my imagination and I prayed Marcus knew what he was talking about.

"The width of the boards under all that old carpet, for one thing," Marcus replied turning toward the far corner of the now empty room where part of the old carpeting had been pulled back.

"What does the width of the boards have to do with insulation?" I followed him to the patch of bare floor.

"Boards this wide haven't been used in general construction in over a hundred years. Closer to two hundred years." He pointed to the floor which, to my eye just looked like old wood with several coats of paint on it.

"Come here," he straightened and headed to the other side of the house.

I followed, still puzzled about how wide boards made any difference.

"See here?" he gestured to the totally bare expanse of unpainted boards that were much narrower than those in the other room.

"I still don't get it." I shook my head.

"I'll try not to be too preachy. But here's the story in a nutshell. The original house was built almost two hundred years ago. Wide boards were easy to get and quicker to install in the eighteen hundreds. When this addition was put onto the house, wide planks were a premium even when they were available. Hence the narrower boards. Also, back when Murray House was built, they didn't even know about

Asbestos. They used layers of newsprint between the outer wall and the shingles or clapboards. This is the only part of the house with the narrow boards on the floor. So, I'm guessing it's the only part with asbestos. If you find the place drafty and cold come January and decide to insulate, there are other options."

He walked over to the window where trim had been removed and pieces of insulation showed. Not that this meant anything to me given that what he was pointing at looked more like rotting cardboard than the bright pink fiberglass insulation I was more familiar with.

"Do you know when this addition was built onto the house?"

I shook my head. "I found some old photo albums in the attic. They might give us some idea if there are any images of the house itself."

"Well, maybe. I have the guy coming tomorrow. He'll poke about and hopefully this is all he'll find. I just thought you'd want a heads-up."

The workday was over, and Marcus had apparently waited for my return considering his apprentice was gone.

"Thanks, and please, keep me informed," I said after Marcus tossed the last of his tools into his tool chest and started for the stairs.

As soon as I'd closed the door behind him, I hustled to my computer and googled asbestos and mesothelioma.

"How's the project going?" Sam sat at the kitchen island while I fried up some summer squash to go with the rotisserie chicken I'd brought back from the grocery store.

I scooped the squash into a serving bowl and carried it to the counter while I dithered over how much to reveal of the last few days. He'd made that loan offer, and I still didn't want to take it, so I hesitated about sharing the financial setbacks lest he renew the offer and put serious temptation in my way.

"That good, huh?" he asked with that disarming tilt of the head.

So, I explained about the asbestos but bit my tongue over the other unexpected expenses.

"Let's hope Marcus is right about it being just that addition that's involved," Sam said when I'd finished serving dinner and my explanation. "He's experienced with old houses, so I'd be inclined to bank on his judgement."

With my mind still randomly calculating expenses, I asked, "Do you have any new detailing jobs coming in?"

If Sam guessed at my major concern, he didn't let on. "Yup. I would have told you before you left today, but I got caught up on a phone call from the assisted living facility where my Aunt Phe lives."

"Is she okay?"

"Nothing alarming. They just wanted me to schedule her annual checkup and let them know when to transport." He dished up a second helping of potatoes and squash, then went on. "Anyway, that rich dude that bought the big house up on the bluff by the Giant Staircase came in to schedule both his own and his wife's cars. He'll bring his wife's Mercedes in tomorrow and his Range Rover will come in on Tuesday. He's a good tipper, too."

He'd better be an uber generous tipper. I could use the extra cash. Of course, I'd have to go above and beyond to meet the guy's expectations. Maybe this new gig doing detailing would keep me in the black after all. Not that I was ready to share that hope with Sam.

Sam and I were becoming a thing. At least in the eyes of our island neighbors and my boys, while I was still clinging to my independent status. Complicating that resolve, I enjoyed Sam's company far too much to say no when the opportunity arose to be with him. What did that say about my state of mind?

He'd started coming to my place on Thursday nights and he often took me out to dinner on weekends when he wasn't out straight at the shop. I wasn't sure why Thursday had become our night. Maybe because it was toward the end of the workweek, and we were both ready to relax a bit. Maybe it was because there was absolutely nothing on television either of us cared to watch and sitting in front of a crackling fire was far more entertaining. Never mind pleasant.

I wasn't immune to his knock-your-socks off kisses though, and they were maybe the most pleasant part of those nights by the fire. I had begun to wonder if or when he was going to try to take things to the next level, but so far, he hadn't pushed. And I was happy to just enjoy the status quo.

What would it say about me or my determination to remain unattached if I let him take me to bed. Or rather, if I took him to bed, which given the desire rushing through me at times, might even happen before he made his move.

CHAPTER THIRTY

Kenzie Ross – Present Day

For all the time spent in front of the fire, or sharing over a meal, I still didn't know very much about Sam's life before he came into mine. That thought ran through my head as I sipped coffee at my desk at work and tried to decide if I should work on inventory or bills.

Sam had revealed that his wife of seventeen years had lost her fight with breast cancer some three years earlier. He had been in the military and not even in the country when his daughter Becca was born. He'd spent two years at Bowdoin College before enlisting, but never finished his degree, preferring, when his military service was up, to return to his father's shop and tune up cars for a living.

He was a moderate conservative, happy with neither party as far as politics was concerned. He liked to read, but nothing too literary. He preferred Tom Clancy and Lee Child and their ilk. All action, no romance. Which was odd, considering how thoughtful and caring he was as a person. He liked the NCIS and FBI series on television, football both pro and college. But that was the sum total of what I knew about this man who'd so easily invaded my new life.

Sam was personable, handsome, and available and it seemed hard to believe he hadn't dated since his wife passed. But if he had, he never mentioned it. I hadn't heard any scuttlebutt to that effect, but I was still new man on the block and maybe locals didn't tell tales.

I had noticed that Mainers would give you the shirt off their back if you were in need, but they also gave you your space and didn't seem to have a need to know everything about your life. Or maybe they did know more about me than they let on, but kept their sources close to the vest. Where I had lived most of my life, if you disappeared for two days everyone wanted to know if you were okay. Now I could be gone for a month and when I resurfaced not a soul would ask where I'd been. This was a whole new concept for me.

Maybe I needed to start hinting for info about Sam from Evelyn or Dawn. Or just be upfront and nosy when I was with him. It was a two-way street, though, and I hadn't shared much about my former life either. It made me wonder how a man could be willing to loan me a twenty or thirty grand and not want to know more about my trustworthiness? It wasn't like I'd worked for him for years.

Interrupting my thoughts, the desk phone rang, and I answered, ready with the automatic, "Hank's. Who needs our help today?"

"It's Marcus," my contractor said with a chuckle. "And mostly good news. Like I suspected, it's just that new addition that has the evil stuff in it. But we are talking a few grand to remove it. Should I give the guy the go-ahead?"

What choice did I have? "Sure. Did he say when he could get to it?"

"Pete came prepared to isolate the area, so he'll get that done now. It will be Monday, maybe Tuesday of next week before they can do the job, but it won't take more than a day."

"How long of a delay are we talking about for your work?" I had hoped most of the disruption would be done by Christmas and the way things were going maybe we were looking at Easter. Or maybe that was too pessimistic.

"I already talked to Haley and she's fine with camping on the couch in the great room if it's okay with you. We can finish removing the old carpet in her space, strip all the old paint and put in the new doorway. So, no delay. Just a change in the of order tasks."

"Tell her I owe her and thanks. But she doesn't need to sleep on the couch. No one's using the either of the bedrooms across from my room until Christmas."

Marcus rattled off a few more things he planned to get underway, then we hung up.

I had considered both tile or some kind of artificial wood for the new apartment floors, but Marcus had pointed out that the wide planks were without knots and would be stunning just refinished. Now I'd get to see that transformation sooner than expected.

Jack stuck his head in the doorway. "The Mercedes is here whenever you're ready."

I shoved both the inventory and bill folders into the top drawer. Then changed into the L.L.Bean work boots Jaycee had insisted I needed and headed over to the detailing bay with Duffy on my heels.

Four hours later, after I processed Mr. Kemp's credit card, I took my take which included a rewardingly hefty tip, out of the till, and collapsed into the old easy chair.

"You all tuckered out just washing a car?" Jack stepped in to punch his timecard and give me some good-natured ribbing. He was an easy kid to like. All Sam's employees were fun guys. It made coming to work a pleasure. Something I'd enjoyed all the years I'd worked for Bill and Sara but hadn't expected to find again so quickly, if ever.

"Take home the extra brownies," I told Jack pointing at the half empty container. "I don't need to finish them myself."

He snagged the container, sent a kiss my way and disappeared.

Next in was Ed, who was followed by my dog. Duffy had abandoned the detailing bay halfway through that job and had been hanging out with the mechanics. "Say hi to your kids for me," I said as he turned to leave.

Paul reached around the corner, plucked his card from the rack, and jammed it into the timeclock, then left with just a wave.

I was considering hauling myself out of the comfy chair and gathering my stuff when Sam arrived.

"Where did you put the Napa invoice?"

"Where did you last see it?" I responded, knowing full well, he wouldn't remember.

"I put it on the desk but when I came in looking for it, you had moved it somewhere."

"You left it under a stack of shop towels on the bench in the garage." I shook my head. It was a wonder anything had ever gotten paid before I started work for Hank's. "It in my bills file now." I got up and went to the desk, pulled the drawer out and handed him the Napa invoice.

He studied it a moment, grunted and handed it back.

"How about supper up town?" He asked on a completely different tack.

I looked down at my soiled and still damp garments.

"After we both clean up," he said noting my hesitation. "If you're up for Thai, we can head up to Bangkok Gardens. Full disclosure? I need to stop at Walmart on the way home, though."

An hour later, while we enjoyed a tasty dinner of salmon curry, Sam asked about the progress at Murray House. I told him about the wide boards and apparently, he knew more about their significance than I did and whole-heartedly approved Marcus' plans to leave them with nothing more than a protective coat of top-quality polyurethane.

We followed the curry with Templar cheesecake, a dish I'd never tried before but instantly became a convert. Then it was off to Walmart and the mundane and very unromantic job of purchasing supplies for his shop and my kitchen.

While Sam was getting bulky stuff for the shop, I decided to do my weekly grocery shopping and skip a trip up later. We grabbed separate carts and parted with a promise to meet back at the door. It wasn't like Brunswick Maine was a dangerous place at night, but Sam vetoed meeting at the car. He didn't want me loitering alone in the parking lot that late at night.

Chivalry wasn't dead after all.

We were unusually silent on the trip back down the peninsula in the dark, but it was a comfortable silence. Sam turned the radio on and tuned into an oldies station, to which he hummed along. It felt like the whole town had gone to bed. Even Cook's Lobster House was dark as we crossed the Bailey Island bridge. Fishermen keep early hours and pretty much everyone else in my new neighborhood does, as well. Another change for my lifestyle of being a life-long night owl who never had trouble finding places open and people up until well after midnight.

Sam pulled his truck right up to my back door to make unloading easier.

Duffy greeted us enthusiastically, then went about his business while we carried groceries in.

"Do I get to enjoy a snifter of brandy and a fire?" Sam asked after he'd let the dog back in and I'd finished unpacking at least the refrigerator items in my bulging grocery bags.

"I don't have any brandy, but I can offer you some Bailey's Irish Cream."

Sam tipped his head at me and grinned. "Excellent. I'll go start the fire."

My heart skipped a beat like it always did when he was being cute. And sexy. We were beginning to act like a couple. But despite the underlying excitement, a couple who'd been together a while. Maybe it was time to start probing for more information.

"Have you dated anyone since Tansey passed?" I asked once we were ensconced in front of a toasty fire with drinks in hand.

"Jealous?" he asked taking a sip.

"No." Maybe that was too abrupt. "I'm not jealous, just curious. A good-looking guy like you and no one has tried to catch your eye?"

"Wasn't like they didn't try," he admitted with no false modesty. "I just wasn't interested until you showed up."

"Why me?" I wasn't fishing for compliments, but I wanted to know. Or maybe I just wanted to feel wanted.

He considered the question a moment before answering. "You're feisty. You're pretty. And you have a great dog."

"How romantic!" I couldn't help chuckling at his reply.

"Well, then, how's this for romantic?" he leaned closer, kissed me a few times, then whispered, "And you make my heart race just thinking about you."

"And Becca likes you," he added after the next round of kisses. We were both more than a little breathless.

"God, you do know how to diffuse a sexually tense moment, don't you?" And I just said that out loud, for Pete's sake!

"How about I refill these glasses. Then we can discuss sex."

Before I could reply, he leapt to his feet and headed for the kitchen.

Was this the night we'd end up in bed? Or was he buying time to cool off?

CHAPTER THIRTY-ONE

Sam Philips – Present Day

Sam added fresh ice and started to divide the last of the Bailey's Irish Cream into the empty glasses, but then set the bottle down again. He leaned hard, pressing his palms on the cold granite counter, head bowed, trying to regain his sense of cool, calm, and collected.

Things between him and Kenzie suddenly seemed to have escalated, and he wasn't sure what he should do about it.

His body knew exactly what it wanted. It was all about taking Kenzie's hand and hustling upstairs to her room, with the bottle and glasses to be filled and consumed while he slowly and deliberately disrobed her. Or maybe there would be no slow and deliberate. Depending on how she reacted, it might become a frenzied race to see who could undress the other first.

Was that what he wanted? What about Kenzie. She hadn't been single all that long. Just a few months. Well, half a year, but who was counting. He'd been celibate for almost four years. And he was a guy. Big difference.

He also sensed she was still finding out what she wanted for herself. A part of that appeared to be some new level of independence. The chance to make her own decisions. If he were to take her to bed now, it might be him making the decision and Kenzie going along for the ride. That wasn't exactly fair to her.

He took a few more deep breaths, picked up the bottle and emptied it into the glasses. Equilibrium more or less intact, he headed back to the great room, the fire and Kenzie.

She leaned over and kissed him as he sank back into the nest of pillows he'd created with intimacy in mind. Then she took her drink before settling comfortably at his side. "Thank you."

"So, are you going to be a Patriots fan now that you live in Maine?" It was the first innocuous topic he could think of that didn't remotely touch on either of their lives. And especially not sex.

"Maybe," she muttered softly.

"You don't follow football?"

"I like watching it, but if you haven't got a dog in the fight, it's less stressful."

"But less exciting." He couldn't imagine not getting energized about a play, even to the point of jumping up and shouting at the TV when you were the only person in the room.

"But no nail-biting and no big disappointment, either."

"I guess you have a point there, but still." He took a sip of his Bailey's and tried to decide where to go next since football wasn't working."

"Have you missed being . . ." Kenzie set her glass on the floor, lifted her shoulders in a sigh and turned to face him. "Have you missed being intimate since Tansey passed?"

Sam swallowed hard. So much for small talk.

"Not at first," he answered honestly. "I was too busy grieving. Then I was too busy being a single parent. But then . . . I don't know. Yes. I miss sex. But until . . ." He almost said, until you, but was doing his level best not to back her into a corner.

"Until now?" She whispered in a husky voice that seemed to mirror what was coursing through his body. A moment later without a hint of what she was thinking, she was sitting astride his thighs. She lowered her face to his and he was lost.

Sam barely had time to set his own glass out of harm's way before Kenzie was beginning the process of disrobing him that he'd imagined happening in her bedroom. With their lips locked and her hands seemingly everywhere, all his good intentions went to hell in a handbasket.

He slid her down his thighs until they were touching. Clothing still separated them, but there was no disguising his need. Nor, apparently, hers.

"Maybe we should take this upstairs," he gasped as her lips left his to trail a row of kisses down the side of his neck to the skin she'd just bared below his shoulder.

"Yeah. Maybe we should," she agreed, between the parade of kisses she continued to lay down.

Good idea, but she didn't seem inclined to let him up, and he was quite certain he couldn't pull them both out of the nest of pillows on his own. He gave up wondering what next and began unbuttoning her blouse.

Amazing! His brain registered the lack of a bra, but his hands didn't hesitate to take advantage. Her breasts were small but perfect and the feel of them turned everything hot and heavy. His dick strained at the confines of his jeans. He pressed harder into her warm welcoming crotch.

"Kenzie," he gasped.

"Yeah, right. Upstairs." She was on her feet in a heartbeat and reaching for his hand.

"Will Duffy mind?" Sam asked, trying to chill things off just a bit.

Her gurgle of laughter was enchanting. "He's been fixed. I don't think he cares." Then she was dragging him toward the stairs.

As they lay cuddling in the afterglow, Sam considered his next move. Should he stay the night? Or find a way to leave gracefully? He wanted to stay. He wasn't that kind of guy who took what he wanted then couldn't wait to be gone. On the other hand, he didn't want her to feel like he was presuming too much either.

"Please stay," Kenzie murmured, curling into him.

That answered that problem. Sam rolled onto his side and pulled her against his chest, curling his knees up under hers. She layered her arms over his and sighed contentedly.

The. Best. Sex. Ever. Not that he was comparing her to Tansey. Just that she was different. And those differences made it even more exciting. Never mind his return to a sex life had been a long time coming. At least he hoped it was a return, and not a one-night-stand.

Two things barreled into Sam's mind the moment he opened his eyes to sunlight streaming across a strange bed. The sex had been magnificent. And he'd not been wearing protection.

They were both in their forties but that didn't mean Kenzie couldn't get pregnant. What if the unthinkable happened? Would she resent going back to giving up her independence? Sam couldn't imagine not being part of the life of any child he fathered. Maybe he was borrowing trouble that wasn't going to happen.

He had no idea how long it had been since Kenzie left the bed, but the scents of bacon and coffee hung in the air. Time for him to get up and face the music.

Please God let it be happy music. He prayed Kenzie was not at this minute regretting last night. It didn't matter that she'd initiated it and had been more than an equal partner in bringing the attraction he'd felt for her from that first day to its natural culmination.

He found his clothes neatly folded in the seat of an old rocking chair and put them on. Raking his hands through his hair, he wished he had a toothbrush. But it was what it was. He stopped in the bathroom before heading down to the kitchen.

As he crossed to the bedroom door, he noticed a long fat garment bag hanging on the back of the door. The clear window that ran down one side revealed a lot of white. Lacy, beaded white. He unzipped the bag and tipped his head. Why would Kenzie have a wedding dress hanging in her room? He probably had no business asking but he knew curiosity would get the better of him.

"You're up bright and early," he said as he arrived to find breakfast just being set on the island.

"Duffy needed to go out or I'd still be lounging in bed with you." She grinned and crossed the kitchen to go up on tiptoes and plant a lingering kiss on his mouth. "You hungry?"

"I wasn't, until I until I smelled the bacon," Sam answered with relief. Judging by that welcome, she wasn't regretting last night, whatever that nuptial gown might mean.

Duffy got up from the door mat where he'd been curled up with a battered old toy and came over to sniff Sam's hand.

"Good morning to you, too, old man," Sam said, bending to ruffle the dog's ears.

"So, what's with the wedding dress?" he asked, giving in to his snooping curiosity.

Kenzie frowned, then her expression cleared. "Oh! The one hanging on my door? I found it in the attic and brought it down out of curiosity."

Apparently, Sam wasn't the only one who snooped.

"It was never worn, but I have no idea whose it might have been or why it wasn't worn."

"How do you know it never got worn?" Sam took a bite of bacon.

"There are still pins in the hem." Kenzie shrugged. "It will likely be one of those mysteries that never gets solved."

"Too bad you're not an author. You could make up your own story to explain the dress."

"I don't mean to hurry you along," Kenzie said sliding onto a stool. "But I have an appointment uptown to pick out cabinets for the two apartment kitchens. Haley was supposed to go with me, but she must have stayed at Marcus' place last night. She texted to say she'd meet me there."

The mystery forgotten, Sam looked at his watch and realized he was going to get a boatload of ribbing when he showed up late for work. He was never late, and his mechanics were going to jump to conclusions about where he'd been. They'd be right, of course, and it would be impossible to deflect.

"I'll consider myself lucky you delayed long enough to make breakfast, then. But I need to eat and run, myself."

"If you're headed to the shop, maybe you'll take Duffy with you. He hates to be left behind and I don't know how long I'll be. He's not a fan of being left in the car, either."

"Done," Sam answered filling his fork. "I'll enjoy the company. And knowing his mistress will be stopping by even if it is her day off." There wouldn't be any kissy-face stuff at Hank's unless they wanted to listen to the taunts. But just seeing her brightened his days.

Twenty minutes later, Sam closed Kenzie's car door and blew her a kiss as she pulled away onto the lane and headed for the Harpswell road.

Then he opened his truck door and invited Duffy to jump in. The lingering doubts about unprotected sex came back to haunt him as he drove to work with his lover's dog playing co-pilot.

Chapter Thirty-Two

Kenzie Ross – Present Day

It was hard to concentrate on the issue of making choices. Sam had introduced me to lovemaking like I'd never experienced in my life. Compared to Sam, Garrett had been about as exciting as watching paint dry. And he'd never been very concerned about me or what I wanted.

Once upon a time, I must have found sex with Garrett exciting, but that had been a very long time ago. For the past few years, intimacy had been more obligatory than something to look forward to. Which was half the reason I'd lost it last night.

At least, that's what I kept telling myself.

The surge of needy desire had been irresistible. For a few lengthy minutes while Sam was in the kitchen refreshing our drinks, I'd been afraid he wasn't as interested as I'd thought. I'd gambled and won when he returned, all the while praying he wasn't the kind of guy who needed to be in charge.

The result of my brazen behavior had been more than I could have ever imagined. Sam was fierce and sexy, yet gentle and considerate. He made me feel things I'd never felt in my life. Sam was a lover to cherish, and I couldn't wait to explore where else our shared passion might take us.

"What do you think of these?" Haley asked, pulling me back from the land of Sam and sex.

"I—" What did I think? What was the question? Or rather, the cost?

"They're on sale," Haley said. "Not the cheapest, but not the most expensive. The pale blond finish will be good because those new kitchens will be small. A light color will make them feel bigger."

"Good point," I agreed, forcing myself to concentrate. I could day-dream about Sam once this task was done. I looked to the salesman who was punching numbers on a calculator.

"A basic small kitchen as you outlined in your plans would be about two K," he said looking up from his calculator. "The slab ones we saw are a little cheaper, but you wouldn't be saving enough to make the sacrifice of style worth it. With tax and delivery for two sets, we'll call it four grand even. Does that seal the deal?"

Four grand. Good grief. I still didn't have a quote on the asbestos. But this was an expected expense, I reminded myself. Already in the budget.

Haley stood watching the wheels turn in my head, being respectful in a way that impressed me. Jaycee would have been talking my head off trying to either take the deal or trying to convince me the more expensive option would pay off in the long run.

"Done," I said. "When can they be delivered?" They could all be piled downstairs until the asbestos issue was taken care of. I just want-ed the bulk of the work done sooner rather than later. Partly to give

Haley her space. But partly because I didn't need her walking in on Sam and me getting it on in front of the fire. That was just one of the new experiences I wanted to explore. I'd lived a life of strait-laced stricture, and I was determined to break the mold forever.

Originally, Haley and I were going to look at flooring while we were here, but with Marcus' suggestion about the old boards, that would be one savings I could count on. He'd be in charge of picking up whatever he needed to finish the original wood floor, but even the most high-end floor finishes couldn't come close to a whole new layer of artificial wood or tile. Maybe that would help to offset the asbestos removal.

We puttered about the big store, looking for anything else we might have forgotten to put on the list, but apart from shelving for the new closets which Marcus had already assured me he could create from leftover pieces of lumber from other parts of the rebuild, nothing leapt out at us.

I took Haley to lunch and then we headed home. I would invite Sam over for dinner again when I stopped to pick up my dog. I wondered if he liked lobster or if he was so used to its easy availability that he preferred other things.

More things I didn't know about this man I'd become intimate with. His favorite foods. His favorite color. Where he liked to go on vacation. What was on his bucket list. So many exciting new things to explore. I turned into Hank's lot with eager expectations for the night to come.

Duffy was laying in the open bay doorway, but when he saw me coming, he leapt to his feet. He trotted across the lot and shoved his face into my hands for a greeting, his tail beating an eager welcome.

Sam appeared shortly after the dog.

"He was a good boy. Played ambassador to all the folk who stopped in, begged bits of lunch from Jack and Paul and kept us company."

I saw Jack lurking in the doorway watching. "Jack expecting me to do a few cartwheels or something?" I asked.

"He knows where I was last night, and he's hoping for a demonstration so he can rag me some more."

A flush crept up my cheeks. I might be eager for a repeat, but it was unsettling to know there were no secrets in this small town.

"Sorry," Sam said. "I'm not very good at deflecting and I was very late coming in to work this morning. They've had a grand time roasting me. Otherwise, I'd be kissing the stuffing out of you right now."

If the whole island already knew, or would know before much longer, I wondered if there was any point in acting like nothing was going on. But I'd respect his reticence. "There's always later. I was going to invite you to dinner anyway. I was going to ask what . . ."

Sam shook his head, and I stopped talking, my heart sinking. All day I'd been looking forward to tonight. I'd even stopped to get some protection once free of Haley. Taking a chance once, okay, twice, so soon after my last period was maybe okay, but I couldn't keep daring the fates. I put a stop to the whirring doubts and waited for him to explain.

"Tonight is Aunt Phe night."

"Aunt Phe night?" He'd mentioned his aunt before, but never an Aunt Phe night.

"Bingo night at Avita. My aunt looks forward to it. I usually join her for dinner at the dining hall first then hang around while they play bingo, but the last couple weeks, I've taken you out instead. Tonight it has to be Aunt Phe or she'll think I've abandoned her."

My happy plans for the evening ahead imploded. I did my best not to let my disappointment show, but I guess the effort wasn't all that successful. Even if Jack was still watching, Sam took two strides and folded me into his arms, resting his chin atop my head.

"I'm sorry, Kenzie. I'd far rather be having dinner with you, but Phe's family and I'm all she's got now." He leaned back and tipped my chin up. I tried to resist, but he persisted. "Forgive me?" he asked with that endearing tip of his head.

"Of course," I forced myself to say. Then I went up on tiptoe and kissed him, not caring if everyone on the island was watching. Before it got too far, I stepped back and looked down at Duffy, waiting patiently at my side.

He wagged his tail tentatively. As if he wasn't sure of my mood either.

"I guess it's just us tonight, Duff."

"I'm sorry," Sam said again.

"See you Monday?" I tried for a happy lightness I wasn't feeling.

"Can I have a rain check for tomorrow?"

"Sure. But for penance, you bring dinner."

"You're on."

Before I said anything else that might make me sound needy or selfish, I blew Sam a kiss, ruffled Duffy's ears and headed for my RAV 4.

I took Duffy for our usual evening walk down to Garrison Cove but wouldn't let him swim. If dogs could shrug, I'm sure he would have done so when it became clear I was not going to change my mind about the water. We walked over the bridge and back, then up the hill to Murray House.

I started to heat up a few leftovers, then decided I should have stopped at the candy store for a consolation indulgence. The shop would be closing over the weekend so maybe I needed to stock up to tide me over until they reopened in the spring. I grabbed my purse and headed for the door.

Duffy beat me to it. He sure wasn't about to get left behind if anything good was happening.

"You can go with," I told the dog as I held the door open for him. "But you know dogs can't have chocolate. Right?"

He trotted ahead of me, tail wagging. Maybe I'd get him an ice cream pup-cup. Once again, I had to wonder how I'd managed to go my whole life up to this point without knowing what I'd been missing by not having a pooch to share life with.

There were bare spots on some of the shelves, but thankfully none were where my favorites usually reside. I ordered up a two-pound box. It wouldn't last until spring, but if I behaved myself and didn't have a pig-out, then I'd have some until Christmas. Then I'd have to satisfy my chocolate cravings with Christmas candy.

With Duffy's pup-cup in one hand and the indulgent box waiting on the counter, the owner and I chatted as she rung me up. I wished her a lovely holiday and promised to be first in line when she reopened.

I let Duffy out of the car to consume his treat, then it was off to home and a night without Sam to fill somehow. Duffy shoved his head over the seat back and rested his chin on my shoulder as if to remind me I wouldn't be all by myself. I patted his head and then had to pay attention to driving over the bridge that still had me clutching the wheel with both hands.

Once back in my kitchen, I set the box on the shelf, contemplated having just one now, but shook my head and refrained. Instead, I put the leftovers in the microwave and grabbed Duffy's bowl.

I carried my second-hand dinner to the great room to eat in front of the TV. Not much of interest to choose from with all the fake reality stuff currently in vogue, but I didn't have the heart to start a fire that Sam wouldn't be here to share.

My pity party led to an internal debate about my so-called, new-found independence. One night in Sam's arms and I was ready to dispense with being happy on my own? Talk about conflicting goals and desire. By nine pm, I had zero idea what I'd watched on the boob-tube and wasn't tired enough for bed. I reached for a paperback I'd found on the shelf, thinking I'd read that, but instead found a folded bit of paper where I'd left the book.

I picked it up, thinking it might be a fun little note Sam had left for me to find.

But the folded paper wasn't just a scrap of paper. It was an elegant note card with the initials EMK embossed in silver on the front. I opened it to find the cursive script inside as elegant as the notepaper.

My dear Eleanor, the writing began. *How sorry I was to hear that your wedding was called off just a few short weeks before the big day. I know how much you were looking forward to your special day and now to have Jeff enlist so unexpectedly must be heartbreaking. While I won't be using my train ticket to travel north for your wedding, perhaps you can use it to come to me for a visit. We can go shopping and visit some of the many museums to take your mind off your sorrow for at least a short while. I would love to have you come.*

Your loving Aunt Emily.

I glanced back at the top and noted it was dated May 1943.

Could the dress Sam had asked me about just that morning have belonged to this young woman named Eleanor? And where had this note come from? I read it again. Written halfway through the last century, it didn't just appear out of thin air. I'd have to ask Haley if she'd found it somewhere and left it on the table.

And just maybe that was the mystery of the unfinished wedding dress solved. The young bride who had been planning to wear it had been left behind while her fiancé went off to war. And apparently never returned. How sad.

I didn't feel like reading the book that had gone missing. "Maybe I need a nice long walk in the fresh air," I announced out loud.

Duffy scrambled to his feet. He'd heard the word walk and was always an eager participant no matter what time of day or night.

I wrapped my arms about the dog and nuzzled his soft fur with my face. "Maggie thought she was asking me a favor when she begged me to take you in, but it's the other way around," I told the dog. "Having you in my life is one of the biggest favors she ever did for me."

CHAPTER THIRTY-THREE

Eleanor Murray – 1944

Eleanor rushed up three flights of stairs to her Aunt's apartment as soon as the driver pulled up to the apartment building. She couldn't wait for the elevator.

"Aunt Emily!" Eleanor shouted as she let herself into the apartment gasping for breath. "Aunt Emily. An invasion . . . has happened. They talked of . . . nothing else . . . at work today. . . It began this . . . .morning."

"Eleanor, dear. Calm down and catch your breath." Aunt Emily emerged from her sitting room with a concerned expression pulling at her features.

"Turn on the radio, Aunt Emily. Hurry." Eleanor dropped onto the bench provided to remove her work boots which were never allowed on any of her aunt's carpets. "Turn it on. I'll be right there."

Aunt Emily shrugged and crossed the wide front hall to the parlor. "Such a fuss, dear."

Eleanor couldn't imagine how her aunt could have gone through the whole day without hearing about the invasion that had begun while they were still sound asleep in their beds that morning. Jeff might be among the thousands of men who rushed onto those beaches. He might even be one of the unlucky ones. She shook herself. Jeff could not be one of those. He promised her he would come back to her, and Jeff always kept his promises. She shoved the boots out of sight under the bench and dashed into the parlor.

Aunt Emily fiddled with the tuning knobs while the radio made screeching noises, then a few deep bongs.

Eleanor sank onto the ottoman to wait with barely contained impatience.

At work there had been so many conflicting bits of information, she was keen to hear the whole story. She leaned closer as a familiar voice crackled to life and began describing the events of the day with sounds of the actual invasion in the background. What had happened to the censorship Mike mentioned if they were broadcasting from the warfront?

Eleanor wrung her hands as she listened to the account. Maybe Jeff had been in the thick of things. He'd always wanted to be wherever the action was. If there was any way to be part of the invading force, he'd have been first in line.

Her heart felt like it was stuck in her throat as the sounds of cannons and machine guns accompanied the reporter's words. When he finished and the radio went silent, Eleanor slumped, her mind in turmoil as she digested the news.

Her aunt was similarly quiet. She hadn't even known what went on that day before Eleanor got home and urged her to turn the radio on. She had even more to digest even if she didn't have a fiancé to worry about.

"Seventy-three thousand soldiers," Eleanor repeated the detail in barely more than a whisper.

She turned to her aunt. "I can hardly believe there are so many America soldiers in just one place, and all of them rushing into the face of death from the guns of the Germans." This must have been what Jeff tried to tell me about that got blacked out in his letter.

"Why is it so hard to believe, My Dear, when we know there are almost twelve million men in uniform right now?"

"That's everywhere, Aunt Emily. Everywhere all over the world. Today, this very morning thousands and thousands of American soldiers ran ashore in Normandy with the Germans trying to shoot them down from fortifications up above those beaches. Thousands more soldiers parachuted from airplanes. How amazingly brave they must all be."

Eleanor went suddenly silent. The man reporting the day's events had claimed thousands of Americans were wounded or killed. What if one of them had been Jeff? Never mind his promises. Jeff had no magic shield to keep him any safer than the next man.

"We will pray for him," Aunt Emily said as if reading Eleanor's mind.

"Of course we must pray. The fighting has only just begun, and the man said it will be days or weeks, maybe even months before the war is over." Eleanor struggled to stay positive. Jeff would come home. He was too ornery to let himself be killed. Maybe wounded. Like Mike. Mike had probably assured his family he'd come home in one piece, and yet, he hadn't.

Every night, Eleanor perched on the ottoman, glued to the radio for the latest reports of the Allied advance through Europe, but details were scarce. Jeff must definitely be where the fighting was now considering he'd likely been among the thousands pouring ashore on that fateful day in June. Even more troubling was the letter she'd received from Mike. A fellow Mike knew who had also gone ashore in Normandy, had managed to get news sent home weeks ago. Mike had relayed all the information his friend had imparted and reassured Eleanor that if anything had happened to Jeff his family would by now have heard. No news was good news in this instance. So she could set her angst aside.

That Mike's friend had cared enough to let his family know weeks ago, while Jeff hadn't written, worried her. She tried to reassure herself that his letter was probably still somewhere between Europe and home, but surely written.

His letters to her had begun to sound more like he was writing to his sister instead of his fiancée. Did he still love her as he'd professed before he left? Was he still eager to return home to get married and start a family?

She buried her disappointment and apprehension with ever more effort in her work each day at the Brooklyn Navy Yard. Just days after the invasion, Eleanor had watched the USS Missouri leave the navy yard on her initial cruise. She wished she had been in New York in January to see her being launched which everyone told her was the most exciting event of their time working at the yard.

Her grandfather used to tell tales of the ships built on the Kennebec River, a little north of where she lived, but she had never been to see a ship launched there. If Bath Iron Works was still building Navy ships when this war was over, she was going to make sure to watch one get launched.

"Eleanor? Are you ready to go?" Aunt Emily called from the hall outside Eleanor's door.

Tonight, they were attending a charity event. Her aunt had insisted all work and no play made for a very dull boy. Or girl, in Eleanor's case. But a letter had finally come from Jeff and instead of finishing her preparations for tonight's event, she'd been re-reading Jeff's letter at least a dozen times.

My dear Eleanor,

I am sorry it has taken me this long to reassure you that I am still among the living. By now, I am sure you have learned of the invasion in Normandy, and I know you must be greatly worried.

It was a terrifying day. I was eager to go, but the reality was worse than any of us feared. I lost two close friends and three more have gone to hospital in England.

I cannot tell you where I am presently, but I am safe and whole. A very kind priest agreed to carry this letter and be sure that it got posted home to you. I can report that it is very hot. Far hotter than our lovely island home in Maine. I wonder if New York City is hot now that summer is at its height.

Your most recent letter sent months ago, finally caught up with me two days ago. I was interested to learn of all you have accomplished. How proud I am of you, taking on a man's job and learning how to run a big lathe. I expect you are very pleased to have a part in supporting the war effort. It is most certainly of vital importance to keep the shipyards launching new ships, and you are creating some of the parts that make them run.

I must sign off now and keep this short, but I wanted to reassure you.

Jeff

When her aunt called out a third time, Eleanor jumped to her feet and raced to put the last touches to her hair and face. She didn't expect to enjoy herself. But then, she hadn't expected to enjoy her last community gathering on Bailey Island, either. And that time, she had ended up kissing Mike as if Jeff didn't exist.

She simply had to behave and be faithful until Jeff came home again. But what if he didn't return home? Had he written a similar letter to the Irish family he'd been billeted with? Did he even still love her?

CHAPTER THIRTY-FOUR

Kenzie Ross – Present Day

It was a good thing Duffy was allowed to come to work with me because the beginning of the week meant Murray House would be overrun with experts in the process of removing Asbestos. We were told it was okay to be in the sections outside of the containment perimeter, but I didn't think the dog would be happy shut up in my room while he could still hear the sounds of men working just down the hall. Haley had been able to move her gear into my smaller guest room for the duration, but she had to drive up to Brunswick for a few days so she couldn't keep an eye on the pooch either.

Thankfully, by quitting time on Wednesday, the men were done. Not so thankfully, I was presented with the bill for the work. The total was about what Marcus had quoted so not a big ugly surprise. But not all that welcome either.

I sat down at my desk, pulled out my checkbook and considered my options. I had just enough to cover the check, but it would be slim pickings for a couple weeks unless I moved all of the currently available income from my investments and some of the buffer my severance had left me out of savings and into the checking account. With Christmas coming, this was going to have to be my answer.

Liam had a new friend whose family owned a ski lodge in Killington. His buddy assured him the night life in Killington would be awesome. So, of course, Liam had asked for a weeklong lift pass and cash for the social whirl. The best part of this deal would be that after spending Christmas itself with his father and brother in Virginia, Liam would spend a few days with me before his buddy picked him up for the week in Vermont. I was going to let Garrett fund all the airfare and the pocket money. I'd spring for the lift pass.

Luke planned to head out to California after his time with Garrett. Judy was a gymnast and had to return to campus and regular practices the day after Christmas even though classes wouldn't resume for another two weeks. Luke would just be able to catch her first meet of the year before returning to Brown. In the meantime, Judy wanted to show him around her school and maybe spend a weekend in San Francisco. More airfare and spending money for Garrett to contribute, while I was left trying to decide what I should offer.

I took a steadying breath and went online to purchase the ski pass. Then I did the transfer and wrote a check for the asbestos company, as well as a check for Marcus for ongoing work and supplies.

When I was done, I put away the notebook where I'd started to keep track of Murray House expenses, sat back, and sighed. At least I wasn't paying exorbitant rent for an apartment somewhere in Virginia.

That satisfaction was quickly challenged on Sunday when Duffy came home from our walk limping. And bleeding all over the kitchen floor.

I plopped down to inspect the foot he was favoring and discovered a slice in two pads of his right paw.

You might know. I hadn't yet found a vet in the area. Besides, even if I had, who was likely to be open on Sunday? I tore up an old T-shirt and tied up the wounded appendage.

I called my new friend Dawn. She had dogs.

"So, where do I take him?" I asked once I'd explained the problem.

"Portland is the closest I know of. There's a woman up in Brunswick that sometimes comes out to see pets who aren't feeling well on days when the clinic isn't open, but I think she's away. She has a daughter living in Aruba and she wanted to fly down for the holidays. She's half retired anyway. How bad are the cuts?"

I did my best to describe them.

"Best call the Portland clinic then. You need me to drive you down?"

"I hate to put you out."

"Heck, I need to get out of here. George and the boys are watching football on TV and all three are yelling at the refs like they could be heard all the way from here to wherever that game is being played. I'll be up in a few. But call and let them know you're on the way and what the problem is."

Dawn had clearly been to this clinic before because she navigated the many turns as if she could do it in her sleep. Made me doubly glad for her offer.

There was a signup table out front where I collected a clipboard and began filling in all our information. Before I was done a cheerful lady in green scrubs appeared. She squatted down to speak to Duffy who lay with his head on his paws doing his best to look pathetic and in need of sympathy.

"And what's a good boy like you doing here on Sunday when you should be out playing?" She scratched him behind his ears, which he took to be an invite to get up and go wherever she was going. I stood as well, but the woman reached for the leash. "I'll be right back with a report."

Not that I'd had that much experience, but back home in Virginia, I'd gone with him the first and only time I'd taken him to the vet. Guess it was different at a twenty-four-seven clinic. Dawn appeared, having parked her car, and we sat down to wait.

"When we get out of here, do you know any places where people eat outside, and dogs are welcome?"

Dawn raised her brows. "In December? In Maine? I doubt it."

"I guess we'll have to be happy with take-out then." Duffy was fine in a car by himself so long as it was cool and I left my moonroof open, but for some reason, I didn't want to abandon him after he'd been injured and then had to spend time being prodded and poked in a strange clinic.

"Bet you wouldn't turn down a good lobster roll," Dawn said with a wink.

"And I wouldn't bet against you."

"There's a tavern in Freeport. Can't take Duffy in, but we can order to take out, and the little detour through Freeport won't add much time to the return trip at all."

"My treat then. Should we get some for your guys while we're there?"

Dawn laughed. "They're chowing down on tacos and beer. Don't waste the bucks."

Not that I had bucks to waste, but still. Before I could reply Duffy came trotting out ahead of the nice technician who'd come to claim him earlier. His paw was bandaged halfway up his leg, but he wasn't limping.

"He's all set." She handed me a small bag with paw prints on it. "Looked worse than it was. Leave the dressing on for the first twenty-four hours. Then put the salve on it a couple times a day and keep him from licking. I'd order up a cone of shame, but I don't think it would work. My best advice is to get some toddler socks at Walmart and some sticky gauze at Rite-Aid to hold them on. Cheaper than the cone, and less stressful for the animal."

Duffy was mugging it up with Dawn, so I thanked the woman, and headed to the counter to pay the bill.

Another staggering, unexpected expense. The old Duffer would have to keep on keeping on with the pile of old quilts in my room instead of the fluffy new bed I had planned to get him for Christmas. Dog ownership came with a lot of perks, but it also came with a price.

Sam's truck sat behind my Rav when we finally arrived home. Had I known, I could have brought him a lobster roll.

Dawn swept in an arc, to head back out before stopping. "I'd come in, but it looks like you have company." She winked. "Besides, I need to get home and make sure my crew hasn't destroyed my house."

I leaned across the console to give her a hug and press two twenties into her hand. "Thanks for taking us. Fill your tank on me."

She tried to push the money back at me, but I ignored the gesture and got out, opened the back, and let Duffy hop down. Then we both watched as she pulled out, before heading to our own door.

Sam greeted us halfway across the lawn. "You've been gone awhile," he said as he stooped to pet the dog, then straightened to honor me with a kiss.

"Long story." I filled him in on my day. "Did you know it's almost three hundred dollars to visit an emergency vet clinic on a Sunday?"

"Still worried about money?" He asked holding the door for me, before whistling for the dog.

"Of course, not," I lied. "I was just . . . a little surprised."

"Jerks that toss beer bottles out to get broken on the rocks should be fined."

"How do you know it was a beer bottle?"

Sam shrugged. "Ocean tossed stones are not sharp enough to cut a dog's paws."

He had a point, and I knew I was going to have my eyes glued to the ground in the future. For the near future anyway.

"I was going to ask if you wanted to go to dinner, but I'm guessing not. Considering..." Sam started to suggest.

"We could spend the night in," I offered, hope blossoming in my chest. "I made soup yesterday. And I can pop some biscuits in the oven."

"With a fire in the fireplace?" He wagged his eyebrows at me.

"And s'mores?"

"And maybe a sleepover after?"

That head-tipping thing he did was going to be my total undoing.

"And maybe a sleepover," I replied hoping he didn't see the eager longing in my eyes or the blush I felt creeping up my neck.

CHAPTER THIRTY-FIVE

Sam Phillips – Present Day

Sam hoped Kenzie didn't notice his uncertainty or his eagerness.

When she'd come to his shop a week ago with an invite for an encore of the night before, he'd had to beg off. It had killed him to do it, but his aunt had been counting on his visits far longer than Kenzie had been on the island. He might have found a way to get himself invited during the week that followed, but work had been busy, and Kenzie had been gone by the time he knocked off. Every day but one.

On that one day, he'd had a dentist appointment, but Kenzie was deep into a detailing job when he left. For some reason, it just seemed crude to call her on the phone to invite himself over. So, he hadn't called. But he had missed her. Which is why he'd driven down today and waited for her to show up.

He'd spied her Toyota in the drive, but when there was no response to his knock, he'd taken a side trip to the Hamilton's house in case she'd walked down to visit them. That had elicited the information about where she'd gone and with whom. After sharing three tacos and as many beers with the Hamilton men, he'd decided to return to Murray House and await her return in the hope she'd give him a second chance.

It appeared luck was with him.

"How did the asbestos deal go?" he asked as she bustled around the kitchen preparing a tray of muffins to shove in the oven.

She swung away from the stove after shutting the oven door. "Want to see how things are going?"

He nodded.

"We've got time before the muffins are done and heating up some of my leftover chowder won't take but a couple minutes. If you're hungry for some chowder, that is. Dawn and I had lobster rolls in Freeport so I'm not all that hungry. A muffin and a cup of tea will do it for me."

"Muffins and tea does it for me, too," he replied as he followed her out of the kitchen. The Hamiltons stuffed me with tacos. I went down to see if that's where you'd gone when I didn't get an answer at your door."

They headed for the stairs. Another flashback to a week earlier. Sam did his best to curb that thought and pay attention to her description of the work underway.

"That kid is a genius," Sam said as she led him through the partially framed new rooms.

"He's hardly a kid," Kenzie pointed out.

"He's a lot younger than me," Sam conceded. "Anyway, I'd never have thought of splitting things up like he has. He took advantage of every nook and cranny this old house possesses."

"Makes me glad you suggested him," Kenzie said as they returned to the kitchen after the tour. "Your cousin is no slouch when it comes to interesting suggestions, either."

"What's Haley up to now?" Sam asked as he came to lean against the counter while she checked the muffins. He loved just looking at her and while she had a lovely backside, he preferred to watch her face while she spoke. So much enthusiasm and enjoyment.

"What hasn't she been up to might be a better question. But honestly, she thinks I should open an afternoon coffee and tea parlor in the great room where we could build a fire and let people enjoy all the old books."

Kenzie handed him a jug of honey and the butter, while she turned back to dump the muffins into a basket.

"If you'd prefer, we could have this in the other room by the fire. I found a set of old TV tables at a yard sale last week."

"Like that idea," he agreed. The fire had been a good starting point before. "I'll go start the fire."

Few minutes later they were ensconced in the big room with mugs of tea that held hints of vanilla and the warm, honey laden muffins on the old new tables. Duffy curled up in front of the cheerfully crackling fire while they ate and chatted about everything but what had happened between them a week earlier.

When the muffins were gone, Kenzie collected the dishes and disappeared telling him to stay put and she'd be right back.

Sam considered rebuilding the nest of pillows, but Kenzie hadn't said if there was another course to come, so he waited.

She returned at last carrying a white candy box in one hand and a bottle of Bailey's in the other with two glasses trapped between the bottle and her fingers. She paused and looked at him, then at the fire and back.

"What no pillows?"

Sam scrambled to his feet and whisked the tables shut. "Your wish is my command." And my personal favorite.

A few moments later, things were just as he'd envisioned them. He quickly poured the Irish Cream liqueur into the I love Maine glasses and handed her one.

Kenzie flicked the lid up on the box and offered it to him. "I was really torn about inviting you to share these," she said as he chose one. "The Island Candy Shop is closed for the season, so this is it until sometime next spring. I was going to make them last, but I decided to be nice and share."

"There's a place called Wilbur's in Brunswick," Sam said before popping a chocolate covered cherry into his mouth. He savored the unique and lovely flavor before swallowing. "Not as good as our candy store, but better than store-bought."

"Good to know," Kenzie said before taking a bite out a piece of chocolate coated toffee.

Sam ransacked his mind trying to think of some bit of small talk they hadn't already visited to fill in the gap between now and what he hoped would come later. Truthfully, he was hoping later would come sooner, rather than later. But patience is a virtue, he reminded himself.

He suddenly recalled that it was Kenzie who had initiated the love-making the last time, after he'd done his level best to rein in his libido. But the chances of that happening twice were zip to none. If anything was going to happen tonight, it was his turn to make it happen.

"Are we a couple?" he blurted. So much for sounding casual.

"What makes a couple?" She peered at him over her shoulder as she put her glass to her lips.

He set his own glass on the floor beyond where it wouldn't get knocked over, then reached for her free hand. "Two people who enjoy each other's company?"

"That's all?" She stared steadfastly into the fire.

"It's a start," he replied.

This time when she looked back at him, he thought he saw a flicker of the same yearning that churned in his gut. And enjoy each other's bodies, he wanted to add, but didn't.

She rolled onto her side and propped her head on one palm, elbow on one of the pillows. She stared at him for a long pause during which his heart seemed accelerate while his breathing went on hold.

"Are you afraid this is all too fast? What's happening between us?" he finally found the breath to ask.

Another long pause. She blinked slowly, looked down at who knew what, and then back at him. "I'm afraid of getting hurt."

The admission stabbed him. He would never hurt her, but she couldn't know that. A man who had promised love her until death did them part had hurt her. A man she'd entrusted with so much of who she was. She had a right to be afraid.

What was he supposed to say to that?

He swallowed hard, trying to decide where to go next.

Slowly she set her glass behind her and inched his way. She laid her head on his chest and cuddled closer, snaking an arm across his waist.

He wrapped both arms about her and held her. He could promise he'd never hurt her. At least not on purpose. But maybe that wasn't what she needed right now. He could tell her he understood why she might be afraid to trust him. He'd lost his wife, but it wasn't the same. Tansey hadn't left him for someone else. It had hurt to lose her, but he hadn't lost her love.

His heart thumped in his chest. Surely, she could hear it, and maybe even guess at his growing feelings for her. Maybe it was too soon to offer those kinds of feelings or promises.

The shock of it, to him, at least, was that he was already in love with her.

It had been so different with Tansey. He and Tansey had grown up with each other and drifted into loving. Had cancer not taken her from him, he'd have loved her for the rest of his life, no doubt. But Tansey was gone and God, in His infinite wisdom, had brought Kenzie into his life.

And he was in love with her.

CHAPTER THIRTY-SIX

Kenzie Ross – Present Day

What had possessed me to be so up front about being afraid of a being in a relationship with Sam? Twenty-four hours later, and I was still shocked at my unvarnished confession. Nothing like opening myself right up to the very thing I fear most. If I'd said I was afraid of spiders or heights, I could have recanted and easily disproved the lie if it later turned inconvenient. But NO! I bare my soul. I had promised myself I was never going to be that vulnerable again.

Sam had only asked if we were a couple. He hadn't asked for any kind of declaration. Yet, instead of giving him an easy, lighthearted answer, I'd just blurted out the fear that clouded my emotions about what was clearly growing between us.

Sam hadn't said anything. He'd let me bury my face against his chest and held me. He hadn't made any promises or even suggested that what he felt for me went beyond the physical. Whatever he'd been thinking as we watched the fire die and the embers fade had remained locked in his head.

Tonight, I was curled up beside Duffy, asking myself what I'd expected Sam to say. Had I wanted a promise? One I'd have, in all honesty, had difficulty accepting after knowing each other such a short time? Had I wanted Sam to say he wasn't that kind of guy? I hadn't thought Garrett was that kind of guy, and yet he'd betrayed my trust. Another promise I'd have been wary of.

I wrapped my arm over Duffy's furry warmth, thankful that here, at least, was unconditional love and devotion. Maybe I should just stick to being buddies with a dog. But still...

Despite the question and my answer, Sam had come to bed with me last night, and stayed until morning. I'd enjoyed every minute of his company and his lovemaking. Even the atrocious coffee he'd brewed this morning. Although, I'll admit, he's a genius with French toast. I needed to ask him what he adds to the eggs to get that delicious flavor.

But that isn't my big problem right now.

"Let's face it," I told Duffy. "I'm just a big bag of conflicting emotions and mixed messages. Sam wants to know if we're a couple and I tell him I'm afraid. Then I let him take me to bed again. Like we are a couple. If he's confused, he has every right to be with me sending mixed signals."

Duffy lifted his head and licked my cheek.

"At least you love me without any promises or qualifications." I buried my face in the dog's silky fur for a few minutes, then laid back on my pillow.

Tomorrow would be another busy day. I needed to stop brooding and get some sleep. Maybe I should read a book. On the other hand, my mind probably wouldn't stay with the action on the page.

A soft snore sounded from beside me. If only I could turn my brain off that easily.

"The Escalade is here." Jack stuck his head in the office doorway to let me know my next detailing gig had arrived.

Sam had suggested that detailing cars would likely be more lucrative in the summer when the island was hopping with tourists who had money to burn. But it turned out the guy who'd come in last week with the Lexus had connections in Brunswick. And beyond. If I recalled correctly, the Escalade belonged to an upper-level manager from Bath Iron Works.

"Tell him I'll be right with him," I said, trying to straighten the paperwork I had strewn out across the desk.

"Take your time. He just left it and said he'd be back at quitting time. You've got all afternoon." Jack tossed me a salute and disappeared.

I managed to corral my paperwork and headed for the detailing bay.

"How many dogs does this guy have?" I asked out loud to no one in particular, as I began to gather up the loose dog toys that cluttered the back of the car. Everything behind the driver and front passenger seats had been removed, except one bucket seat on the right side. That seat supported a youth booster. I decided the guy must have a wife, one kid and half a dozen dogs.

Job number one was to vacuum up the gallon or two of sand. His dogs clearly liked the beach and got to go regularly. Or maybe he just never hosed them down. But wondering wasn't going to get the car cleaned. Even if I did have all afternoon.

Three hours later, I stepped back and surveyed my work.

"You're the most thorough person I've ever known," Paul commented, stopping on his way to grab an oil filter off the shelves beyond my workstation. "Word gets out and you won't be able to keep up. Either that or Sam goes back to doing his own books."

"Don't even suggest it," I said laughing. "Do you have any idea how long it took me to sort them out when I started?"

"I can guess." Paul bounced the filter box from one hand to the other. "He's the best boss in the world, but more than a little disorganized. Anyway, Connors is going to think he's got a whole new car."

With that Paul turned and headed back to whatever he was working on, and I began cleaning up my gear.

"You up for two more this week?" Jack called out to me as I headed back across the mechanics' bays to collect my purse and boogie on home. He was chatting with a man I'd seen before but couldn't recall where.

"You bet," I answered without stopping. Haley and I were headed to Freeport to do a little Christmas shopping on Saturday, and I could use all the extra bucks I could collect. If I didn't stop to chat, Jack would just add the guy to the schedule, and I'd refresh my memory without having to admit I'd forgotten the customer's name.

I grabbed my jacket off the chair and my purse from the bottom drawer. Duffy scrambled from the comfy dog bed Sam had insisted my pooch needed while I was busy at the office.

"Are you in a hurry or something?" Sam asked as I headed back out the door.

I jumped. I hadn't noticed he was in the office when I stepped in to get my purse and Duffy. "Jeese. You startled me. What are you doing messing around in my office?"

"Your office?" He tipped his head and grinned at me.

I looked at the dog who also tipped his head. I squared my shoulders. "Yes. My office. At least until you fire me."

Sam reached past me and shut the door, then bent his head to kiss me. "Not planning to fire you any time soon," he said when he lifted his head again. "I guess I'll just have to concede it's your office."

"Damn straight." I did my best to keep the breathlessness out of my reply. This man could push all my buttons. At least all the exciting ones.

"Becca asked what you were doing for Christmas. I think she was angling for a repeat invite and a chance to hang with your boys again."

"You're both welcome to come over." Which would mean I didn't have to spend Christmas alone for the first time in my life. "But it will only be the three of us unless Haley and Marcus are around. The boys will be with their father in Virginia."

Sam's face registered regret. Or was it pity? I didn't need pity, but Sam spoke again before I could come up with a suitably pithy reply.

"I can only imagine how hard that's going to be. Do you get to see them at all during the break?"

I nodded. "For a few days between Christmas and New Year's. Then Luke flies out to explore his girlfriend's California campus and watch her compete. She's a gymnast," I explained. "And Liam goes to Vermont to ski with a new friend from school."

"Becca will be disappointed. I'm pretty sure Marcus is headed home with Haley to her parents' place for the holiday, but I'd still love to spend the day with you. And Becca, of course."

The earlier expression that might or might not have been pity was gone. Replaced by a hopeful one. And that damned endearing tilt of the head.

"I'd love to spend the day with you, too. And Becca." His smile lit up like a hundred-watt bulb and did a lot to banish the feeling of dread I'd had over the upcoming holiday.

CHAPTER THIRTY-SEVEN

Eleanor Murray – December 1944

Another Christmas without Jeff.

As the war dragged on despite the successes of D-day and in the months since, the hope Eleanor had been clinging to that Jeff might be home for in time for the holidays dwindled. The only encouraging news lately had been the sinking of the Tirpitz, pride of the German navy, in early November. The man reporting that bit of news on the radio had been jubilant. But it didn't bring the day Jeff would be home any closer.

In the Pacific things seemed to be a mix of good and bad. One island after another had been reclaimed, yet on other islands the enemy was dug in and determined to stay that way. Hundreds of Japanese aircraft had been shot down by American hellcats, yet the Japanese seemed undeterred. So, that half of the war ground on, as well.

Each day, Eleanor reported to her job at the Navy Yard and created endless parts on the lathe she'd been assigned. She'd even given her machine a name since they spent so much time together. The woman who drove the forklift had nicknamed that bit of equipment Bumblebee because it was yellow and black. Eleanor's lathe had become The Moose because it was big and ugly. But The Moose kept her occupied and feeling like she was doing her bit to win the war.

She missed her big Victory Garden, but Aunt Emily had allowed her to plant some tomatoes in pots on their little balcony. They'd enjoyed fresh tomatoes until the October frost had killed the plants off. Eleanor was already planning what she'd start indoors as seedlings come March. Her bedroom faced east, and the big window would be the perfect place to get a head start.

Mike reported that he'd put her garden to rest for the winter and stacked the big windows in the shed where they wouldn't get broken. That was thoughtful of him considering he was kept busy with the government project that kept getting more involved as time went on. She knew all this because Mike had begun to write to her regularly. More regularly than Jeff. And despite her promises, both spoken and left unspoken, she'd become addicted to reading Mike's letters.

Did that make her unfaithful? Mike was her friend, she kept telling herself. No one would think anything of it if Priscilla wrote every week. Except Priscilla's letters were as rare as Jeff's. Mike had begun to share things with her that she suspected he didn't tell anyone else. And, whether it was faithless or not, she'd begun writing back.

Her first reply had been posted with a hint of rebellion. Even if Jeff came home and they married as planned and he never mentioned Bridget again, Mike was still her friend. She had every right to write to him.

She'd shared with him how she and Aunt Emily went to the Red Cross building to help pack care packages for soldiers. Which, she'd also admitted, was a lot more fun than knitting socks. She'd told him of the new friends she'd made. Bella, who called her forklift Bumblebee and Sally who answered phones, ran errands, and manned the lunch cart when it arrived outside their shop at noon each day.

In one recent letter, she'd told Mike about becoming a volunteer at the USO. How once a week Aunt Emily's driver delivered her to Grand Central Terminal where she spent four hours at the USO lounge welcoming service men passing through. Mostly, it was just serving them snacks and coffee, she told him, but more importantly, it was being willing to chat or listen when lonely men a long way from home needed someone to talk to.

She didn't tell Mike that when the young men flirted with her, she flirted back. To her it was a game, but she didn't know if Mike would agree. Jeff surely wouldn't. But she hadn't told Jeff that she volunteered at the USO at all. Despite his more and more distant letters to her, she had a hunch that he would think her unfaithful just being there with all those other soldiers.

Christmas day finally dawned. Eleanor and Aunt Emily began the day with a visit to St. Patrick's Cathedral to celebrate the birth of Christ and pray for all the soldiers and sailors still a long way from home. Back at the apartment, Eleanor discovered that Christmas at Aunt Emily's was more lavish than Eleanor had ever experienced on Bailey Island, even before the war. Where Aunt Emily found the meat that was served, Eleanor couldn't guess, but she enjoyed it thoroughly.

After dinner, Aunt Emily bustled in from the kitchen with a tray bearing a plate of Christmas cookies and a teapot with steam curling from its spout and two delicate porcelain cups.

"Smile child. It's Christmas, and I've a gift for you." Aunt Emily set the tray on a small, lacquered table. She went to the tiny green tree Eleanor had acquired from a vendor on the corner and decorated with cranberries strung on thread. Her aunt had added a delicate glass star for the top. "Here," Aunt Emily said returning with a slender package wrapped in red paper.

Eleanor bounced from her place on the settee and retrieved the package she'd wrapped for her aunt. It had taken some time to decide what to get for a woman who seemed to have everything. Then she had chanced to see a copy of *Forever Amber* on sale. Wildly popular and banned in some cities, it had been proudly propped on the counter at Eleanor's favorite secondhand shop. Eleanor had eagerly turned over the hard-earned cash to honor a woman who had given her so much.

"For you," she said placing it on Aunt Emily's lap.

Slowly, making a big deal of it, Aunt Emily peeled back the silvery paper the store owner had wrapped it in. "Oh! My!" she breathed as she revealed the book and its title. "I am to be titillated at last!"

"It's all the rage, Aunt Emily. I hope you will enjoy it."

Aunt Emily pressed the book to her chest and grinned. "I just know I will. Now open yours. There are two. The one you set on your chair and another under the tree."

Eleanor returned to her seat, picked up the red wrapped gift and sat down. She squealed with delight as the paper fell away revealing a brand-new pair of nylon stockings. "Wherever did they come from?" She asked as she launched herself toward her aunt to bestow an energetic hug.

Eleanor had been wearing trousers to work, but with the loss of silk from Japan and nylon being set aside for parachutes, new stockings were almost unheard of. She and her friends had begun shaving their legs and staining them with coffee to make them look like they were wearing stockings when they reverted to dresses for their social outings.

"I have my ways," Aunt Emily said with a sly smile. "Now open the other."

Eleanor retrieved the second package and returned to her seat again. This one was bigger but not by much. As she carefully folded the wrapping and set it aside, a white bit of silky fabric slithered across Eleanor's knees and onto the carpet. Eleanor grabbed it up. She let the folds fall free and beheld a beautiful satin nightgown with embroidered flowers decorating the bodice and tiny pearl buttons down the front.

"Oh, Aunt Emily," Eleanor crooned as she ran shaking fingers over the delicate fabric.

"It's for your wedding night," Aunt Emily said, the smile no longer sly but full on.

"Jeff will love it."

"He will not love it more than who is wearing it, I pray. I just thought—"

The doorbell interrupted her aunt's thought and both women jerked their heads toward the door. No one was expected.

"Please, do answer it, Dear," Aunt Emily finally broke their surprised thrall. The cook had gone home to her own family as soon as dinner had been served and their man servant given the rest of the day off after he'd delivered them home from church.

Emily bundled the nightdress back into its box and set it aside, then hurried to the door. She threw it open and stared in total shock at the man standing in the hallway.

"Have I been gone that long that you've forgotten your own brother?" Raymond Murray asked opening his arms wide.

Eleanor gazed, jaw sagging, for just a second longer before flinging herself into her brother's arms.

"You're home. He's home, Aunt Emily. Raymond is home. How? When did you get here? How?" Eleanor babbled when Ray set her back on her feet. "Come in. Come in," she repeated flinging the door wide and ushering him into the foyer.

Raymond followed his sister back into the sitting room and moved to envelop his aunt in an embrace only slightly less exuberant than the one he'd given his sister.

Once back on her feet, Aunt Emily gestured to the divan. "Sit. I'll get us a fresh pot of tea. Or would you prefer coffee?"

Raymond smiled at her. "I've been drinking tea for four years, and while I'm used to it now, coffee would be lovely if you have any to spare."

Eleanor and Raymond barely had time to get started on all the things they desperately wanted to catch up on before Aunt Emily returned with a fresh pot of tea and a coffee pot, both of which she set on the coffee table along with some scones and a third porcelain cup.

"Why are you home?" Eleanor finally got to ask. "The war is not over yet, the last we heard."

"Well, it is for me, Sister. I've flown my twenty-five missions. Now they are sending me to San Antonio to train new pilots."

"Twenty-five? Why twenty-five?"

"Actually, it's a lot more if you count the missions I flew with the Royal Air Force before Roosevelt got the US into the war. But I wasn't counting. I just suited up and buckled myself in whenever I was told to. Now they're telling me it's my turn to train new pilots to take my place." Raymond took the cup his aunt was holding out to him and sipped. "Ambrosia!" He closed his eyes and sipped again.

The three of them talked over each other as the afternoon wore on and the tea and coffee grew cold. So many things the women wanted to hear about what Raymond and his fellow soldiers had endured. So much Raymond wanted to learn about life back home in his absence.

"Let's go for a walk," Eleanor suggested. Then glanced at her aunt. "You won't mind?"

"Not at all," Aunt Emily said making shooing gestures with her hands.

Ray looked at the enormous watch on his wrist. "I wish I could, but I have to be back at the train station soon."

Eleanor's heart fell. Ray was leaving again so soon? He'd just gotten here.

"But before I leave, I have a package to deliver." He snatched a paper bag he'd left sitting on the table just inside the living room door. "Save it for later. Right now, I need another hug."

After a hasty, but hearty, round of hugs and wishes for safe travel, Eleanor closed the hall door and returned to the sitting room and the bag Ray had given her. He'd been home to Bailey Island for a few days before coming to New York so it must be a gift from her parents.

"What is it, dear?" Aunt Emily asked when Eleanor seated herself on the hassock again.

Eleanor unfolded the top of the bag to reveal two packages wrapped in the comic section of the newspaper. That made her smile. Then she read the tags.

"This one is for you, Aunt Emily," Eleanor said handing the heavier of the two to her aunt.

She watched while her aunt removed the paper to reveal a little round pot of honey. Honey? Her mother had sent her sister a jar of honey? How odd.

"It is from your friend," Aunt Emily said. "From his Grams' bees."

Mike had sent the honey. With a start, Eleanor glanced at the tag on her package. It wasn't from her parents after all. It, too, was from Mike. Her fingers trembled as she peeled the comics away to reveal a soft pair of deerskin gloves lined with rabbit fur. A folded bit of paper slipped from between the pair. Eleanor unfolded it to see Mike's bold hand. *For your poor chapped hands. I pray these will keep them warm since I am not there to warm them for you. Love, Mike.*

CHAPTER THIRTY-EIGHT

Mike Hamilton – 1944

Surrounded by the laughing, joyful crowd of Grampa and Grams, Ruthie, Bert and their parents who had arrived just two days earlier, totally unexpected, Mike felt like only one thing could have made him happier.

Eleanor.

He'd been bold writing her that note and signing it 'Love, Mike'. But her recent letters had given him hope. Hope for what, exactly, he couldn't say. Should Jeff return from the war, Eleanor would honor her promise to marry him; even if she no longer loved him. Eleanor was faithful and she would remain so. No matter what it cost her.

But she was so much more. She was giving, generous, patriotic, loving, and fun. And he was hopelessly in love with her.

He'd just never had the courage to tell her.

All the while he was fashioning the gloves for her hands, he kept thinking of her slender fingers wearing them. He'd traded gas rations for the deerskin, and he'd killed and skinned the rabbit himself. The idea had come to him moments after reading her letter when she told him of how red and ugly her hands had become working in the shop.

Her hands would never be ugly to him, but her words had inspired him to create the gift and given him the courage to send it to her via Ray. Knowing it would look odd to send a gift to just Eleanor, he'd bartered a jar of Grams' honey for a cord of split wood for her cookstove so he would have something to include for Eleanor's aunt.

Then Ray had cornered him to come clean about his intentions toward Eleanor.

At first, he'd thought to dodge the question, but in the end, he'd admitted to his friend that he loved her. But he had also promised not to come between her and Jeff. Ray had grumbled something about wishing he would. Apparently, Ray held the same poor opinion of Eleanor's betrothed as Ray's father and Mike himself. But he knew Eleanor would think less of herself if she failed to keep her promise while Jeff was overseas fighting the Germans.

"Mike! Mike!" Ruthie chortled, dragging his attention back to his family. "Look what Daddy brought me." She held up a doll that she couldn't see but could definitely feel as her fingers slid over the doll's limbs and the velvet dress trimmed with lace.

"And I got a new rifle," Bertie said, the note of pride clear in his young voice. "Now I won't have to borrow yours." Bertie's hand caressed the wooden stock with as much care as Ruthie's had her new doll.

"Here, son" Mike's father leaned across the gap to hand Mike a slender box. "I heard yours disappeared while you were in hospital."

Mike lifted the lid to reveal a brand-new Omega pilot's watch, the leather strap still stiff and shiny. He gasped at the gift. His parents didn't have money for watches like this. But saying 'you shouldn't have' was just wrong. Before he could utter the wrong thing, he just got up and gave his father a hug.

"Thank you."

"It's from your mother, too."

"Aw, Mom." Another round of hugs.

"We're just glad it was only your watch that didn't come home," his mother said when they'd all resumed their seats.

"I hope you find my gift as useful," he said slipping a package with a pair of gloves just like Eleanor's into his mother's hands.

"For you, Dad," he handed a bulkier package to his father. "Your old one was getting pretty stinky."

His father guffawed as he revealed a pipe that Mike had carved himself that featured a nearly naked woman sitting astride the stem with her arms around the bowl.

"What about Me, Mike? What did you get for me?" Bert asked.

"Ammunition for your new gun, Squirt." Another heavy box was handed over.

"And for my favorite girl, not counting Mom," or Eleanor. Mike slipped a square wooden box about half as big as a shoebox into his sister's hands.

Ruthie shook it and jumped at the sharp rattle from inside.

Mike put his hands over his sisters and guided them to two holes. One in the top and one in the bottom.

"It's a maze inside a box that no one can see. Not even me. There's a marble inside and if you keep tipping it in just the right direction, the little ball will eventually find its way out of one of the holes."

A crease formed between Ruthie's eyes as she tipped the box one way, then another. She held it up to her ear and listened. Then tipped some more. For a while the whole family watched but eventually their attention drifted. Ruthie's look of determination just grew.

Mike had heard about this kind of puzzle and realized that with her loss of sight, Ruthie would eventually develop a more keen sense of touch and sound and she'd have an advantage over people who could see in solving the riddle.

"Can I go try out my new rifle?" Bertie asked, losing all interest in his sister's gift.

Mike's father hefted himself to his feet. "Sure. I'll go with you."

"I'd better start putting dinner on the table or we'll never eat," Grams said as she abandoned her rocker and headed for the kitchen.

With one last glance at her daughter, Mike's mother got up, as well. "I'll set the table."

Mike stayed where he was, his hand lightly ruffling Rascal's ears and watched as Ruthie continued to work on her new puzzle.

It had, in fact, been Eleanor who had told him about seeing such a puzzle box at Macy's in New York and wondered if it was something Ruthie might like. She had even offered to purchase it and mail it to him in time for Christmas.

"I got it!" Ruthie shrieked, holding up a red marble for Mike to see.

"Congratulations, Sis! You did really good."

She held the box out. "You try it, now."

With a tip of his head that Ruthie couldn't see and a sigh she surely could hear, he accepted the box. "Okay. But if I get stuck, then you have to rescue me."

Ruthie laughed as he dropped the marble into the hole.

He was still trying to figure out where inside the box the marble might be when dinner was called. He set it aside and offered his sister a piggy-back ride to dinner. She declined.

"Rascal will take me to dinner."

Which, of course, Rascal did. They were a pair now and the dog took her everywhere, even down to the cove where she could toss rocks into the water just to hear them splash. At least that was one good thing that came out of this awful war. His sister had gained both confidence and a sense of independence she might never have known, had Mike never encountered that dog in Grand Central Terminal in New York.

When dinner was over, Bertie took off to show his friends his new rifle. His father and grandfather walked down the street to visit with a neighbor, and his mother and Grams were cleaning up the kitchen. So Ruthie and Mike were alone while Mike tackled the puzzle box again.

"Can you feel it?" Ruthie asked.

Mike shook his head. "Nope. I mean, I can feel it bumping into walls, but I can't feel where it is."

"Keep trying," she encouraged.

Her now nearly sightless eyes were gazing past his hands and the box, but her head was tipped as if she was listening.

"How did you know to get me the puzzle box?" Ruthie asked.

"It was Eleanor's idea," he admitted. "She saw it in a big store in New York and asked if I thought you would like it."

"Well, I love it," Ruthie said with a nod.

"I'll have to tell her, then."

Mike continued turning the box this way and that doing his best to figure out where the ball was without being able to see it and failing.

"You love Eleanor, don't you?"

Mike almost dropped the box in surprise at his sister's question.

"I like her very much," he prevaricated.

"But if she wasn't supposed to marry Jeff Winslow, you'd ask her to marry you, wouldn't you?"

Mike set the box on his knee and looked at his sister. Her eyes might be sightless, but her heart saw way too much.

"Yes, maybe I would," he finally answered.

"I like Eleanor, too."

CHAPTER THIRTY-NINE

Kenzie Ross – Present Day

A truly joyful Christmas without Garrett should have shocked me but didn't. As I had done so many times in the last few months, I reflected on how I'd spent my married life and once again realized I'd always deferred to Garrett and never insisted on anything I preferred.

I grew up attending church at midnight on Christmas Eve where the highlight of the service was singing *Silent Night* in a church filled with candlelight. Yet, for all the years of my married life, we'd always attended on Christmas morning with Garrett's mother. Once they were past infancy, that tradition had disrupted two excited little boys eager to check out their stockings and burrow under the tree hoping that all the things they'd put on their wish lists would be found there. Instead, those childhood things always had to wait until the afternoon; after church and after a formal and stilted dinner with Garrett's parents. Jaycee had escaped that tradition, having opted instead for the more casual celebration at her in-law's home.

This year I'd taken myself up to historic old St Paul's in Brunswick. Being alone didn't feel nearly as sad as I'd expected. At midnight, with each parishioner holding his or her own candle, faces lit by the glowing flames, our voices had been raised in the familiar words of Silent Night. I'd come home feeling fulfilled by the arrival of Christ's birth for the first time in two decades.

Only having Sam along to share the night could have made it any sweeter, but he'd worshipped at the assisted living home with his aunt. Another cherished tradition he didn't want to break, for his aunt's sake more than his own, he'd told me. That had always been Garrett's excuse. The first pang of disquiet in the comparison of my ex and Sam.

But now it was Christmas morning and Sam would be along soon with his daughter. He'd informed me that Becca would make Monkey Bread. Something I'd never tasted before. Of course, I googled it, and I was looking forward to the confection. Every indulgent sugary bite of it. My food offering for the day's events was a tradition of punch and finger food surrounding a turkey that had been roasting in the oven all night. Another of my parents' traditions I'd not enjoyed during my marriage.

As I sat at the kitchen counter with my first mug of coffee, trying to decide what to wear for the day, a knock sounded on my door and Duffy raced to greet whoever was there.

I was still in my jammies and robe with no time to change, so I followed the dog and hoped Sam wouldn't mind the informality. He'd seen me in less, truth be told. But still. Becca would be with him.

I shushed the dog and swung the door wide.

It wasn't Sam.

Evelyn with her grown kids and a few school-age ones I had to assume were the grandkids I hadn't met yet shouted, "Merry Christmas." Thank God I had the forethought to make cookies and lay out the supplies for plenty of my grandmother's Christmas punch.

Evelyn turned to the tall man at her back. It was her son whom I had only met the week earlier. He stepped around her and produced a glass jug filled with an amber liquid.

"Mark has his own sugar maples and makes his own syrup," Evelyn explained as Mark pushed the jug into my startled hands.

"Will you come in?" I asked, stepping back.

"Oh, no. We can't. We just wanted to bring you the syrup and say Merry Christmas. We have dozens of stops to make." Evelyn began to hum and a moment later the entire entourage broke into a rousing rendition of Jingle Bells, followed by one about going over the river and through the woods to Grandmother's house.

As soon as the last note faded to a stop, the youngsters scampered off to the line of cars waiting on the other side of the wall. Evelyn pulled me into a hug.

"We wanted to make sure your first Christmas on Bailey Island was as merry as it could be. I expect Sam will be over soon. Right?" She winked and turned away to the car before I could reply.

As I returned to the kitchen with my precious jug of real homemade maple syrup, my phone chirruped. I answered without checking the screen.

"Merry Christmas, Mom," my twins voices shouted out in unison.

"Happy Christmas to you too, my sweet babies." Tears threatened, but I blinked them away.

"We aren't babies," Luke boomed with a laugh.

"You'll always be my babies. I don't care if you end up growing to seven feet tall."

My equilibrium restored, we chatted for a while. Bits of how their exams had gone and demands to know how the renovations were proceeding. I didn't bother to enlighten them about the asbestos debacle. Long before any of us were ready to end the conversation, I heard their names being called. Time to leave for church, no doubt. Better them than me.

"Have a wonderful Day," I told them. "I'm blowing you kisses."

"We love you, too, Mom."

And then they were gone.

If I didn't hurry up, I'd still be in my jammies when Sam arrived. I headed for the stairs but was only halfway up when another knock sounded at my door. Duffy turned and nearly knocked me over hurrying back down the stairs to greet the new arrivals.

Sam looked me up and down when I opened the door, then grinned. A grin he quickly wiped off his face as he glanced at Becca who stood to his side with a cake tin balanced on her palms.

"Please. Come in and excuse my pajamas. I keep heading up to get dressed and someone keeps coming to the door and interrupting me." I stepped out of the way so they could enter.

"No need to get gussied up for me," Sam said, the grin back in place despite Becca's presence.

"Gussied up?" There was a new one. Mainers seemed to be full of terms I was struggling to learn.

"Dressed up," Becca supplied the definition. "My Gramma used to call it that. It's kind of old fashioned, but Dad has a bunch of words he likes to use that most people have never heard of. He especially likes hornswoggle and fudgel."

Two more new terms I'd be googling next time I sat down at my computer. "You'll have to give me a crash course, but first, let me take the monkey bread off your hands so you can hang your coat up and get comfy." I reached for the cake tin and she handed it over.

"Your dad can start the fire I haven't gotten to, while I get dressed. Then, I'm eager to try this yummy smelling monkey bread. Would you believe I've never had it before?"

Becca raised her brows, then shook her head. "They don't make it in Virginia?"

"Oh, probably. But I've just never had any." I left them in the living room and dashed to the kitchen, left the cake tin on the counter, and started a fresh pot of coffee. Then back to the stairs.

Duffy's tail wagged tentatively. He wasn't sure if he should hang with Sam and Becca or follow me. He ended up choosing Sam when he saw the box of Milk Bone biscuits Becca rattled to get his attention.

Stuffed to the gills with the gooiest, most decadent Christmas morning treat I'd ever tasted, I unhooked the stockings I'd stuffed from their places on the mantle and handed them out. Sam didn't waste any time before he shoved a hand into his, but Becca got a little teary. While she didn't say anything, I wondered if it had been her mother who remembered things like stockings, and Becca hadn't had one since Tansey's passing. I was glad I'd taken the time to find stuff to fill the old woolen socks I'd found in the attic.

Once the wrappings were gathered up and burned down to ashes, we decided on a walk to the cove and back. Partly to help me digest all those Monkey Bread calories and partly for Duff to have a chance for a romp. I spread the buffet of food out on our return, and we noshed on that while watching *It's a Wonderful Life* on the television.

"I wasn't sure what to get you," Sam said as we returned to the fireside after cleaning up the kitchen. "But I thought these wouldn't be out of place." He handed me a box suspiciously shaped like the ones from my new favorite candy store.

When I saw the Island Candy Company logo, my gaze jerked up to meet Sam's grinning face. "But how? They closed a month ago."

"The owner is a friend of mine. I promised her a free tune-up and she made them in her kitchen at home. She even remembered the ones you liked best."

I launched myself at Sam and gave him a hug meant to cut off breathing for at least the duration of the hug. Then I started to slide a thumbnail under the seal.

Sam covered my busy hand. "Save them for later. No need to share."

Then he slid a far smaller box from his pocket and handed it to Becca. Her gift was a pretty bracelet wrapped in silver paper, and beneath that, the newest iPhone. Her squeals of delight said he'd hit two for two with his daughter. Batting a thousand if you counted my chocolates.

Next, Becca went hunting through the boxes under the tree that Sam had cut and helped me to trim the week before. I thought all the remaining boxes were things for my boys when they came, so you can imagine my surprise when Becca chortled with glee and fished out a box I didn't recognize. She handed it to me with a flourish.

I stared at the unfamiliar writing, then at Becca.

"A little bird told me to give this to you."

"A little bird?" What little bird had she been listening to?

"So, open it, already," she urged, settling on her knees in front of me.

I looked at Sam, but he just shrugged.

I did as Becca asked and began tearing away the paper covered with gnomes in red and green hats.

Inside the square box was another box. And inside that, a third. I laughed. My boys used to love wrapping the tiniest of things in numerous boxes to make me wonder what they could have gotten for me.

The fourth box finally gave way to a wealth of tissue paper with an oddly shaped glass bowl nested in its midst. I lifted it out and held it up to the light.

"There's more," Becca said reaching to pull more of the tissue from the box to reveal a gnarled, polished piece of driftwood. "They fit together," Becca said.

As I inspected the bowl and the wooden cradle, I realized the glass had been specifically formed to fit the exact contours of the driftwood.

"It's perfect, Becca. Wherever did you find it?"

"Land's End," she stated as if I should have guessed. "And this is to go inside." She dropped something into the bowl that almost sounded like a wind chime. "You can put flowers in it if you prefer, but I thought it would be perfect for keeping sea glass in."

"And how do you know I've been collecting sea glass?"

"Because Dad saw you picking a piece up a few times and slipping them into your pocket."

With one last flourish, she handed me a folded piece of paper, which I opened to read:

Sea Glass is a symbol of renewal and healing, a metaphor for life. Sea Glass was once just a bottle, or perhaps a dish that was no longer needed because it had served its purpose, outlived its usefulness or was broken. But now each unique piece can become a promise for something new to come your way.

Now I was the one with tears smarting in my eyes.

"Oh, Becca." I was touched beyond words. "I love it." We both hesitated another long moment before I opened my arms and pulled her into a hug. Was this what it felt like to have a daughter?

CHAPTER FORTY

Sam Philips – Present Day

His daughter's gift was so perfect for Kenzie. It surely put his own choice of bartered chocolates to shame. He had considered a number of other options for Kenzie's gift, but all of them suggested a relationship he wasn't sure she was ready for. So, he'd just gone begging for the chocolates he knew she loved.

Watching Kenzie and his daughter as they hugged, then went back to admiring the unique glass bowl, Sam wondered what had been printed on the paper that had brought tears to Kenzie's eyes and a breathless declaration to her lips.

Something to do with sea glass, he surmised. But what had passed between the two women that he'd missed?

Sam knew how much Becca still mourned the loss of her mother. Perhaps even more than he did. Not that long ago, he'd still woken thinking of Tansey and fallen asleep still missing her presence beside him. But now, many of those thoughts had been taken over by Kenzie.

He knew Tansey would be happy for him. She had made him promise to do his mourning and then move on when she was gone. If Kenzie was the woman he was meant to spend the rest of his life with, Tansey would be cheering.

Becca hadn't had nearly as much time to get to know Kenzie, and no one, however wonderful, would ever replace her mother. But maybe, just maybe, this was the beginning of a friendship that would be nourishing for both of the women he loved.

He smiled at the lovely warm feeling that crept over him. Despite the fact that he'd be driving home with Becca tonight instead of crawling into Kenzie's bed and making love to her, he was a happy man. And a patient one. He could wait.

"Hey, Dad," Becca interrupted his pleasant thoughts. "The fire's dying and there's just a couple more logs in the box."

Sam pulled himself to his feet with a nod. "Shall I take Duffy out for pee break while I'm fetching firewood?" he asked of Kenzie.

"Or teach him to fetch firewood." She laughed. He loved the sound of her laughter.

He whistled to the dog and headed for the door, grabbing his jacket on the way. Duffy pranced out ahead of him, tail wagging happily.

They walked up to the end of the road while Duffy checked out any new K-9 calling cards that had been added to his usual stops, then turned toward the cove. Once he'd done his business, they meandered along a tide line rimmed with ice.

A bit of bright blue caught Sam's eye and he bent to check it out. Sea Glass. An unusual deep blue – the color of a Vick's bottle except he thought that stuff came in plastic in today's world. Maybe it had once been a wine bottle. He slipped it into his pocket, and they turned back, up the hill toward Murray House and the woman who claimed his heart.

Duffy went directly to the door, then turned to follow when Sam continued around to the side yard. Sam gave the dog a brief pat, then loaded his arms with firewood from the rack piled with logs he'd split and stacked a month earlier.

When he elbowed his way back into the warm room redolent of fir and turkey and other holiday scents, neither Becca nor Kenzie were anywhere in sight. He kicked the door shut, dumped the firewood into the box beside the fireplace, then removed his jacket and tossed it over the back of a chair. As he crossed back to the fireplace to add logs to the dying fire, he noticed the bit of paper that had accompanied Becca's gift laying unfolded beside the bowl.

"Curiosity is going to get me one of these days," he muttered as he picked up the slip of paper to read it. Maybe it was none of his business, but he couldn't help himself.

"A promise," he said, barely above a whisper, but the dog heard him anyway and tipped his head. Sam fished in his pocket and brought out the bit of bright blue glass worn smooth by the sea. He dropped it into the bowl and silently promised Kenzie he'd love her the way she deserved to be loved when she was ready.

Becca was off for a sleepover with friends she'd had since she was in grade school, and Sam was right where he wanted to be. With Kenzie.

It had been a busy week, both at the garage and outside of work. Seemed like half of Bailey Island had car troubles this past week, but he really shouldn't complain. The work paid Becca's tuition. In his off hours, he and his daughter had enjoyed hanging out with Kenzie and her boys twice during the precious few days they were on Bailey Island.

For New Year's Eve, there had been some discussion over the merits of driving up to Brunswick for dinner, or to the Bar Crawl in

Lewiston. In the end, Kenzie had voted to experience the bonfire and fireworks right here on Bailey Island.

Along with dozens of islanders, they were seated on a collection of beach chairs and wooden crates surrounding a blazing bonfire with coolers full of beer and wine. Sam smiled at the firelit faces of men and women he'd grown up with, while George told tales that no one believed, but everyone encouraged.

"Is he putting on this show for me?" Kenzie asked. "Because even if there's a nugget of truth to his stories, there's no way he isn't stretching it beyond all recognition."

"Well, he did catch a big tuna one summer that won the annual tournament," Sam conceded. "And it's belly *was* full of squid."

"But?" Kenzie asked. "There has to be a but."

Sam chuckled. "The fish wasn't nearly as ginormous as he's claiming. The biggest catch on record was at least a hundred pounds less, and I don't think George was even born when that fish was caught.

"Ginormous is another of those words?"

Sam laughed. "I guess."

Kenzie was silent for a bit, then spoke again. "I'm pretty amazed that anyone can catch a fish that weighs several hundred pounds with just a fishing pole. How do you not get pulled into the water when it tries to swim away?"

"Next summer I'll get us a prime location to watch them when they bring their catch in to be weighed. I don't own a boat, but I can borrow one, and we can anchor in Mackerel Cove to watch. That is, if you're still planning to be here next summer?"

Sam held his breath awaiting her answer which seemed like a long time coming.

She squirmed under the arm he had draped over her shoulder to look up at him. "And where else would I be next summer?"

He breathed again. "Just checking. I know you've been worried about finances and the detailing has tailed off some now that winter has set in."

"I spent a bundle on winter clothes at L.L. Bean. I'm kinda committed now. I am a little disappointed, though. Everyone kept talking about how much snow we'd get, but there hasn't been a single flake so far."

"Wait until January and February. But it must snow in Virginia. It's not like you've never seen snow, before."

"It never lasts long enough in Virginia, which is why my winter wardrobe wasn't up to keeping me warm if even half what Dawn and Evelyn claim is true. Did I tell you how much fun it was shopping with Becca?"

"Becca enjoyed herself, too. I'm the one who was worried when the two of you took Luke to the airport and didn't get home for hours."

Kenzie gave Sam a teasing elbow to the ribs. "Girls do like to shop. We only started at L.L. Bean. Then there were other outlets with enticing sale signs that we just had to check out. A stop to refresh ourselves at the tea house was also a must, but I am sorry you worried. I thought Becca texted to let you know we were stopping in Freeport."

Sam pulled Kenzie back against his side again. He liked the feel of her cuddling there. "To be honest, I should have guessed. And Becca did text me, but my phone was dead and I had to put it on the charger, then forgot it when I came over to walk Duffy and get a fire started for your return home."

George had given up on the fish stories and was busy with two other men readying boxes of fireworks for lighting at the moment midnight arrived. A fourth man with a skiff hovered just off the point, his outboard engine idling. Finally, one of the men threw a line out to the skiff, which the driver cleated down before pulling the raft filled with boxes safely away from the partygoers.

"What happens to the guy in the boat? Isn't he a little close to the fireworks when they go off?" Kenzie jumped to her feet to watch the progress of the skiff and the raft.

"Nah! He'll toss an anchor overboard to keep the raft in place and row like crazy until he's safely out of range." Sam stood and consulted his watch. "Five minutes."

A few minutes later, the skiff reappeared and rattled up onto the rocky beach behind the dying fire. Then the chant began.

"Ten. Nine. Eight. Seven . . ." Sam pulled Kenzie into a half embrace as they counted with the crowd. "Three. Two. One!"

The timing was spot on as the fireworks began launching with little poofts that could be heard over the lap of waves. The sky overhead lit as dozens of fireworks blossomed against the inky dark. It wasn't to be a long show with one explosion, then another with spaces in between. Like every year Sam could recall, they were all set to go off nearly at once in one crazy, shower of color and noise.

Sam looked down at Kenzie. Her eyes wide as she stared up at the awesome display.

"Happy New Year, Kenzie." Then he kissed her.

CHAPTER FORTY-ONE

Eleanor Murray – 1945

Eleanor gaped at the radio in shock.

Their president was dead.

Horror and sadness gripped her, and for several long moments she forgot to breathe.

Roosevelt, for all his faults, had been a rock leading their country through this awful war. Now he was gone.

Just like that, America was rudderless. What would Hitler or Hirohito think? What further atrocities would they decide their armies could get away with now?

Eleanor didn't know much about Russia or if Stalin was to be trusted. Churchill didn't think so. At least that was the impression she'd gotten from reading reports of his speeches, but she had trusted Roosevelt and Roosevelt had trusted Stalin. With Roosevelt gone, would Stalin's Russia try to take America's place? What about Great Britain, America's main ally?

"Our president is dead," she said, in a voice filled with all the alarm coursing through her veins. "I didn't even know he was ill. Did you know he was ill, Aunt Emily? He was only sixty-three. How could this happen?"

"We have a new president," Aunt Emily said in a calm voice, although Eleanor felt no reassurance in the words.

Eleanor knew almost nothing about Harry Truman. He'd only been vice-president for a few months. Before that, he'd been a senator from a state she knew even less about.

"I suspect the late president has been ill for some time, but with the war going on, no one wanted to replace him," Aunt Emily said.

Where her aunt gleaned such knowledge from, Eleanor had no idea. All she could think now was how reassuring Roosevelt's voice had sounded during those fireside chats. Even though the war ground on without an end in sight, she'd been confident they would eventually win, and the evil forces of Nazi Germany and the Empire of Japan would be vanquished once and for all.

"You must trust in our new president and keep the faith, Eleanor," Aunt Emily said as she got to her feet. "I'm going to go make us a nice pot of tea. That will warm you and hopefully you will find the serenity to go on, just as we all must."

Eleanor watched her leave the room, wishing she had half her aunt's confidence that all would be well. Eleanor couldn't even remember a time before Franklin Roosevelt had occupied the White House. Back when she was ten, the world beyond Bailey Island hadn't existed. At least not for her.

She was a teenager before she understood the depth of the depression and began listening to her father talking about Roosevelt and the New Deal. Not that she always agreed with her father. He was staunchly against many of the presidential decrees issued by Roosevelt, and Eleanor never did understand his point of view. As a banker, her father had been fortunate not to lose his job, or his stature.

But now Roosevelt was gone. Replaced by a man Eleanor had little knowledge of and no faith in. Tea was not going to help.

I am shocked. Jeff's bald statement in black and white on the page echoed what Eleanor herself had felt just a few weeks ago.

She reread all of Jeff's letter a second time, but it had been written just days after Roosevelt's death. Before Hitler had committed suicide. Before Germany had conceded defeat. Before victory had been declared in Europe. Jeff had had no idea how close he might be to coming home again as he'd penned the sentiments that had gripped Eleanor such a short time ago.

It hadn't been Aunt Emily's tea that put starch back into Eleanor's spine, though.

Roosevelt had died less than a month before victory was declared in Europe. How sad that he had never known how close they were to triumph.

What had reassured Eleanor was all the talk at the Brooklyn Shipyard. Her fellow workers there had helped her to regain her focus.

She'd listened carefully to all the discussions about President Truman, some staunchly positive, some hopeful and others less flattering. Eleanor had learned why Wallace had been dumped as Roosevelt's running mate, and she had gained a new sense of confidence that what Roosevelt had begun and fought for with his last years of life, Truman would bring to a successful conclusion.

Mike had echoed that confidence his weekly letters. Maybe he had painted a rosier picture to reassure her, but she'd believed him and taken heart. Truman would see them through.

Only Japan continued to hold out in spite of defeats like the American triumph on Iwo Jima and the loss of other strongholds across the

Pacific. With the war over in Europe and the thought of losing Jeff fading, Eleanor had begun to pay more attention to what was going on in the Pacific.

When Jeff had written from Paris, his reports of that city had been triumphant and encouraging. Major portions of his letter had been blacked out by censors, but the war was over. Jeff was safe and would soon be on his way home to her.

Laying in her bed at night, though, she'd begun to have misgivings. In Jeff's absence, she'd let herself begin to care too much for Mike. It was partly Jeff's fault, though. He'd continued to comment so often about his time in Ireland that even when he didn't mention Bridget, she began to wonder if he still felt the same way about her and their marriage. She didn't feel the same, but she'd made him a vow. An unspoken one, but still. She'd promised to wait for his return. No matter how she felt about Mike, or Jeff himself, she would keep it.

The knock on the door on a quiet Sunday afternoon while Eleanor and Aunt Emily were finishing their afternoon tea caught them by surprise.

No one ever came to their door on a Sunday afternoon.

"Would you please see who is at the door?" Aunt Emily asked, looking up from a section of the newspaper she had been reading. "You are quite presentable."

Eleanor looked down at the lovely house robe her aunt had given her for Christmas, presumably to cover the skimpy lingerie that was meant for Jeff's pleasure only, and decided her aunt was correct.

She slid from her seat and headed for the front hall.

It never occurred to Eleanor to put her eye to the peephole to see who might be knocking on the door, so it was a bit of a surprise to see a young man in an olive-green uniform standing in the hall when she opened the door.

Then she noticed the bright yellow envelope he held in his hand.

Eleanor's head began to buzz.

A telegram could only mean bad news. The worst possible news anyone with a beloved soldier far from home could receive.

Heart hammering, hand shaking, Eleanor reached for the envelope, but her fingers never closed around it as she slumped to the floor.

CHAPTER FORTY-TWO

Kenzie Ross – Present Day

I'd never spent New Year's Eve on a beach in jeans and a winter parka but there's a first for everything and I thoroughly enjoyed the new experience. I'd especially enjoyed welcoming the new year with Sam's lips on mine.

A mere six months ago, I'd have told anyone who asked that I was not going to date anyone on the rebound. Or maybe ever. Yet here I was, welcoming Sam into my life and my bed, and it didn't feel like a rebound.

Sam was so very different from Garrett. Maybe that was why everything felt so very different and new. So far, the only thing about Sam that I found troubling was that he was a disorganized slob.

Laying here with moonlight streaming in my window and Sam snoring softly at my side, I itched with the knowledge that his clothes were strewn everywhere about my room. On the floor, draped over the antique mirror, tossed onto a chair. Probably there were bits in the bathroom, just as his boots were kicked off inside the back door and his jacket tossed on a stool in the kitchen.

I'm not OCD. I'd just been converted by Garrett into obsessive neatness, and I was still having trouble ignoring this less than stellar quality in my new love. Which should have been easier given he was totally laid back about everything else, including my total disruption of his office at the garage.

I also knew he was eager to cement our growing relationship but was patiently waiting for me to catch up.

He was not aware I was even in the room when he picked up the note that came with Becca's gift at Christmas, and he didn't know I saw him drop that beautiful bit of sapphire blue glass into the bowl. The following morning, I'd plucked the bit of glass from the bowl and rubbed the sea worn smoothness between my finger and thumb. Had there been a promise to go with it?

Sam was such a romantic, I told myself there must have been a promise, and I wondered what it might have been. But I also knew, whatever unspoken promise he might have made, he would never break it.

Sam was a light at the end of my tunnel of rediscovery. Actually, he was doing a pretty good job of shining that light into the tunnel and helping me find my way. Did I even deserve a man like Sam in my life?

The idea of committing myself to anyone again scared the crap out of me. But if I made that leap, it would be with Sam. Of that, I was sure, even if I wasn't ready to make any promises, beyond the one I'd made to myself.

Be strong. Be yourself. Be free.

"Hey Kenzie."

I woke to Sam jostling my shoulder.

I rolled over and opened my eyes, surprised he was already up. He liked to sleep in on days he wasn't working. And up to now, he'd been eager for a round of morning lovemaking before getting up. But he was fully dressed and looking worried.

"What's up?" I asked struggling into a sitting position and gathering the comforter around my nakedness.

"There's no water. I'm not sure if the circuit breaker is off or what, but I'm headed down to check. And I got a call-out for a tow."

My heart jerked. No water! I was on a well. Another new thing I was coming to terms with after having had city water reliably piped into my home all my life. Maybe it was just a circuit breaker. "Please, God, let it be just the breaker." I tossed the covers aside and stood.

Heat flooded Sam's eyes. "You trying to put me off my game?" He ran a finger down my cheek and neck to my chest, tracing the curve of my breast.

"The breaker?" I reminded him doing my best to ignore the answering response in my own body.

"Yeah. Sorry." He shook his head and bent to kiss me. "I'll check the box on my way out." With another quick kiss, he headed for the door and didn't turn back as he disappeared into the hall.

His being up before me meant none of his discarded clothing was laying around waiting for me to fuss over, but considering the reason, I'd have preferred his messiness. I hurried to put on my own jeans, carefully folded and left on the window-seat. I grabbed a sweatshirt and a fresh pair of socks and followed Sam downstairs.

He met me in the great room.

"Not the breaker. Possibly a leak somewhere. If I wasn't already late, I'd stay and check. Give Marcus a call. If he's around he'll come over and look for possible causes. In the meantime, check all your fixtures and make sure nothing was left running. Including the new builds.

The water level might just have gotten too low and needs a few hours to recover."

He headed for the door, shoving one arm into his parka as he went. At the door he turned back. "Duffy is out in the yard taking care of business."

I hurried after Sam's disappearing form and caught a glimpse of him giving Duffy a pat before climbing into his truck. The dog plopped onto his butt and watched the truck disappear.

"Come, Duff." I had leaks to look for and a water situation to check into. I didn't need to be worrying over a dog that might decide to follow Sam's truck.

Duffy took one last look at the diminishing truck, then got up and came back to the house.

"I'll get your breakfast in a minute, but first I gotta check a few things," I told the dog as he came in and went directly to his food dish. Thankfully his water dish was full. I couldn't say the same for the coffee maker. I'd have to live without a caffeine fix until I got the trouble sorted out.

Alarm was tightening my gut as I finished checking every single bit of plumbing I could see. No water running anywhere. No toilet tank float stuck open. No sink with water running endlessly. No dripping pipes anywhere. So, if there was a leak, then where was it? And if it wasn't a leak, then what?

I ached for Sam to find a reason to return, but I squared my shoulders and hunted down my phone. Be strong. Be free. I repeated the mantra. I could fix this without relying on Sam.

I called Marcus, instead.

An hour later Marcus suggested two possible issues I might be having. Neither of them sounded good. Especially since it was New

Year's Day and well maintenance companies would be closed. I wasn't even sure who my well maintenance company was.

"I looked at the pressure setting but diddling with that didn't make a difference. Could be a bad switch, which would be an easy fix but none of the stores where I could buy one are open today." Marcus shook his head, a regretful look on his face. "That's the easiest answer. As far as a leaking drop pipe, I couldn't fix that on my best day. You'd need a professional for that. I did find this tucked under a connection on the tank in the basement."

He handed me a business card. Temple Well Drilling was printed in bold black letters with a phone number under that.

"Give them a try. They probably have someone on call who could get out today. If not, call again first thing in the morning. Looks like they've been here before and should be willing to come out and troubleshoot."

With my heart in my brand-new L.L.Bean boots, I thanked Marcus for coming over on his day off and doing his best to figure out why I had no water coming out of my taps. Haley had packed herself a small bag and was going home with Marcus until the water was back on at Murray House. She gave me a quick hug and followed Marcus out.

Belatedly, I realized I'd flushed my own toilet without thinking before coming downstairs and had not heard the tank refilling. Did that mean I couldn't flush again until this was fixed? I did my best not to panic, pulled out my cell phone and tapped in the numbers on the card.

After five rings the call went to a recorded message that included an emergency number. But I wasn't quick enough to catch it. I raced to the kitchen, found a pen and paper and dialed again. Listened to the five rings, pen poised, while a no-nonsense, Downeast voice announced the office was closed and to call back during regular hours which were Monday to Friday between eight am and five pm. "If this is an emergency, please call," I stabbed my pen at the paper and scribbled down the digits.

Two minutes later I reluctantly tapped end. So much for emergencies. That number had just rung twice as many times before a taped voice announced that the party I was calling was not available.

I hurried to my desk and opened my laptop, typed well companies in Brunswick, Maine into the search bar and came up with two additional well companies. With new heart, I tried again.

With the same disheartening lack of success. The first on the list announced the number had been disconnected and the second just rang without being picked and without any announcement of the recipient not being available.

Now what?

So much for being strong and free. For the first time since my marriage had formally ended, I wanted to call Garrett and let him sort things out. My ex wasn't much of a DIY guy but he always knew who to call and how to make things happen.

One thing I did need was coffee. If I was going to cope at all, I needed at least a gallon of the stuff. I had a tank full of gas and I'd just drive as far as I needed to get some caffeinated restorative juice. Then I'd add a few gallons of bottled water and come home to regroup and decide what to do next.

There was still the problem of a toilet I couldn't flush again, but there were five other toilets in the house. I'd just have to play musical toilets.

I found both coffee and bottled water at the little convenience store on my way up the peninsula and was headed home when my RAV 4's audio system announced that Sam was calling.

"Hi, Sam," I answered injecting as much cheer as I could into my voice. "You get whoever needed a tow back to the shop, okay?"

"Yes and no. I got him picked up, but he wanted to be taken to the dealer so I'm in Bath. I called to see how the water situation came out."

I was determined I was going to cope with this problem on my own, but that didn't mean I couldn't share my frustration with a friend. And Sam was a friend. If Jaycee had called, I'd have poured my whole disquieting day out on her ears. Belatedly, I realized that maybe I should have tried calling George. He was kind of a jack of all trades. Maybe he could have figured it out. But then, Marcus's efforts hadn't resulted in a fix. So likely neither would anything George could do.

I replayed what Marcus had told me and whined about all the unsuccessful calls to local well companies.

"Are you home? Sounds like you're in the car."

"I was desperate for coffee so I came out in search. I'm headed home now."

"You can stay at my place tonight and we'll get in touch with someone in the morning."

It sounded reassuring when he said we would get in touch with someone in the morning. I was still determined to deal with this on my own, but there wasn't any reason I had to turn down his offer of alternative shelter, just to prove my independence.

"That would be nice, Sam. I assume Duffy is welcome to come with?"

"Woof, woof," Sam replied with a chuckle. "Of course. See you in about thirty minutes. Unless you'd like me to stop at that Chinese take-out place you like. Then make it an hour."

"*If* it's open," I replied with emphasis on the *if*. It wasn't like I'd been batting a thousand today. More like zero.

"It will be. See you at my place." What sounded like a kiss was followed by the end of the call.

Chapter Forty-Three

Kenzie Ross – Present Day

I hugged myself as I watched the men working out at the perimeter of my side yard. I had told them I didn't want to get in the way, but truth to tell, it was damned cold out there and I was happier to watch from my kitchen window.

"Cold as a witch's tit," the man who was the boss had said, seconding my decision to wait inside while they assessed the situation. Wind whipped up off the icy blue waters of the bay, tugging at the men's clothing. They seemed not to notice as they went about figuring out my well problems.

Watching them wasn't getting the answers any quicker, but somehow, I couldn't tear myself away from the tableau. Three trucks parked at random angles. One with equipment I couldn't even begin to identify appeared to be the tool of choice at the moment. Every once in a while, one of the men would fetch a tool from one of several trunks lining the bed of a pickup with the Temple Well logo on the door panels.

Finally, whatever had been going on stopped and all three men stood, arms folded while a discussion ensued. Then all the tools were gathered up and returned to their respective trunks. The big rig was folded down against the bed of its truck, and the boss headed my way. Apparently, a diagnosis had been reached.

I took a deep breath to steel myself for the verdict and went to let him in.

I pulled the door open before the man reached the top step and gestured for him to come inside. No one should have to stand outside any longer than necessary on a freezing day like today.

"Waaeellll," the man drawled the word as he rubbed his hands together, likely trying to get blood circulating again.

My heart bottomed out. That introduction didn't sound good. Not good at all.

"The drop pipe is good, and the pump appears to be okay. It's old, but functioning. There's just no water for it to pump."

"What do you mean, no water? It's a well. Wells are meant to have water in them," I protested. My city-girl knowledge at a disadvantage here in the sticks.

"Your well is pretty shallow to begin with, and I'm kinda surprised you haven't had a problem before now." The man shrugged. "There's plenty of water out here to tap into. Your well just doesn't go that deep."

I swallowed my apprehension. "You mean drill a new well?"

"Ayuh." He nodded several times and then scratched at the thick beard covering his face. Probably half the reason for growing a beard up here was that it kept the face warm if you happened to have a job that required being outside very much of the time.

"Can't do her today," he went on. "But I can have my men down here first thing in the morning. We'll have you hooked up and back in business before the end of the day. Otherwise, it will have to be next week."

What choice did I have? I couldn't wait until next week for water. I guess I should consider myself fortunate that he could drill a new well the very next day.

"How much?"

"Depends . . ." another long pause and more chin scratching.

"Depends on what?" I prompted. I had a strong premonition I was not going to like the answer, but I had to ask.

"On how deep we have to go before we get a decent flow. Don't do no good to cut corners and stop before we get a reasonably acceptable gallons-per-minute flow. Elsewise, we'd just be back out here in another year or two. Might's well do the job right the first time."

"Any ballpark figure?" A hint at the disaster would be nice.

"We drilled one for a fella just up the road just last month. Hit a good aquafer at a hundred eighty feet. Likely about the same here. It could run between six and fifteen k depending. And you'd want to install a new pump which would be another fifteen hundred. Not likely to go over twenty thousand. Best guess is a lot less than that. Maybe fifteen total with casing, and pump. We'll get it tested to ensure it's potable. That comes with the deal. But if there are excessive minerals. Iron and the like, you might end up wanting to add a filtration system. But that's your option down the road."

He finally finished with his rambling quote and my head was reeling. Where was I going to come up with twenty grand? But what alternative was there? Maybe now I would qualify for a loan. Now that I was working pretty much full time. But this well was going to take the last of my generous severance and I hadn't even paid Marcus off yet.

"You want for us to get started in the morning, Mrs. Ross?" The man glanced at the door, clearly eager to be gone, the sale made.

I swallowed, trying to wet my mouth and find my voice.

I started with a nod, but finally did manage to croak out a yes.

The man handed me a card. "My cell's on the bottom if you need to reach me before then. My crew will be here first thing tomorrow."

"When—" I started to ask when I'd be expected to fork over the dinero, but he was already through the door and halfway to his truck. The other truck and the rig had already disappeared from my yard.

I closed the door and retreated to the coffee machine. Coffee wasn't going to cure my problems, but without it I wasn't going to think straight. Duffy got up and padded over, pressing his nose into my thigh as if he understood that I was troubled, and he was offering his support.

I had enough in my account to pay for the well. Provided the ending cost was not above the outlined quote. I'd paid Marcus a generous advance, but there would still be a final reconning with him when he was done. The asbestos people had been paid as well.

But what else might rear an ugly dollar laden head going forward?

My phone rang. A new tune I'd picked out for Sam. A tune called *Treat You Better* by a singer I'd never heard of before.

"Hi Sam," I answered doing my best to sound upbeat.

"Good news?" he queried.

"Depends on what you call good news. I need a new well drilled. That's the bad part. But they can do it tomorrow. That's the good news. So, Duffy and I won't have to invade your space for more than another night."

Sam laughed. "I enjoy being invaded. Any time. But," he cleared his throat. "I have a guy who wants his car detailed tomorrow. He's transporting guests for a wedding on Saturday and Ben Kemp gave him your name. I'm guessing you don't have to be on site for them to do their thing. What shall I tell this guy?"

Like I was in any position to turn down a paying job. Especially not one that came as a referral from my best customer and hefty tipper. "I'll take it. See if you can schedule not first thing so I can be here when the well crew arrives, at least. Then I can head up to the shop."

"You got it, Kenzie. How about I thaw out a couple steaks for supper. I'll grill them while you toss a salad."

"Grilling? Outside? It's cold as a witch's tit." I took fiendish pleasure in using the obscene reference the well boss had used.

Sam guffawed. Apparently, he thought it was funny, too. "Grill's hot even if the air five feet away is arctic. See you at my place when I close up here. Door's not locked."

With another chuckle he was gone and I was left to return to my financial pondering. Maybe I would revisit the offer Sam had made about a loan two months earlier. Might be easier than facing the disapproving bank officer I'd sat with last time.

Cuddled against Sam's big frame, and even languid with lovemaking, the problem of money flooded to the front of my mind from the dim corner I'd relegated it to since arriving at Sam's place. Twice, I almost started to speak but finally decided that hitting a man up right after sex seemed too much like demanding payment. I'd wait until tomorrow to ask him if he was still interested in making me a loan.

"Something on your mind?" Sam asked.

"No." I did my best to make my voice sound sated and relaxed. "Just not sleepy yet."

His hand closed around my breast, one finger and thumb rolling the nipple between them. A flash of fiery desire shot through me despite the previous round of sex and my worry over money. "Maybe I could fix that," he growled.

In my entire married life, I'd never had sex more than once in a night. With Sam multiple rounds were becoming a habit. When his other hand reached down to fondle my crotch, I growled back. "I dare ya!"

I woke to a silent house and sun streaming through the windows. Duffy sprawled across the foot of the bed as if he was okay with sleeping in for another hour or two. Sam was nowhere in sight. I turned my head and saw the bright blue numbers on Sam's alarm clock.

Appalled, I jumped from the bed and hit the floor with a thump. Duffy languidly raised a head, then dropped it back onto the mattress.

"It's late, Duffy. How did it get this late? I have to be at home for the well guys." I struggled into the clean jeans and T-shirt I'd set out the night before, then dashed into the bathroom.

Why hadn't Sam woken me. Clearly, he'd been up long ago. He'd probably taken the dog out to do his business considering how content Duffy was to remain where he was. I called the dog and headed for the kitchen.

A note sat propped against the coffee maker.

You looked so peaceful I decided to let you sleep. Walked the Duffer and scrambled him an egg. I left early enough to check on the well crew, so if your phone hasn't woken you, then consider that project well underway and no need to head down to Murray House. Just come into work when you're ready. Kemp's friend is bringing his vehicle in at one. Dinner later? Hugs, Sam.

He'd left the coffee maker busy brewing a fresh pot by the looks of it and a plate with fresh baked muffins sat wrapped in plastic on the table. I could get used to this kind of pampering.

I still had to discuss that loan business but felt easier about approaching it in the light of day. And after I'd put in a full day of work.

I polished off two muffins, filled my thermos with coffee and whistled to the dog. Now it would be my turn to arrive very late at work and live through the knowing looks and snickering.

It turned out easier than I'd expected, given all the various heads were either under hoods or on rolling boards under cars when I arrived at Hank's. Late as I was, the bills needed to be paid and files still needed updating, so I got to work and quickly got them all done and put away with plenty of time to get to the big forest green Navigator that sat parked in my brightly lit detailing shop.

It was a big vehicle and not all that clean, but I had it completed well before the owner showed up to claim it. I hesitated, not wanting to be interrupted while discussing money with Sam. While I stood, uncertain about what to do next, the owner hurried in.

His pleasure at the sight of his car made me glad I'd gone the extra mile. His tip made me doubly glad. I opened the electric door and waited as he backed out, waving with a big grin on his face. I waved back and brought the door down again.

Time to get to it.

Ed and Paul were already gone. Jack pointed toward the office when I walked through the maintenance bays. Then he waved and left, as well. It was just me, the dog and Sam.

It's not really groveling, I told myself as I headed for the office. So why did it feel that way? Duffy stopped to check out something on the floor, probably a tidbit left over from someone's lunch. I left him to it and started down the hall.

Sam's voice sounded friendly but concerned. I hesitated. Jack would have mentioned it if someone was in the office with Sam? He must be on the phone.

The words were soft, but clear.

"You know I would if I could, Kitkat."

Kitkat? Who was Kitkat? Sounded like a pet name. For a woman. But Sam had told me there was no woman in his life. And what did she want him to do that he would if he could?

"Yes, I'll come. I always do, don't I?" Sam's voice. Still gentle and full of caring.

Eavesdropping was not a habit of mine. I didn't know who Kitkat was. Or why he would hurry to her side when asked. I stepped away from the door. I needed to talk to Sam now, more than ever.

I leaned against the wall to play a game of Words With Friends, but I wasn't concentrating so I gave up and just stared at the screen pretending. The door opened in a rush, surprising me.

My presence in the hall appeared to surprise Sam, as well. "What's up? You get Jenkin's car done okay? I hope he tipped well." Like nothing unusual was going on in his life.

"Yes and yes, and I hope he becomes a regular. Everything okay with you?"

Sam plowed a hand through his hair leaving it standing on end. "Yup. I'm good, but . . ." He stopped speaking and ruffled Duffy's ears. "Look, I hate to do this last minute, but I've gotta take a raincheck on dinner tonight. I've got some personal business I need to deal with."

He turned and walked back into the office, rounded the desk and started fiddling with a stack of inventory lists I'd left to go over in the morning.

I followed him in. "Stop messing with my stuff and tell me what's wrong."

He dropped the papers and shoved his hands into his pockets. "Nothing's wrong."

He didn't act like nothing was wrong. And he hadn't brought the name Kitkat into the conversation either. He was hiding something and the dreadful feeling of being betrayed again began to creep into me.

"You sure everything's okay?"

"Positive. Nothing to worry about. See you first thing tomorrow." Barricaded behind the desk and he wasn't even offering me a goodbye kiss.

I started to back out of the office, nearly fell over my unsuspecting dog and righted myself. "Sure thing."

Then I beat a hasty retreat.

Something was most definitely off and Sam hadn't leveled with me. Nothing to worry about was one of Garrett's pet lines. I'd bought it back then. I wasn't buying it now.

And there was no way I was asking Sam for a loan now. If he couldn't trust me with whatever was going on with the unknown Kitkat, no way was I going to ask him to trust me with money. For that matter, I was suddenly very sure I had almost made another colossal mistake in trusting Sam with my heart.

Chapter Forty-Four

Eleanor Murray – 1945

Eleanor opened her eyes to see Aunt Emily staring down at her with a frown creasing her brow. Her head felt strange, and it took her a moment to realize she was stretched out on the parlor divan with a crocheted throw pulled up to her chin.

"What am I doing here?" Eleanor didn't remember laying down. She'd never consider taking a nap in the parlor anyway. She tried to sit up and her aunt put a hand under her elbow to assist.

"You swooned, my dear," Aunt Emily answered when Eleanor was upright.

"I don't swoon," Eleanor protested. At least she never had before. Why now?

"You did and the nice man from Western Union carried you in and laid you here."

Western Union!

It all rushed back to her. The familiar uniform and the reason he might have been standing outside her aunt's door. "Where . . .?"

Aunt Emily thrust the bright yellow envelope into Eleanor's hands, then moved away to give Eleanor privacy.

With shaking fingers, Eleanor opened the telegram and brought it close enough to read.

"Shipping home on RMS Queen Mary. Arrive on 14th. Meet me out front of Carnegie Hall. Jeff"

The telegram still gripped in one hand, Eleanor pressed her palms to her cheeks. "He's not dead," she uttered with a mixture of relief and dread. "He's coming home."

"Oh, my. That is indeed good news." Her aunt held her hand out and Eleanor put the missive into it without question.

As soon as Aunt Emily had scanned the contents, she put on her business face. "The Queen Mary. My, my, my. He travels in style. I will have my man find out what time and what berth she will dock at so you can be ready to meet him."

"Thank you, Aunt Emily. I hadn't even thought about finding out when that might be. Today is the first. Right?"

"Last time I checked," her aunt responded with a harumph.

"What shall I wear?" Eleanor blurted. Her Sunday go to church dress was just too starched up. And the dress she'd been wearing to the USO lounge was nearly worn out. Working in a shop, she'd been wearing trousers and those wouldn't do, at all. She would see Jeff in just two weeks. For the first time in four years.

The dread returned. Would Jeff still feel she was as beautiful as he had when he left. She'd been working in a machine shop and no matter what she put on them, her hands were always chapped and red. Her hair had grown longer but was always pinned up, and she'd lost weight. She must look like a scarecrow. What if he didn't love her the way she was now?

"We shall go shopping," Aunt Emily declared with a firm nod of her head. "And of course, we shall plan a lovely welcome dinner. I'm quite certain he hasn't had a decent meal in ages."

Eleanor was about to protest about her aunt springing for a new dress, then didn't. Her aunt had more money than she knew what to spend it on, and she appeared to enjoy spending it on Eleanor. Jeff might has well have the benefit of seeing Eleanor at her very best, and Eleanor could use a little boost of confidence.

The fourteenth dawned clear and welcoming. Eleanor stood on a wooden walkway well back from the pier itself. Thousands of people crowded the span between her and the river, awaiting the arrival of the Queen Mary. She was glad Jeff had thought to suggest they should meet at Carnegie Hall. It was only a few blocks from here and once the ship had docked, she would have plenty of time to walk there before Jeff could free himself of the crowd. Trying to find him in this crush of people would have been impossible.

The ship's horn blew the long-awaited announcement of its arrival and tugboats tooted as they guided the luxury cruise ship into its berth. The crowd erupted in shouts and whistles. Eleanor gaped at the sight. Thousands of men, a sea of army green covered every inch of the Queen Mary's many decks. It was a wonder the ship didn't sink under the weight, and remained upright with nothing to balance the men on deck.

Not that Eleanor blamed the soldiers. Most of them had not seen home in as much as five years. Of course, they would be eager to see home. Even if home wasn't New York and even if their loved ones were still miles away. She was doubly glad Jeff had mentioned an alternative meeting site.

As the tugs eased the big ship up to the dock, crew members on deck tossed fat hawsers to men waiting on the pier. Those men quickly snugged the lines down, and inch by inch the Queen Mary was brought to rest. The shouts of the crowd grew deafening. Eleanor scanned the hundreds of faces, but from where she stood, Jeff could have been any one of them. Even so, she shouted along with everyone else.

It seemed to take forever for the gangways to be rolled up and secured to the ship. Finally, the gates opened, and the men began to pour down onto the dock in a river that seemed to have no end. Most of the men bore big canvas bags on their shoulders that were quickly tossed aside if someone they knew appeared out of the crowd. Everyone hugging. So many ladies being kissed.

How long before Jeff left the ship and headed to Carnegie Hall? Eleanor finally turned her back to the welcoming scene and began to weave her way down the crowded walkway to the stairs that would take her out to the street.

Even once free of the mob of revelers on the dock, Eleanor still had to fight her way through sidewalks teeming with excited humanity. She elbowed her way and was elbowed in return, but everyone was in such a celebratory mood, no one cared if they were being rude.

Things didn't begin to be any better until Eleanor had reached 10th Avenue and turned up 52nd Street to zigzag her way to Carnegie Hall. Finally, after what felt like hours of shoving her way through crowds of people, she saw the main entrance to Carnegie Hall. New York was always a bustling place. Nothing like Bailey Island on a normal day, but today it seemed more bustling than ever.

She gazed at the wide expanse of Carnegie Hall and wondered which corner Jeff might have been thinking of. The one closest to her now? Or the one closest to her aunt's apartment? She decided the closest to where she stood since that's where Jeff would arrive first.

She took a moment to survey her reflection in the glass covering the posters of the shows to be seen within. Her hair was nearly as tidy as Aunt Emily's maid had made it just hours earlier with combs holding the curls that fell to her shoulders in place. She slid her hands down over her lovely new dress.

A lovely rosy peach that brought out the color in her cheeks, the dress clung to her bosom and waist, then flared into wide, luxurious skirt that went half-way down her calves. She hadn't owned a dress this splendid in her whole life. Even the wedding dress that still hung in her closet was not this fine.

Instead of the patriotic red she'd worn on her lips throughout the war, today her lipstick matched the rosy hue of the dress. Part of the reason it had taken her so long to arrive at the meeting point was the height of the heels on the shoes Aunt Emily had insisted she needed to go with the dress. Finishing off the picture was the smart little hat, decorated with tiny roses that sat at a jaunty angle on her freshly curled locks.

Ever critical of her own looks, she liked the picture she presented. With a sigh, she turned away from the posters and began her search of the milling groups of people for Jeff's familiar face.

At first it was just the usual people seen on the sidewalks of New York in the middle of the day. Most of them worked in the area and were out for lunch. Some women pushed carriages with babies napping inside, headed toward Central Park. Men with briefcases in a hurry to meetings here and there. But finally, men in olive green began to appear.

Just one or two at first, bulging bags still perched on their shoulders. Some with an arm around a woman smiling happily up at their man. Some of them disappeared down to the subway platforms below.

Occasionally one would whistle for a cab, climb in, and be whisked away. But Jeff was not among them.

Time seemed to slow to a snail's pace as the crowds thickened with still no sight of Jeff. Fifteen minutes. Then a half hour passed. Eleanor checked the pretty little watch pinned to her bodice that Aunt Emily had given her. Forty-five minutes. When the hour finally came and went, Eleanor wondered about the corner she stood on. Maybe Jeff was at the other end of the building, shielded from her view by all the people on the bustling sidewalk.

She began to make her way through the crowd, glancing behind her every several feet, then back to her front. A man bumped into her so hard she would have fallen if he hadn't grabbed her shoulders to steady her.

"So sorry, Miss. You are all right?"

"Yes. Thank you," Eleanor replied stepping free of his grasp. He nodded and went around her.

Where was Jeff?

She spotted a man who might have been her fiancé, but he had his arms about a woman and was kissing her soundly. Jeff would not be kissing another woman. Would he?

Then the man set the woman free and tossed his head back with a hearty laugh. It wasn't Jeff.

Eleanor peeked at the watch again. More than two hours had passed since the gang planks had been run up to the big liner, and soldiers had begun to stream down them to the pier and their welcome home.

Her feet hurt and there was nowhere to sit and give them a rest. She shouldn't have let Aunt Emily talk her into wearing such impractical shoes. Of course, when she'd buckled them onto her feet, she hadn't thought she would be standing around in them for hours.

Five o'clock had come and gone and even the bustling throng of workers had mostly disappeared. And still no Jeff. No other soldiers in sight either. She'd give him another half hour, then go back to the apartment.

As Eleanor gazed out at the thinning crowd, her mind saw the ocean as it appeared from the widow's walk at home and her ears heard the echo of the whispered words that had come to her all those many months ago after reading her aunt's invite. When she'd wondered if Jeff would know where to find her if she came to New York.

How can you be sure Jeff will come looking for you at all?

But he'd told her where to meet him and she'd followed his direction. Why wasn't he looking for her?

He's alive, my child, but your father might be right about some things.

Where had those words come from? Eleanor had never believed in the stories of a ghost who appeared on that widow's walk. She'd believed the words were in her head. In her imagination. But Jeff wasn't here. Maybe he wasn't looking for her after all, in spite of the telegram that said otherwise. Had her promise to wait for him been kept in vain?

Eleanor's shoulders sagged and the confidence that her appearance in the mirror had given her fled. She turned away from Carnegie Hall and began limping in the painfully high heels toward her aunt's apartment that she'd called home for what felt like an eternity.

With Central Park in sight, she heard someone call her name and whipped around so suddenly, she'd have fallen had not two strong arms caught her.

"Hey there. I didn't mean to startle you."

The breath caught in Eleanor's throat as she looked up into Mike Hamilton's concerned blue eyes.

"M-mike?" she finally managed. "What are you doing in New York?"

"I came to see you, of course," he replied setting her free and stepping away to sweep her with an admiring gaze that brought a flood of heat to her cheeks.

"But . . ."

But she was supposed to be meeting Jeff. Not Mike. She'd abandoned Bailey Island to avoid falling in love with this man, yet here he was and her heart didn't seem to have gotten the message. Jeff hadn't come looking for her, but Mike had.

"Let me escort you back to your aunt's apartment and I'll explain," he said offering her his arm.

She hesitated, still overwhelmed with doubt and confusion.

Mike tipped his head as if puzzled.

"I'm supposed to be meeting Jeff," she finally answered the unspoken question.

"Well, that's kind of why I'm here. I have news I wanted you to hear in person."

If Mike knew Jeff was due home, why had he come to New York?

Mike glanced toward the street, then to her. "Let's go find a place to sit and I'll tell you everything I know." He offered his arm again and this time she slipped her hand into the crook of his elbow and let him guide her across Fifty-ninth Street and into Central Park.

He stopped at the first bench they came to and gestured for her to sit. Then he settled beside her and sighed.

"There's really no good way to tell you bad news, I'm afraid. I just didn't want it to come in a phone call from someone who didn't care."

Eleanor's heart thundered in her ears. "My father? Is he okay? Or mother?" It couldn't be Ray. She'd just seen him and he was home and safe. At least as safe as anyone could be flying those little aeroplanes every day.

"Your parents are fine."

Was the bad news connected to Jeff not being where he said he'd be? "Jeff?" she managed to say his name without choking up, but the most telling thing was that her heart had stopped its frantic hammering. *He's alive, my child.* Those whispered words again. Eleanor looked up into Mike's eyes, waiting for the bad news he didn't know how to tell her.

"Apparently he took a little side trip on his way to America," Mike said with a frown.

Ireland. *But he isn't looking for you at all.* The words popped into Eleanor's head like fireworks on the fourth of July. "He went to Ireland, didn't he?"

"Yes. I'm afraid he did. Three days ago, he called his parents to tell them he was staying in Ireland. Indefinitely. I'm so sorry to be the bearer of bad news."

Why hadn't Jeff called her with his change of heart? Coward. He'd sent that telegram before his return to Ireland. Before he'd gone to see Bridget on his way home to the woman he'd promised to marry.

She should be crying right now. Sobbing over his faithlessness. But that wasn't the case. There was a feeling of relief filling her breast.

"I thought you might wish to return home," Mike said.

Eleanor tore her thoughts from the jumble of mixed emotions to consider his comment. "I can't go home right away," she told Mike as if being dumped by Jeff wasn't important. Her father had been right all along. Jeff wasn't to be trusted. And she was free. Except for the job she had promised to do to aid in the war effort.

Mike gathered her hands into his. "I promised your parents I'd bring you home with me."

"But I can't just walk off the job without notice," she argued. All the women were hired on a temporary basis with the idea they would be let go as soon as the men came home and were ready to go back to work. But it would be a while before that happened. Or so she assumed.

"Then I'll just have to wait. How long before you might be able to leave?"

"Two weeks," Eleanor decided with a nod. Two weeks was plenty enough. Even if the men didn't start returning to work for a month, or even longer, she was only going to give the Navy Yard two more weeks. It was time for her to go home.

CHAPTER FORTY-FIVE

Kenzie Ross – Present Day

I studied the numbers again. For about the hundredth time. I was having a hard time concentrating. The sound of Sam's voice assuring someone named Kitkat that of course he would come, followed by his breezy assurances to me that everything was 'just fine' kept intruding into my thoughts.

Somehow, I was going to have to make my new life here on Bailey Island work even if Sam was no longer going to be anything other than my boss.

For the first hour after arriving home and feeding Duffy, I'd seriously contemplated leaving Bailey Island for good. The idea of putting the historic old house up for sale and running home to Virginia like a dog with his tail between his legs hadn't been pretty. But neither was the idea of seeing Sam every weekday and pretending I'd not been duped again.

The next hour had been spent poking through my belongings trying to decide what to pack first and what could be collected later.

Preferably by the agent who'd been in charge when the house was a rental. She could just ship it home to me.

Then the reality hit me. *Here* was home now. Not the house I'd called home in Virginia for the last twenty years. That was Garrett's and his new love. Home could never be the old Craftsman dwelling I'd grown up in that had been sold years ago after my parents passed. Home was right here. This beautiful old house on an island in Maine that needed a little TLC.

And if here was home, then I needed to finish what I'd started with the rebuild and pay off Marcus. That done, I'd need to rent out the second apartment and start bringing in more dollars to help pay for the place.

So, it was back to the money. If I wasn't going to run, I needed to get my finances squared away. The new well was in and drawing plenty of water for the whole house, new apartments and all. Probably half of Bailey Island could survive on the gusher the well guys had tapped into. But paying the well company for the drilling and the new pump had taken most of the cash in my savings account.

Truth be told, I had grown fond of Murray house and all its fun little nooks and features. I liked the people I'd gotten to know on Bailey Island, too. All of them, save Sam, seemed to be far more genuine than the neighbors I'd had in Virginia. That high-end neighborhood where Garrett grew up had been populated by people just like Garrett. Always concerned with appearances and making their way to the top.

I didn't want to go back to that narrow existence. I liked it here.

I just didn't like having my heart broken.

Again.

The admission brought tears to my eyes. I slashed angrily at them, but they only fell harder.

We'd just been having a great time. At least that's what I'd told myself. Sam was funny and undemanding. He was thoughtful and kind to everyone. Easy to work for and be around. And the sex was off the charts.

I hadn't realized I'd let myself fall in love with him.

Tears continued to flow down my cheeks.

I was in love with Sam Phillips.

When had that happened?

I pressed a fist against my chest trying to still the pain blossoming around my heart.

Duffy appeared at my side and nuzzled me. I bent in the chair, wrapped my arms around his warm body and wept into his soft fur.

Eventually there were no tears left in me. At least for now. When I pulled away Duffy licked at my cheeks. "I should have just stuck with you as my main man," I told the dog as I got up to grab the tissue box from my bedside table. "You'd never betray me. You'll only break my heart when yours stops beating."

His tail swept back and forth gently, as if he was agreeing with me.

"And you like it here, too. Right?"

More tail swishing.

Okay, then. I needed to suck it up and make it work. Somehow.

I bent to kiss the top of the dog's head and squared my shoulders.

First thing tomorrow, I'd return to the bank, fill out another application with updated employment information and apply again. On second thought, perhaps I should wait until next week. A few extra days wouldn't make any difference and no way did I want to skip work tomorrow and give everyone the impression I was hiding. I lifted my chin.

We can do this, Mr. McDuff. Together we'll figure it out.

It was Sam who didn't show up at work the following morning. Ed reported that Sam was off on family business. No idea how long he'd be gone, but likely not until Monday.

His Aunt Phe was just up in Brunswick at the assisted living home, which made it doubtful that Sam would have had to take a whole day to tend to anything she needed. Becca was at school, and I had to presume everything with her was okay since I'd never heard Sam call her Kitkat. Neither of them had ever mentioned any other family. Sam was an only child. His parents deceased. So, who was Kitkat if she wasn't family?

Two more detailing jobs had been scheduled, which kept me too busy to spend much time dwelling on Sam's dishonesty. Once again, the tips were sizeable and welcome. I was beginning to feel a twinge of hope.

Perhaps it was a good thing that Sam didn't show up today. It gave me some space to process my disappointment and determine how I'd go on if I remained employed at Hank's.

Duffy and I were on our evening walk to the cove when my phone buzzed. It was Sam and I let it go to voice mail. The second time it buzzed I was about to answer with a chilly, unwelcoming greeting when I noticed it was Jaycee.

"Hey there, Island Girl. How's life in this new year treating you?"

"You don't want to know," I responded after taking a moment to throw a stick down the beach for Duffy to chase.

"That bad, huh? So, other than the well fiasco, what else has gone wrong?"

I wanted to keep my broken heart to myself. At least for a little longer. But this was Jaycee, the lady with Xray vision even at a thousand miles.

"Sam?" she asked, all the bright breeziness gone from her voice.

"Yes," I said, dropping down to sit on a section of telephone pole that had washed up onto the stony little beach.

"Let me guess. Another woman he failed to mention before?"

"A woman named Kitkat," I confirmed. Now I was going to have to tell her everything.

As I recounted the overheard conversation, a blast of icy wind found its way down my neck and reminded me that long chats on the beach did not happen in January in Maine without me turning into an icicle.

I got to my feet, whistled for Duffy, and headed for home. On the way up the hill, I outlined my cowardly initial reaction and the logic that had changed that decision. By the time I followed Duffy into the welcoming warmth of the Murray House kitchen, I was on to the need to apply for a loan come Monday.

I started to put the kettle on for a cup of tea. But then I changed my mind and poured a generous serving of Bailey's Irish Cream into my mug.

"I thought Sam offered to make you a loan," Jaycee said.

"I can't borrow from him. Not now," I said as I added ice to the mug.

"But he made that offer before you two got chummy."

"I can't, Jaycee. I don't even know how I'm going to greet him when he shows up for work again. When we both show up on the same day, that is," I corrected myself.

"Okay, Kenzie. I'm going to lay this out for you, and I want you to keep your trap shut until I'm done. Got it?"

A lecture was coming. Jaycee lectures were not always comfortable, but they were generally filled with wisdom. Sort of like when the priest at church gave a down-to-earth sermon on what the gospel demanded of us instead of a fluff piece about peace and tranquility.

"Got it." I settled at the kitchen table to listen as instructed.

"You two need to talk. And I don't mean about money. It's up to you if you'd rather owe the bank than Sam. But—Uh-uh. No interrupting." She made warning tsking sounds.

I shut my mouth, which had, indeed, been open to protest.

"I've only met the guy a couple times, but I've listened to you talk about him for months. Since practically the day you got there. I know you have other new friends that you've mentioned from time to time and I'm glad for you. But Sam has been the one you talk about the most. Everything you've told me about him and how he treats you has been night and day different from the way my dickhead brother treated you.

"I feel it in my bones that you two were meant to be together. But that can't happen until both of you level with each other. Have you told him you're in love with him?"

I shouldn't have been shocked that Jaycee knew. Even before I realized it.

"You haven't, have you?"

"And I'm never going to. Not now," I protested.

"Maybe not. But if you ever want to put this behind you, you need to get the whole of it out in the open. You need to ask him who Kitkat is and what she means to him.

"Be willing to listen and not jump down his throat before he gets a chance to explain. He just might have an explanation that is so far from what you're thinking right now that it would be a shame not to know what it was."

"What if I really don't want to know?"

"You do. Deep down, you really do. You love him. You feel like he betrayed you because he didn't level with you. But what if the explanation involves a story that wasn't his to tell? I'm pretty damn sure he never told you he loved you, because if he had, I'd have heard about it. So, maybe he doesn't love you. He never made you any promises, so he hasn't broken any. And he deserves a chance to explain."

"I gave him a chance."

"Okay. Then he needs a second chance. He might have been struggling to put things together in his own mind at the time and not ready to open up to you."

I reviewed the brief exchange between me and Sam two days previous. I'd seen the unexplained look of pain and resignation on Sam's face, but I'd been more focused on my own feelings of being used and lied to. I swallowed. Jaycee was right.

"So, what are you going to do next?" Jaycee prompted.

"I'm going to let him explain," I replied like a good student.

"And?"

"And what?"

"How do you plan to give him a chance to explain?"

Having just reviewed the conversation, I recalled his first words. 'I'm going to have to take a raincheck on supper.'

"I'm going to invite him to supper."

"Atta girl. Just don't jump all over him the moment he walks in the door, all judgmental and ready for a fight. Promise?"

"I promise." So many unspoken promises of late, but this one I put into words and even if Jaycee wasn't here to enforce it, there was no way I would go back on my word to her.

"Lecture over," Jaycee announced with a triumphant chortle. "Now, let me tell you what's been going on in my life. Did I tell you about my new year's resolution?"

"We haven't talked since the new year," I reminded her.

"Okay, then..." And Jaycee was off on a happy discussion about the cruise she'd finally convinced Vance to take her on.

My phone was nearly dead when we finally hung up. Before it could completely die, or I could change my mind, I brought up Sam's contact and tapped message so I could invite him over for a meal on Sunday night.

CHAPTER FORTY-SIX

Sam Philips – Present Day

The unforgiving bare wooden pew in the silent, empty nave of a church Sam had never been to before hurt his butt. It wasn't his first time praying outside an AA meeting waiting for his childhood friend. He'd lost count ages ago.

Several times it had involved bailing Reggie out of jail and then having to follow-up and make sure he got to court to answer for the pugilistic behavior that gotten him kicked out of whatever bar he'd been in at the time. The past weekend hadn't been the first time he'd rescued Reggie from some alley where he'd finally passed out, either. Nor was it the first time he'd spent the following day sobering Reggie up.

Every time, Reggie had promised to stop drinking and get his life squared away, but so far that promise had never been kept for very long.

Sam could only guess at the number of times Reggie had promised Cathy the same thing before she finally took the kids and called it quits. Sam wondered if Reggie might have stayed sober longer had his marriage not failed, or his kids not been moved to Montana where Cathy had grown up. Eventually, he'd have had to consider the fact that he needed to set a better example for his sons.

But this time, the dive seemed to have been deeper. This time he'd lost his job, his apartment, and his car. Reggie might have just disappeared into the land of the homeless and never been heard from again if his sister hadn't loaded an app on her own phone that allowed her to track his phone which she had been paying for.

A rustle at the back of the church interrupted Sam's prayers. He turned to see Kitkat tiptoeing down the aisle. She slipped into the pew beside him.

"How'd you make out?" he whispered. Even though the church was empty, he felt like he needed to keep his voice to a whisper.

"The Beacon will take him, if he agrees to their contract and they will come to terms on costs since he no longer has any insurance," Kitkat whispered back. "Will you drive him up there?"

Sam nodded. Of course, he'd take him. Provided Reggie agreed to go.

Kitkat pressed an envelope into Sam's hand. "This is a start on the fees. It's all I can scrape together right now, but . . ."

"I can help, Kitkat. Please don't worry about money. You've got your own kids to worry about and with Frankie headed off to college, you'll be stretching as it is."

"What about you? You've got Becca and UNH isn't cheap for nonresidents."

Sam gave her shoulder a hug. "But you have two more after that. Becca is the only one I have, and she earned a really good scholarship. If this place can bail Reggie out of the hole he's dug for himself, then it will be worth it. I owe him. And you."

"I think you paid us back years ago," Kitkat protested. "But I won't pretend your help isn't greatly appreciated. As always."

"You better skedaddle before the meeting's over. You know how he gets when he thinks his kid sister is trying to run his life. Even when he's not in any shape to run it himself."

Kitkat twisted in the pew and gave Sam a hug. "You're the best Sam Phillips. Reggie is lucky you still care." Then she stood and slipped silently from the church, leaving Sam to his lone vigil again.

Sam pulled out his phone thinking he should call Kenzie. He'd tried to reach her earlier but gotten no answer. He hoped it was because she took the dog for a walk and forgot her phone at home, and not because she was upset with him.

He hadn't leveled with her, and she'd known it. He'd seen the look in her eyes, but it would have taken too long to explain, and he'd needed to get moving based on Kitkat's description of Reggie's condition.

He started to put the phone back in his pocket. Even in an empty church it didn't seem right to be chatting on a cell phone. But it vibrated to tell him he had a new message.

When do you want to claim your raincheck?

His finger hovered over the miniature keyboard. It couldn't be tonight. Maybe not tomorrow either depending on how things went with Reggie. Sunday.

He could promise her Sunday. Reggie safely stowed at The Beacon or not, Sam had to be back at work by Monday anyway. And he wanted to see Kenzie before then. Needed to see Kenzie. Any misunderstanding between them needed to be sorted out sooner rather than later.

He loved Reggie like the brother he'd never had, but his heart belonged to Kenzie even if she didn't know it yet. And he had to make things right between them before it was too late.

Sunday?

Got any favorites you'd like me to fix?

Anything Kenzie fixed for him would be just fine and he almost replied as much. But Tansey had always complained when he told her to fix whatever she wanted. Wives don't want to have to make the decisions all the time, she'd tell him.

Lobster stew?

Got it. Duffy misses you.

Tell Duffy I miss him too.

A smiley face showed up on his screen.

The dog missed him, but nothing about Kenzie missing him. He sighed. He had some making up to do. No way could he convince the lady at the chocolate shop for another special order. He'd have to get creative.

Reggie had come out of the AA meeting with a sense of energy Sam hadn't expected. Apparently, he'd heard two stories so similar to his own from men who'd finally managed to tame the demon, that Reggie was determined to follow their example.

Convincing him to check himself into The Beacon and sign any agreement they presented had been far easier than Sam had anticipated. After collecting what clothing Reggie had left at his sister's, Sam had driven him to his new home for the new few months, handed a check to the man in charge and hugged his friend. Reggie had started to make Sam another promise, but Sam had told him to stow it.

"Make the promise to yourself, Reggie. And this time, keep it."

With another hug, Sam had said goodbye and headed home.

***

Nerves got to him as he stood on Kenzie's porch. He had plenty of back up. A special something in his pocket that had once belonged to his mother. His arms were full of an enormous box of chocolates from a shop he'd found in Freeport and an even bigger bouquet of pink roses and daisies. The woman at the shop had told him pink roses stood for promises and the daisies for new beginnings. He didn't know anything about flowers and their meanings, but he liked the combination, and they made him think of Kenzie and her new beginning. He prayed they might lead to a new beginning for them together.

"You could have let yourself in," Kenzie said as she swept the door open. Then she noticed his arms were full. "Oh. Maybe you couldn't have." She reached for the flowers. "Are you trying to butter me up for something?"

"I just liked them, and I thought you would, too." He handed the bouquet over.

Kenzie planted her nose in the flowers, then looked at him with a curious expression in her eyes. "I do. And I'm very sure I'm being buttered up if those are for me, as well." She pointed to the chocolatier's box.

"Well, maybe a little," he admitted bending to kiss her.

As kisses go, it was a disappointment, but he still had fences to mend, and promises to put into words. He handed over the box. "Wilbur's was voted Maine's best Chocolate by Yankee Magazine. I hope it lives up to the hype."

"Dinner's ready, but it won't spoil so, if it's okay with you, I think we need to talk first," Kenzie said setting the chocolates aside and taking another sniff of the flowers.

"We do," Sam agreed.

"I guess I should put these in water, though," Kenzie said as she led the way to the kitchen.

She reached into the island cabinet and came out with a vase which she turned away to fill at the sink. He watched her arranging the blossoms, probably trying to decide how to approach what was obviously bothering her. So many things she might be bothered by, but which was the most concerning? He pulled out one of the stools placed on his side of the island and perched on it while he considered what to say next.

"Kenzie—"

"Sam—"

They both started at the same time.

"I know you're upset, but I'm not exactly sure what I've done. Or not done. So why don't you go first."

A parade of expressions crossed her face. Finally, she grabbed a stool from the end and parked herself close enough that he could touch her, but not so close that he could have attempted another kiss.

"Who's Kitkat?"

"Kitkat? You're upset about Kitkat?" If he was confused before, he was totally at sea now. "She's Reggie's sister."

Kenzie frowned. "And who's Reggie?"

"My best friend from high school. He's like the closest thing I have to a brother. Except he's kind of lost. Kitkat called to ask for help."

The frown lightened but didn't go away all together. "What do you mean by lost?"

"He's an alcoholic. Kitkat called to tell me he was drunk again and sleeping in an alley and . . ."

"And you said everything was just peachy." A note of censure crept into Kenzie's voice.

"I should have explained. But at the time, it seemed like too much to go into when I needed to leave sooner rather than later."

"Maybe you should have taken the time. I just felt like you weren't leveling with me."

"Things were fine between us. At least I thought so. It was Reggie who was in trouble and that wasn't a problem you needed to worry about."

"Do you have any idea how many times Garrett told me it's nothing to worry about? Only later I'd find out there was plenty to worry about. So, when you said it, I just felt like I was being lied to again. Like I'd been duped all over again after I promised I was going to be smarter in the future."

"Oh, Kenzie." Sam reached out to cup her cheek in one palm. "I'm so sorry. I never meant to hurt you. And I promise I'll never lie to you again. Even a lie of omission.

"Here," he slipped off his stool and dug into his pocket. "This was my mother's. I want you to have it. With my heart. It's a promise ring."

Kenzie's hand shook as she took the ring between a finger and her thumb. When she looked up at him, there were tears pooling in her eyes. "What does a promise ring promise?"

"When my dad gave it to my mother, it was a promise that he would always love her. He was headed to Vietnam, but he didn't want to make her commit to an engagement or get married in case he didn't make it home."

"And what are you promising me?"

"The same thing. To love you. Always."

Epilogue

Eleanor Murray - 1945

"I've never heard of a promise ring," Eleanor said as she glanced up into Mike's eyes.

The two weeks she'd told him she needed, had stretched into a month. But sometimes a month can change everything. When Mike held up the wee black box, she thought he was going to propose, and she was ready to say yes. But a promise ring? What did that mean?

"Eleanor," Mike said reaching for her left hand and gesturing for permission to slide the slender band onto her finger. "You must know by now that I love you. I've always loved you but when I first realized it, you were just a kid. I went off with Ray to fly fighters knowing I loved you, but it was too soon to tell you how I felt back then."

Eleanor glanced at his hand, still poised over hers and nodded.

He slipped the ring down over her knuckle, then brought her hand to his lips and kissed it. "Sapphires because we were both born in September. The Infinity loop because I promise to love you for the rest of my life. I promise I'll wait until you're ready to love me back, even if it takes the rest of our lives."

Tears prickled Eleanor's eyes and Mike's face blurred. "It won't take the rest of our lives. I love you already."

***

Kenzie Ross - Present Day

"I have never heard of a promise ring," Jaycee said as she admired the slender silver band with tiny sapphires set twined in a pretty ivy engraving that now graced my ring finger. "Does this mean you're engaged?"

"No. It means we promised to love each other," I explained. "To be faithful. And to always be honest, even if the truth is hard or complicated."

"Can't beat that," Jaycee said in approval. "I knew I liked this guy."

"And I'm glad I took your advice and gave him a chance to explain instead of just believing the worst."

"So, what's next?"

"Well . . ." I gestured to the ceiling above us. "Sam moved in over the weekend, and I gave up half my closet. What's next is that Marcus is going to build a second closet in the master bedroom. And we'll see where it goes from here."

After her fun but all too brief visit, I watched Jaycee disappear through security at the Portland airport and thought about Sam and his promise.

Suddenly eager to get back to Bailey Island, I turned and hurried back to my RAV 4 in short term parking. While the mystery of the wedding dress had been half solved before, another strange bit of paper had appeared that I had yet to explain. It appeared to have been torn from a diary or a journal. As I pushed the button to start the engine, the words written on it played across my mind.

Mother asked why I needed another new wedding dress when the first one was still sitting up in the attic. It's a beautiful dress, but I could never wear it. It was created to impress a man who didn't keep his promises. Jeff survived the war, but chose not to return to me, or even to his home. Mike deserves so much more. Even Aunt Emily thought so when she took me shopping and bought me a gown fit for a princess. Mother said it was a waste of money, but it wasn't her money and Aunt Emily insisted. Mike always makes me feel special, even when I have dirt on my face and my hair is a mess. Thanks to Aunt Emily, I will look especially beautiful on our special day.

The handwriting hadn't been familiar, but the names were. Aunt Emily was surely the woman who'd written the invitation to a niece named Eleanor. And when I'd found a well-worn old family Bible in one of the boxes of books Jaycee had helped me carry down from the attic, I'd discovered the family tree. A girl named Eleanor Murray had married a man named Michael Hamilton just after the end of WWII. Before too many days were out, I'd have to track down my friend Dawn and ask her if that Michael was part of George's family tree.

Then the only mystery would be who had left these hints from the past for me to find.

Acknowledgements

IF YOU ENJOYED THIS BOOK, CONSIDER LEAVING A REVIEW ON GOODREADS, OR YOUR VENDOR OF CHOICE.

Thanks first to one of my dedicated readers who found me on Facebook and discovered I was summering in Maine. As it turned out, on a lovely island she had been to when she was younger. After sharing memories of this unique place, she asked why I didn't write a romance set on Bailey Island. That seed once planted, became this fun new series.

Thanks also to my Sandy Scribbler writing buddies who helped me explore the possibilities and hung in there with critique and encouragement while I put this tale together. And, to my daughter, who was my demanding but very good copy editor, and all my family who support and encourage me.

Also by Skye Taylor

The Camerons of Tide's Way Novels

Falling for Zoe

Loving Meg

Trusting Will

Healing a Hero

Keeping His Promise

Worry Stone

Believing in Mac

Loving Ben (Short Story)

Mike's Wager (Short Story)

Iain's Plaid

(a time travel romance)

The Candidate

Suspense

The Jesse Quinn Mysteries

Bullseye

Crossfire

About the author

Skye Taylor, mother, grandmother, great grandmother and returned Peace Corps Volunteer, loves adventure and lives in St Augustine Florida where she enjoys the history of America's oldest city and walking on its beautiful beaches with Jessi, her four-year old Golden Retriever. She posts a monthly blog and and is currently working on the next book in the Bailey Island series along with book three in her Jesse Quinn Mystery series set in St Augustine. Her published work includes: *The Candidate, Falling for Zoe, Loving Meg, Trusting Will, Healing a Hero, Keeping His Promise, Worry Stone, Believing in Mac, Iain's Plaid, Bullseye* and *Crossfire*. Short stories: *Loving Ben, Mike's Wager and Saving Just One* and non-fiction essays of her experiences in the Peace Corps (Available on her website: www.Skye-writer.co.) She has a page on her website featuring short stories, some set in Tide's Way. She is a member of Romance Writers of America, Women's Fiction Writer's Association, Florida Writer's Association and Sisters in Crime. She loves hearing from her readers at Skye@Skye-writer.com

www.ingramcontent.com/pod-product-compliance
Lightning Source LLC
Chambersburg PA
CBHW071055250626
47159CB00002B/480